ACCIDENTAL
NEIGHBOR

SHARON WOODS

Accidental Neighbor

To everyone who believes in love after loss...

Chapter 1

JENNIFER

THIS HAS TO BE the world's slowest moving line. The shivers running up my arms into my bones have me rethinking my outfit tonight. Cold wind whips around my bare thighs. My teeth chatter, and I shuffle forward. My friends are waiting inside Three Dots Bar and I'm late for my best friend's twenty-first birthday celebration.

It was a struggle to make it here on time, and that was before I had to stay over at work filling in paperwork for a child that had an allergic reaction and vomited on me just before the mom arrived. Loving my job makes these times bearable. I'm scheduled on the late shift at work this week and getting ready for a big night out takes time. The line moves—*thank God*—and I reach inside my bag for my ID card.

Shit. The contents of my purse spill onto the pavement, and I quickly squat down to gather my belongings when I hear a rip. I suck in a breath and freeze. My tight tartan yellow skirt has a new thigh slit.

"Great," I mutter as I scramble to pick up my lip gloss, phone, and wallet.

"That's what happens when you stuff too much into a small bag," a deep male voice comments. I see his black shiny dress shoes and I know he is standing above, watching me.

Wanting to see his face, I rise, careful not to make the situation worse, and tug at the end, trying to add the illusion of more length.

My gaze focuses on the voice's face, and I feel dizzy staring back into a set of dark, brooding eyes. I watch his eyes squint from a smile, causing creases to form near them. His teeth are straight, white, and perfect. And his brown hair is tousled neatly on top of his head. My hand is twitching to see what it would feel like. *What is wrong with me?*

He slowly and seductively slides his gaze downwards over my black bodysuit and over-the-knee boots. And I feel stripped but intrigued by this handsome man. I need to know his name. Before I have a chance to speak, he is turning and walking off inside the bar.

Finally, I make it to the front of the line, but my relief quickly turns sour. The bald bouncer eyes me with heated desire, his stare lingering on me, and I quickly avert my gaze and fight the urge to roll my eyes because I cannot afford to piss him off. I need to get into the bar. My phone vibrates in my hand. 'Olivia' flashes across the screen. I hit decline but type out a quick text.

Jennifer: *I'm about to get inside. In line now. See you soon, birthday girl.*

Olivia and I have been friends since kindergarten; she is the most supportive friend you could have in your life.

"ID, sugar?" The bouncer asks.

"I'm twenty-two."

"I see." He drools and my skin crawls at his unwanted flirting.

Once inside, I'm surrounded by tall wood tables and long booth seats. Sconces with glass globes on the walls create a cozy yellow hue. The stench of hard liquor is evident, but the soft music playing through the speakers in the ceilings keeps me from running outside and into a taxi back home. I'm trying to spot my group when a screech comes from my left.

"*Jen*! Jennifer, over here!"

Olivia waves her arms above her head, the biggest smile lighting up her whole face. She looks radiant in her emerald-green dress and if it was sparkly and had wings, I would think she was Tinkerbell with her blond hair curled to perfection.

My mood instantly lifts, along with the tension I was carrying on my shoulders. Olivia, my little pocket rocket, is everything. I wave back, stepping across the worn wooden floors to join the group. Olivia, cheeks flushed from already having a few, *or more*, drinks, jumps up from her chair and throws her arms around my neck.

A laugh slips out of me, and I hug her back. "Happy birthday. I can't believe it's finally here."

She bounces on her gold heels, green eyes wide and glassy. "I know! I am so fucking happy you're here. Let's get a drink."

She stumbles, and I grab her arm to steady her as a giggle slips from her mouth. "Are you sure you don't want some water first?"

She tips her head back, shaking her head vigorously from side to side. "No way, Mom. I'm fine."

I smile, but don't believe a word she says. "Okay, but if you vomit, do it near someone else," I say. "I've already had vomit in my hair once today."

A few minutes later, we squeeze up to the bar where suited bartenders dash back and forth in front of the bottles of alcohol lining the rows of wooden shelves behind them.

A blond bartender rocking a black vest strides over to us. "What can I get for you, ladies?" he says in a deep voice.

Before I can order our drinks, Olivia cuts me off. "Oh my God, I love your accent. Is it Australian?"

"Correct." His eyes roam her face, and a corner of his lip rises.

She twirls a lock of hair around her finger and flutters her eyelashes at him. Olivia is extremely flirty. It's part of her charm. Men fall for her at the drop of a hat, and women are jealous or want to be friends with her. Personally, I envy her carefree, speaks-whatever-is-on-her-mind attitude. I don't have an ounce of it, keeping how I feel locked tightly away.

He finally takes our order, and they chit-chat while he prepares our trademark turquoise drinks. I take the opportunity while she is distracted, to search for those dark eyes from outside. But with a good peer around and no luck, I sigh and return to listen to Olivia invite the bartender to join us when he's finished, and then we wander through the crowd, back to join the others.

When we arrive at the end of the table a few minutes later, I finally get to see who turned up tonight. Olivia's brother, Jackson, is on at the end of the round booth, already standing up to pull his little sister into a side hug.

I spot and wave to our good friend Katie, who's sitting next to the space Jackson just vacated. A few of Jackson's friends are seated in the booth as well. Tyler, Cody, and ah... *shit*, Nathan. We hooked up once when I had too many drinks at Olivia's.

The guys shuffle further in around the booth to make room and I slip onto the seat next to Tyler, Olivia slides in after me. They throw a few hellos my way before they're back to their beers and banter.

"I thought you weren't going to make it!" Katie says from across the oval-shaped table. Her hair is up in a bun with two pieces out, framing her face, the green headband in her hair making her blue eyes pop.

"Ugh, don't even get me started." The last thing I want to do right now is think about being covered in vomit. "I love my job, but today was just not my day."

"Oh, hon. Well then, a good drink is exactly what you need," Katie says soothingly.

"Darn right it is!" Olivia smacks her lips on my cheek and laughs before declaring we all need to do shots.

Oh God, what have I got myself into tonight?

Jackson returns a few minutes later with a large tray of clear shots, placing it on the table before handing each of us two shots.

Oh, not good.

We all raise our first shot. "Happy twenty-first birthday, Olivia!" we shout and clink our glasses together.

I'll definitely regret this later.

I throw the shot back before I have time to psych myself out, the liquid burning a path down the back of my throat. Screwing my face up, I grab my cocktail and take a long sip, chasing it down.

The second shot isn't any easier than the first, and I can already feel the alcohol working its way through my system. This is why I don't do shots. Give me a nice glass of wine or cocktail and I'm good to go. Although, I must admit, I'm definitely feeling relaxed.

I'm on my third trademark turquoise, the buzz of alcohol well and truly in my veins. The bar's vibe has hit a new level. The music is louder, and they have moved some of the tall bar tables to make a bigger dance floor.

"Hey, I'm going up to the bar to see if I can get some food," I shout, but nobody pays me any attention.

Jackson leans in close and whispers something in Katie's ear, a lazy grin on his face. Katie giggles, a blush spreading over her cheeks.

Well, this is new.

My stomach growls, and I need to get to the bar for some food because my head feels light from the buzz of alcohol. Olivia joins me and we set off through the crowd that is now doubled. We squeeze our way to the bar, then wait behind patrons ordering.

"Just grab me a drink," Olivia yells.

"Are you sure?"

She pops a brow at me. I lift my hands in surrender.

I watch as she heads farther down the bar, already distracted, as the people in front of me move away with their drinks. I step forward and lean on the bar, reading the menu once more.

I flip it over and scan through the drink menu, wanting to try something new.

"Oh, honey or say my name," a deep sultry voice says beside me, close enough I can feel his breath on my cheek, and I suck in a sharp breath at the familiar voice. *It's him.*

My head whips in that direction but connects with a hard jaw. *Ouch.* I peer up into the most magnificent set of deep-brown eyes.

My mouth moves, but no words come out as I rub my head to soothe the ache. The slight buzz from the alcohol is helping dampen the pain, but isn't helping the flush creeping across my skin.

I watch his mouth move and realize he is talking to me. *Shit!*

"Sorry?" I whisper, my eyes still locked on his stunning face.

How can a man be this hot? I don't think I have ever met a man on this level. I still can't form any words. His beauty takes my breath and words away. I just continue my stare until he chuckles.

"I was saying Oh, Honey or Say My Name are excellent drinks."

He moves forward to lean across me, pointing at the menu. The alcohol thrumming through my veins makes my movements slower than usual as his spicy vanilla scent fills my nostrils, causing them to flare and take a deeper inhale. *Shit, he smells good.*

My skin prickles with goosebumps and I blink, snapping my thoughts back to the here and now. *Get a grip, Jen!*

"Ah, I see. I understand now." My voice comes out husky, so I clear my throat, moving to the side so I can face him better. I lean my arm on the bar for support. "Which one would you say is better?"

Am I flirting?

I cringe inwardly, but it's not enough to stop myself in this tipsy state. He is evoking a behavior that is foreign but also refreshing. I didn't think I had desires for an older guy, but this *man* is stirring me up inside.

"Hm, tough call. It depends." He tips his head back and taps his chin, his handsome face etched in concentration. "Let me ask you some questions."

I nod back, unable to say anything. My focus catches on the movement of his finger, which is all too close to his full lips. I want to feel them crushed against mine. I bet they are soft and taste amazing. But I'm not bold enough to make the first move.

"Light and fresh or citrus with hints of sweet?"

Oh, right. He was asking me questions. *Focus, Jen.*

"Definitely citrus with a hint of sweet." My voice is still husky, but at least I'm forming sentences.

"Vanilla and honey or honey with spices?"

Thinking of his sexy scent, I respond without a second thought. "Honey and spices." His lips tip up. And maybe I'm being too transparent. I glance down at the bar before meeting his gaze again.

"And your last drink question." He rubs the five o'clock shadow on his jaw. "Sherry with dried fruit or peaches and lemonade?"

"Easy—peaches and lemonade."

"Good choice." He nods and waves down a bartender. "I'll grab a Redbreast Lustau, and one Say My Name." He winks at me.

"What is it with the names of these drinks? Redbreast?" I blurt.

I roll my lips inward so no other embarrassing words slip out.

He shrugs and throws me a lopsided grin. "I don't know, but clearly they were drunk or horny... or both."

With the mention of the word, my eyes lower to his lips and his tongue comes out to skim across his lower lip. I'm so transfixed with the movement I don't realize I've caught my lip between my teeth until his thumb reaches out and tugs it free.

"Please don't tease," he murmurs.

I freeze and close my eyes at the heat burning beneath my skin.

What is happening to me?

Normally, I only attract playboys who want to have fun for the night, not the older, successful, sexy man.

"Here you go." The bartender places our drinks on the counter.

My mystery man drops his hand and pays, before leaning on the bar, his attention solely on me, which doesn't bother me at all. I want it.

I want more.

I reach for what I assume is my drink, given its colorful appearance compared to the amber whiskey-like liquid in the other, and take a gulp.

A deep laugh leaves his chest. I don't care because I need to cool myself down. I've never reacted to a man like this and feel like I am about to combust.

"Could I order a bowl of fries—delivered to my table?" I ask the bartender, trying to remember the table number, and desperate to get control of myself. "Table four."

The bartender nods, and I take another sip of my drink. "Mm, this is so yummy. Thanks. Even though it would mortify my mom I accepted a drink from a stranger."

I could kick myself for my childlike statement. I must be turning him off now.

"Well, I would have to agree with her there. You shouldn't. But we aren't strangers." He picks up his glass and takes a drink. "I'm Thomas, but most people call me Tom."

"Hi, Tom." I like the way his name rolls off my tongue. "Jennifer... but people call me Jen."

"Beautiful," he says in a way that I'm not sure if he's referring to just my name.

My cheeks flush hotter and I glance away from his prolonged eye contact, needing a distraction. On the dance floor, a few couples dance seductively, kissing. Totally not helping to distract my mind.

"Have you been to Three Dots before?" he asks.

Being this close to him, I can tell he is older than me—probably mid-thirties, judging by the eye creases, the confidence, and the conversation. Older guys have never attracted me to them, but there is a spark between us I can't deny.

"Actually, no. I rarely go out. I work a lot and I prefer to stay home or have dinner with a glass of wine with my friends." I glance around the bar, fiddling with my hair. "You?"

"This is my first time here too. I *can't* normally go out, but tonight I'm with friends celebrating a work promotion."

My brows frown at his comment. "Can't?"

He rakes his teeth across his bottom lip. "Would you like to dance with me?" He doesn't answer my question, but I figure it's rude to push a stranger to talk.

"Yes, I would love to."

I finish my cocktail in a few guzzles while he downs the rest of his drink in one pull. The alcohol buzz gives me confidence when he grabs my hand, pulling me to the dance floor behind him, leading me through the crowd as bodies press all around us, dancing to the music. The last few songs have changed from upbeat to slow, and a dim light over the floor highlights the sweaty bodies all around us.

He pauses in a section of the crowd, spinning me around to face him, stopping me in my tracks. "Are you okay?" he asks, staring down at me.

I nod.

My palms sweat and my heart races inside my chest. This pull toward him is a new feeling for me, but I want to explore it. Explore him.

He skims his fingertips over my forearm, setting the skin on fire. I move my hips to the music. I am not a dancer, but being around Thomas is making me brazen.

I check him out from head to toe, taking in his muscular frame covered in a tight black long-sleeve top and dark low-hung jeans, finishing at his black shoes.

The song changes to "Positions" by Ariana Grande, and Thomas closes the distance, so we have only an inch between us. His hands snake around my stomach to my lower back, causing my insides to flood with heat. Reaching up, I caress his muscled shoulders, skimming my way until my hands link behind his neck.

We move to the beat, our bodies flush. He is taller than me, yet cocoons me perfectly, and I crave more—more closeness, more touch, more of everything he can offer.

I gaze into his heated dark eyes while my heart flutters and beats wildly in my chest. He leans forward, his hand moves to the back of my head, and his full lips take control of mine. When I part my lips, his tongue plunges into my mouth, tangling with mine. He tastes of mixed spice and dried fruit. I groan at the flavor.

My hand thrusts into his hair, pulling him closer, meeting his intensity with hunger. He moans and slides his hand down a little further, settling on my lower back.

I break the kiss and take deep, shaky breaths. His eyes are heated and heavy-lidded. And an idea pops into my brain. I contemplate it for a minute, but the way he is looking at me mixed with the way my body is reacting, I give in to the desire. Grabbing his hand, I find a dark hallway and he must sense what I want because as soon as we are out of eyesight he pushes me up against the wall, and captures my mouth in a savage attack swallowing my gasp into his mouth. His large body covers mine, his hands buried deep in my hair, and our tongues twirl together in a frenzy. I feel his erection hitting me through his jeans, and I move my hips to rub myself on him, chasing friction on my clit. After a few strokes, he lets out a growl and it causes him to snap. *Yes.* His hands move out of my hair and advance to grip my legs, lifting them to his hips, and I lock my ankles over each other behind his back, spreading my pussy over his cock. Our lips are still sealed and our tongues still exploring.

Without warning, he grinds himself hard against me. Breaking our kiss, I tip my head back on the wall with my eyes shut and whimper. The friction on my clit is like a lightning bolt to my body, waking every part of me. He does it again and I moan.

This feels amazing.

He leans forward and trails soft kisses and small nips up my neck, and when his skilled mouth reaches my ear, I feel his breath tickle. "Shhh princess. I need you to be quiet. Unless you want to be heard?"

My eyes pop open.

Holy Shit.

My mouth opens and closes repeatedly, but my brain is misfiring. I squeeze my eyes shut again and shake my head.

"That's what I thought. I will make you feel good. Just relax," he whispers.

One of his hands leaves my hip to dust across my ass, down to squeeze it and then move over to my quivering pussy. Where I'm already wet and ready. I hold my breath with anticipation. He drags his finger under my panties, gently grazing it along my opening, and I hear a hiss leave his mouth.

"You're already wet."

My breath releases, and I pant. "Yes."

My pussy is aching, begging for more touching. His thick finger finds my swollen clit. He circles firmly, and I arch my back off the wall, trying to get more pressure. My body is climbing quickly and when he inserts his finger, my body shudders, welcoming the intrusion. He thrusts his finger in and out, rubbing along my wall. My body convulses and I grab his shoulders, digging my fingers in and grind down, chasing the orgasm that I know is building.

He enters a second finger, and a pinch of tightness is felt for a second before my body welcomes the intrusion. With two fingers he moves faster, and it isn't long until my walls tighten around him and my orgasm ripples through my body, causing me to feel faint. I'm shocked by what I just did but also by how much I enjoyed it... and him.

He pulls his fingers out of me tenderly. Which surprises me after what we just did. I open my eyes and lift my head off the wall to see him studying me with a starved look. My throat squeezes and I watch him bring his fingers to his mouth. They glisten with my slickness and he licks them clean, groaning.

"You taste sweeter than I imagined."

I gape at him, transfixed by how sensual this image is. But also shocked by his words.

I move the leg that he is still holding up back to the ground. His hands move to my waist, and I smooth my hands down my skirt, making sure I'm all covered again.

This should feel wrong, but with him, it didn't.

It felt good.

The only doubt entering my mind, is the fact he's older and more experienced.

"I think I need some water. Uh, it's boiling in here," I whisper.

"Let's head back to the bar, shall we?" He unexpectedly leans down and pecks my lips softly before he leans back, smirking at my mouth hanging open.

Thomas grabs my hand to make our way back to the bar. When we approach, I realize I haven't seen Olivia in a while. I look down the bar to the last place I saw her, but she's not there. Maybe she went dancing or back to the table. I decide I really want to check and make sure she is okay, considering she consumed a lot of alcohol tonight for a small person.

I glance back at Thomas. "Do you mind grabbing me some water? I need to find my friend. It's her birthday tonight and I should really check in on her."

He nods with a smile. "Of course."

I glance down at our joined hands and watch as I slowly remove mine, feeling cool air on my palm. I really wish I didn't have to go right now. I clench my hands.

"I'll be right back," I whisper.

But when I go back to the bar after finding Olivia, I drop my head and murmur,

"He's gone."

CHAPTER 2

THOMAS

Three months later

STARTING OVER IS HARD. I tossed and turned all night, barely sleeping. In the night, Lily must have crawled into my bed, because I woke up feeling her little warm arms wrapped around my neck. She has been waking up with nightmares the last week and seeking comfort from me being nearby. Rose calls out to me. "Da-da, da-da."

Tossing my sheets back, I climb out of bed and stroll toward her room. I open the door and find her standing in her crib with the biggest smile, making me believe at least someone in this house got sleep last night. Lifting her out of her crib, I balance her on my hip and walk to the highchair to clip her in before beginning the breakfast routine. While I mix her oats, my phone rings from my bedroom where I left it on the charger. I run to my room, but as I enter, the covers are moving. Lily's arms are stretching above her head. The ringtone has woken her up. *Shit.*

Snatching the phone off the charger, I move to her side of the bed. "Good morning, sweetheart. Sorry Daddy's phone woke you." I sit next to her on the edge of the bed and stroke her hair. I watch as she rubs her eyes and yawns. "Would you like some breakfast? I'm making some oats for Rose."

Nodding at me, she says, "Yes, Daddy."

I stroke her hair one last time before pushing up off the bed and gazing down at her.

"Okay, I'll meet you in the kitchen." My eyes turn to my phone to check who called, and it's my friend James. Wandering back to the kitchen, I offer Rose a drink and then hit call. I tuck my phone between my cheek and my shoulder so I can continue making Rose's breakfast.

"Morning."

"Hey, sorry I missed your call."

"It's all good. I'm just driving over now. Did you want a coffee?"

My coffee machine is stacked in a box and if I don't take his offer, I won't be getting one today. "Yes, please. A latte, no sugar."

"All good. See you soon."

I'm washing the dishes as a heavy knock hits the front door.

Without leaving the sink I yell out, "Come in, James; the door is open. I'm down in the kitchen."

The heavy door creaks open and then slams shut before heavy footsteps hit the floors.

After I finish the last dish, I dry my hands as James enters the kitchen. Lowering my coffee to the counter, I hold my hand out while James shakes it and brings my chest to his so he can hit my back. I mimic the action. "Thanks for helping this weekend."

"Anytime. Happy to help you. You know that." He surveys the kitchen and the house. "Tell me, what have you started?"

His gaze returns to mine, his arms draped across his chest.

"I have packed the little pieces in almost every room."

He offers a small tilt in his chin. "What are you thinking? Where did you want to start today?"

I hadn't even thought about that. I need to think, to snap out of it. We have little time and I don't want everyone waiting on me all day. I shake my head.

James pops a brow, clearly reading my thoughts. "How did you want to pack the truck?"

I take a deep inhale and scan the boxes in each room. I scratch at my temple. "I think the big items, like the beds and couches. I need to set the girls' rooms up in the new house for Rose's nap today. Let me check on the girls and then let's dismantle their beds."

I set off toward Lily's room with James hot on my heels. I pause at the door, watching them play with their dolls.

"Girls, James is here," I say. Both girls lift their chins in the direction of my voice. Their mouths part into wide smiles. He walks past me into the room and squats down next to the girls in his navy shorts and white t-shirt.

"Uncle Jay," Lily shouts, throwing down the Barbie and jumping into his arms for a cuddle. Rose mimics Lily and cuddles his other side, nestling into his chest.

"Hi, girls. I see you got your Barbies to play with—fun. Maybe after I help your daddy, I can play Barbies? I'm great with Barbies." He turns his face up, catching my gaze, and winks at me. I let out a soft laugh, shaking my head.

Since the first day of high school, we've been stuck together. James is my oldest friend—best man at my wedding, the best uncle to my daughters, even if he spoils them too much. Twenty years later, and we're as close as ever. He's been there for all the highs and the lows of my life, and even though opening up isn't something I do often, besides Victoria, James is one of the few people I'd go to.

I'm excited for the scenery change. I won't lie, juggling my career as a single parent to two kids five and under presents its challenges, but I love my job, and in the end, I couldn't pass up this opportunity that our other friend Joshua offered. I want to be an example for my girls, show them to go after what you want and work hard.

I want to make them proud.

The girls detangle themselves and resume playing again.

"Let's start in Rose's room, shall we?" I take a few steps to the opposite room, with James following behind. We separate Rose's furniture and then carry the pieces and boxes to the truck while we work in silence, which I welcome.

I need the space to think and not talk. I feel numb; packing my family's life up is gut-wrenching.

We need this. It will be worth it. I repeat this in my head, like a mantra.

Once completing Rose's room, I waste no more time. I jog up to my room and walk straight into the bathroom and pack up the toiletries because I want to leave Victoria's stuff until the very end. Finishing up my room, I move on to her belongings, pulling the top drawer open. I stare at it.

What do I do?

I decide at that moment that I can't bring this to the new house. We need a fresh start, to leave the memories of us in this house. I only want to keep stuff I can gift the girls—the wedding dress, rings, and photos.

I head back to the kitchen and grab a garbage bag and jog back to my room before the guys notice me. Opening the lingerie drawer, I hold my breath as I yank the drawer completely out of the frame and tip the entire contents in the bag. I'm not thinking; I am just working on an autopilot to get this done. When I finish sorting out her belongings, I tie up the bag and stalk out to the bin where I put it while letting out a shaky breath. My eyes are glassy and tears are threatening, but I hold them in. Rolling my shoulders back and walking back into the wardrobe, I hear James call out.

"Tom, are you here?"

"Yeah, in the walk-in wardrobe," I shout.

Heavy footsteps hit the tiles, and I glance up as the sound gets louder and I watch as he leans his body against the wall. James is not a short guy, his over six-foot body taking up most of the entry. If he wasn't in real estate, I could picture him in GQ or as a bodyguard.

"You want a hand here? I finished Lily's room and the family room."

That was quick; how long have I been here? I gaze around at the now bare room. "No, I just finished here."

"I gotta fly out tonight. Will you be okay the rest of the week or do you need me to cancel?" he asks.

"Go. The girls and I will be fine. I got it. I haven't got too much to do, and I have plenty of time to sort it out."

"Make sure you call me if you need me to fly back."

I laugh. "I'm a big boy; I'll be fine."

"I don't know about that," he says, his tone light with humor.

I roll my eyes at his comment, and we both laugh.

"You ready?"

James walks to the car while I do a last sweep of the house by myself.

I had this pull to come in and say goodbye.

Say goodbye to my former life. A life I will never get back.

I feel like I need to find myself again. Last year I was a shell of a man. Leaving this house means putting behind some of the best memories. It's soul crushing, but I know there are two girls out there that need their dad. A better version than the empty zombie I have given them. I know grief can't turn off like a light switch and I will never forget Victoria, but I need to live. Really living.

Wandering through the house one more time, I could almost picture Victoria and me curled up on the couch watching Netflix while the girls slept, cuddling beside us. I miss the simplicity of that life before it all fell apart—in an instant.

Closing the front door behind me, I spin and turn the keys to lock it. Walking over, I rip open the door of the car, then slide in silently. Slamming the door shut behind me, I thrust the keys at James. He wants to deal with the sale of the property. I know it will be handed over to a family who will love it as much as I once did.

"You okay?" he softly asks.

I nod, but don't turn to him as I speak. "Yeah." It comes out barely above a whisper as I look down at my ringless finger sitting on my jean-covered thigh.

My heart beats frantically inside my chest and I keep taking slow breaths to calm my body down before I lean toward the radio and turn up the volume, letting James know I'm not in the mood to talk. Sitting back into the leather beneath me, I close my eyes briefly before driving away, and gaze out my window for the final time and watch as the house disappears in front of my eyes and into the faded distance.

CHAPTER 3

JENNIFER

I'M RUNNING MY USUAL loop around the block, not paying any attention to what's in front of me, watching a truck reverse up the driveway next door. There are a few cars parked out front, and standing by the cars is a circle of five men, with an older couple and a young girl. A few of the men have their backs to me, so I can't make them out from here. One has sandy-blond hair, tanned skin, and is wearing black shorts and a t-shirt. The other has brown hair, but he bends down to play with the girl.

My heart leaps and I come to an abrupt stop, not seeing the toy under me until it's too late. I fall flat on my hands and knees.

"Ouch!" I yell.

"Jennifer, are you alright?"

I hear footsteps getting closer and slowly peel myself off the pavement. *God, my hands and knees burn.* I sit back on my heels and peer up to a group of unknown faces etched with concern.

I blush and avert my eyes to my dad, who has kneeled in front of me.

"I think I just grazed my hands and knees. What are you doing?"

"I'm helping the new neighbor move in."

He reaches a hand out to help me up. I snail one leg up at a time, the air stinging my knee. I suck in a harsh breath and stand, mortified I fell in front of an audience.

"Thanks, Dad." I turn my hands over and inspect the damage to my palms. Just the top layer is grazed. I'll need to clean it up inside.

The group wanders off back to unpacking and I glance down at the colorful blocks that caused my fall. I should have been paying better attention, but all I was staring at was the truck.

"I'm so sorry about that. My daughter shouldn't leave her toys laying around."

All the hairs on my body rise. The familiar tone sends my gaze darting to seek the owner. Staring back at me are the deep-brown eyes from Olivia's birthday. My stomach hardens by the knowledge *he* is my new neighbor.

The hot older guy.

Thomas.

He wasn't a part of the group of faces I fell over in front of, was he?

Oh God. How embarrassing.

His gaze flicks over my oversized t-shirt and black running shorts before he squats to collect the little blocks scattered on the pavement. My face burns hot, and I stare with wide eyes, totally mute. *Does he recognize me?* Part of me hopes he doesn't, because pieces of hair are stuck to my forehead, and sweat beads run down my back. I'm standing in front of him looking like a hot mess with my sweat-soaked shirt glued to my back while he's sexy-cool in a gray t-shirt that fits like a glove showing off his rippled muscles and black running shorts showing off his toned, tanned legs.

I squat down and help him collect the remaining blocks and will myself to find my words. "It's okay. They are only kids." My voice sounds higher pitched than I wanted.

When his gaze meets mine, a spark of electricity hits me full force in the gut.

The magnetic pull I feel toward Thomas has me averting my gaze back to the safety of my dad. The sun is hot, but Thomas is making it feel scorching, setting my skin on fire. I bite down hard on my lip as the flash of a memory from the pub slams into me. The feeling of his body pressed against me, his spicy scent, and how his tongue massaged mine. The way he touched my body bringing me to orgasm right there in the bar.

Dad moves closer, all concern removed from his face, oblivious to my flustered state. "This is our new neighbor, Thomas. He just moved in today," he states. "I've been helping them move some things while you were on your run."

Dad interrupts my internal freak-out. "Thomas, this is my oldest daughter, Jennifer."

I glance briefly at my dad and then avert my gaze slowly back to Thomas.

I can't tell my dad we've already met. I'm sure he wouldn't be so polite if he knew how *well* I know him.

"Nice to meet you, Thomas," I choke out.

He rubs the back of his neck. "Nice to meet you, Jennifer. And I'm really sorry about the toys left on the sidewalk."

My dad steps out of ear shot, moving back to the truck. He stands and I follow, both holding blocks.

I take the chance to speak. "I can't believe it's you."

His offers a sexy lopsided smile and I feel my skin tingle in response. My body remembers him and as I get a whiff of his vanilla cologne, my pussy becomes heavy.

"And I can't believe it's you. And you're my neighbor." He inches forward to take the blocks from my hands. Skimming my skin with his, it reminds me what his hand felt like in mine as he held my hand that night. When they empty, I curl and tuck them under my arms.

"Same. What a small world. I must look like a mess." I roll my lips, pinching them together.

His eyes glow under the sun light, "No way. Just as ravishing as that night."

I swallow past the lump that's formed in my throat from his words.

Is he kidding? I'm a bloody mess.

I cast my eyes over my old clothes, not understanding how he thinks that right now, but I don't argue, "Than—"

He glances away when a high-pitched squeal emanates from inside the house.

A little girl with blond braids, wearing a gorgeous frilly pink dress, runs out of the house. "Daddy. Daddy, guess what! Nana said if I go to college, I can be anything I want. I said I want to be a mermaid."

A giggle leaves my lips. She's adorable. Her hazel eyes shimmer as she pauses in front of Thomas. My breath hitches. Does this mean what I think it means?

My flaming desires extinguish and an icy shiver runs through me. A feeling of disappointment and disgust hits my stomach.

"That sounds wonderful, sweetheart, but I need to talk to you." He squats and gently speaks. "You know how Daddy tells you to pack up your toys?"

She nods vigorously at him. "Yes."

"Well, because you left some outside, Jennifer here," he points to me and the little girl's gaze meets mine, "she tripped on some of your toys and hurt herself. You need to pack your toys up from now on, please. Could you apologize to her? For leaving your blocks out."

She looks back toward her dad and then back at me with a frown forming on her tiny face. "Sorry for leaving my toys out. My daddy always says fuck when he trips on our toys." The audible intake of breath has my eyes flicking to Thomas. His face and her innocence have me rolling my lips, biting back a laugh that's desperately trying to escape. The best part of kids is honesty. I peer down at the ground to prevent a big shit-eating grin. When I compose myself, I glance up at her again.

The little girl stares at me, waiting for my response. I squat down and wince when the scrape on my knee pulls with the movement. "Thanks for the apology. My scratches feel much better already." I smile.

Her face drops with relief. "Daddy says shit when he cuts himself." She points in the direction of my chin.

Touching my chin, I feel the cuts of rough skin and warm liquid. I cringe inwardly at the thought of my appearance. I'm sure I must be a real shock to Thomas. He is seeing me at my worst, literally, and compared to the done-up version I was on the night we met, it's like night and day. I need to get away from here. The back of my head is hurting, and I feel a headache coming on.

"Lily, please." Thomas cuts her off, eyebrows drawn together.

"I think I should wash it off and make it better. What do you think?" I ask, trying to calm the situation.

"Do you have princess Band-Aids to put on? My daddy buys them for me. I can give you one."

"No, I don't, but it's okay. You keep them in case you need them. They sound special." I rise. "Well, um, I should head inside and clean up. It was nice to meet you, Thomas and Lily."

I briefly peek at Thomas before darting my gaze back to Lily, then to my dad.

"Bye," they say in unison.

I wave at everyone before dropping my head, unable to glance in Thomas's direction again. I pick up my pace, speed walking to the path that leads to our house. Once I'm in the safety of my home, I take a deep breath. *What the hell was that?*

"Meg."

I sigh, wishing I had enough money for my own place for times I need space but my wage would only cover rent.

"It's me mom, not Meg." Walking further into the house, I find her cleaning the table.

She peers at me with concern. "Oh, I thought you were Meg, sorry love. What happened to your face?"

"I fell on the path running." I explain.

"Let me see."

She walks over, but I wave her off. "Mom I'm fine thanks but I want to shower anyway. I'm all sweaty."

And not just from the run. But a certain handsome man I have a fever for. My body hasn't reacted to a guy like that in over two years and that was with my last boyfriend. We dated for a year, but he wanted to live a single life and go out and party, whereas I want to live a quiet life. We separated on good terms and since then, I have had a few dates who said they wanted to settle down, but then their actions said something clearly different. I'm so over playboys.

"Is your father still next door helping the new neighbor?"

My throat constricts."Yeah, he is."

Her face lightens, "Of course he is."

My dad is the most helpful and polite man. It's probably why my standards with guys are so high. I expect them to treat me the way my dad treats Mom. His love and support toward her are endearing. I would love to find that type of connection. They have been blissfully married since they were fourteen. To have a caring and loving man in my life is a dream. Guys my age are definitely not like that.

I walk to the bathroom and my mind is jumbled with questions.

Thomas has a child?

Where is his wife?

Is he married?

I kissed someone's husband?

CHAPTER 4

THOMAS

THE MOMENT WE LOCKED eyes on the pavement, I recognized her. My heart started beating faster in my chest, my stomach dropping like a roller-coaster dip. *Surely it couldn't be her, could it?*

There was no mistaking those beautiful brown eyes staring back at me, her face free of makeup and a pink flush over her cheeks. She looked radiant and youthful, stealing my breath away. I worry she hurt herself, but she assured us it's only a few grazes, so I don't have any other choice than to believe her.

I wanted the ground to swallow me up right there and then. Trust Lily, my sassy girl, to throw some awkward phrases out without even realizing it. As I watch Jennifer rush back into the house *next door*, it reminds me of the night at the bar. I thought our connection was electric and I know she felt the same, but as I waited in that exact spot at the bar with her glass of water, I realized she is far too young for me and I didn't deserve to move on. I have to be more responsible for the girls, so I got up and left. Thinking she deserved better and that I would never see her again.

Now, seeing her again, I can't seem to shake the memory of how it felt to be with Jennifer. It was an out-of-body experience that night. It was as if we were wrapped in our own world, our bodies vibrating with the strongest of sexual tension. I have never been so daring, but the friction of her body and her intense kiss on the dancefloor had me in a spin. So, when she pushed me through the crowd, my body took over and I caved. Watching her eyes closed, mouth open, succumbing to the orgasm I gave her in the dark with my fingers... blew my damn mind. But the best part was tasting her cum on my fingers. Just thinking about it now makes my balls heavy and my cock hard, wanting it all over again. I stare at her lips, wanting to reclaim them and devour their softness.

I've pleasured women, but this was different. *She left me wanting more.* She is dangerous; her body fits so well with mine. Even in her baggy workout gear, I know the fit body hiding under it. My hands twitch with the reminder of how she felt underneath them.

And now she knows I have children. I'm a dad, but the hardest part is she doesn't know about Rose. It feels like a bomb dropped and I couldn't have a private conversation with her.

My girls are not something I would have wanted to mention straightaway anyway, and Victoria isn't something I find easy to speak about, but with her living next door and knowing I have children, that means I may not have a choice. It makes me wonder how she feels, even though I shouldn't have feelings for someone younger, just starting their life. I'm thirty-four; I need to find stability and I don't want to introduce someone new to the girls since they might leave. They have had enough people leaving from their lives.

"Thomas, where did you want this?" My head snaps in the direction of her dad's voice.

I glance at the large cardboard box he's carrying as he stalks over. "Let me take that. You've helped enough today."

He squeezes the box against his chest. "No, I got this. I have no plans, and the truck is almost empty."

"Okay, just in the garage, please."

He strides off, and I glance over to Jennifer's house before getting back to work.

Thirty minutes later, everything is inside. The big furniture is in place, but the boxes are in each room half-unpacked. Mom watched the girls and put Rose down for her nap, which allowed me to help a lot, meaning I can do less tomorrow.

"Thanks for cooking, Mom." I kiss her cheek as she stirs stew in a pot on the stove. "How can I help?"

"Call everyone to come and eat."

I call everyone in the room and help Mom pass the dishes around. I hand Paul one and stand beside him as I eat mine.

"I can come over and give you a hand tomorrow. What time?"

I swallow the stew that's in my mouth before tuning to face him in surprise. "I appreciate the offer, Paul, but I don't have too much to unpack, and I have all week off."

"A new job?" he asks.

"Yeah, a project manager for my friend's company." I point to Joshua, standing on the other side of the kitchen, talking to James and my other buddy, Benjamin.

"Nice. Smart man." He seems to like my answer.

"What about you?" I ask.

"I have been an accountant all my life."

"Smart too."

He snorts. And that makes me laugh.

"I hope I'm not overstepping here. I don't want to be rude, but are you a single dad?"

My appetite vanishes, and I put my spoon in the bowl and lower it. I can't glance at Paul. I stare down at the stew as I confess.

"Yes."

Chapter 5

JENNIFER

I shouldn't have stayed up until the early morning binge-watching *Grey's Anatomy* on Netflix. Walking through the doors at work with heaviness in my eyelids and lack of energy in my body has made me regret staying up late the last two nights. This is not a good look, since I recently applied to be manager of one room.

A colleague is going on maternity leave soon, and I'm waiting to hear back on my application result for her position. I've been going a little harder, trying to go above my usual role and help, because I want to prove myself to them, hoping it will pay off.

I amble down the hall yawning, struggling to stay awake. I wish I drank coffee. I'm sure the caffeine kick would help me right now. The lights are on in the staff room, and I peek in and spot Emma sitting at the table, hugging a cup between her hands.

"Hi, Jen."

"Morning, Emma," I grumble back as I walk to the cupboard for a cup.

My eyes are still half-closed as I reach for a mug, my mind still distracted with what happened this weekend, or rather *who* happened. Of all the houses, it had to be next to mine. It's going to be hard to ignore the hot neighbor. Shaking thoughts of Thomas from my head, I grab a mug from the cupboard, but as I'm pulling it from the shelf, it knocks into the one beside it. Everything happens in slow motion. The mug hits the edge of the counter, smashing on impact before falling to the floor and shattering into even more pieces.

I wince at the sound and the mess now covering the floor of the break room. *Oh, come on, really?*

A chair scratches against the floor and small footsteps squeak closer.

"Are you okay, Jen? Did the cup cut you?" Emma squats and helps me pick up the pieces from the floor.

"No, it didn't." I place the larger pieces in the bin and step over to the sink, opening the cupboard doors to reach for the dustpan. Once the mug splinters are swept up, I try again to make a cup of tea.

"What happened?"

"Sorry?"

She points to my chin. "What happened to your chin?"

"Oh, that." I blush at the memory. "I fell while running Saturday."

"Trust you to fall." She laughs with a light shake of her head before putting her cup away and heading out of the room. "Take your time. I'll be out here."

"Okay," I mumble back.

If I had more time, and hadn't stayed up so late, I could have dabbed some makeup on it, but I just washed my face and brushed my teeth before driving myself to work.

Emma arrived at the center one year ago, and we bonded straightaway over our love of movies and Netflix shows. She is funny yet kind, always offering to help other staff members. This childcare center is special to me. After my studies and my student time here three years ago, I went to the boss and asked for a job.

I love the way Helen runs the center so efficiently. It's a clean, fun, and happy environment to work. I knew not all centers were like this, so it relieved me to be accepted full time. We have the same set of staff that have been around for many years. It's like a second family to me.

After I've drained my cup, I wash the cup in the sink I head in the direction of the reception desk where I see Emma hunched over, scanning the pages of the assignment book.

"Where am I today, Emma?" I call out as I approach.

She looks over at me. "We're both in the toddler room today."

I smile. The toddler room is my favorite. A lot of girls enjoy babies or the older children. Personally, I love the personalities each toddler presents. Their imagination and the way they grow so quickly at this age are utterly fascinating.

"Okay, great. I'll start preparing the room."

I dash around the center, turning on lights, setting up play stations in each room, and turning on the computer.

At exactly half-past six on the dot, parents arrive for the morning drop-offs.

Emma moves to the room as I welcome them. The next few hours pass quickly, and Helen is due to arrive soon.

The work phone rings, and I lift the receiver and say, "Welcome to the Spring Side Childcare Center, how may I help you?"

"Hi, Jen, it's Helen. I have a flat tire, so I'm waiting for help to come and change it. Do you mind doing the tours until I arrive? I don't know how long they will take to arrive and then fix it," she huffs.

"Oh no, are you okay? Of course, I can do that. Is there anything else?" I offer.

"I'm fine. It's just a big nuisance, really. Just the tours would be great. I'll check the work emails from my laptop and do some work while I wait. I will see you as soon as I get in. Call me if there are any problems."

"Yes, of course. Stay safe. If there is anything else, let me know. Otherwise, I'll see you soon."

We disconnect and I pop my head back into the room. "Emma, Helen has a flat tire, so she needs me to do the tours until she gets here. Will you be okay with that?" I ask.

Concern etches her face. "Yes, that's fine. What time are they booked for today?"

"Nine."

"That's now." She giggles.

"I better get myself organized. I'll catch you soon."

I close the door and power walk to Helen's office. I grab the information packs for the parents today and return to the main desk to fill in the sections required. I'm about to get started when the bell above the door rings and I peer up into the dark eyes of Thomas. *No way!*

I duck my head down to avert my gaze, buying myself time to collect my thoughts and hide the heat rising to my cheeks. I hear the click of fancy work shoes as I pretend I'm absorbed in paperwork. The click stops right in front of me. My heart beats erratically.

He clears his throat. "Good morning... Jen."

He's holding a younger child—one I didn't see the other day.

I'm trying to absorb the new information as a quiet reply leaves my lips. "Morning. I work here."

Duh, I think he knows you work here, idiot.

His brows go from pinched to lifted. My gaze treks over his navy suit and crisp white shirt until I reach his eyes. The outfit isn't what makes me melt—it's the little girl wrapped tightly around his neck, hanging onto his matching tie, wearing a purple tutu dress with the most beautiful blond curls.

Lily is in a school uniform, hugging his leg, but her shy face changes as soon as she registers who I am.

"Daddy." She tugs at his navy pants and repeats it until he lowers his eyes to her. "Yes, sweetheart?" His soft voice causes my mouth to rise in the corner.

"That lady is the one that fell over my blocks."

I inwardly cringe.

"Yes, she is." He doesn't indulge in her further, which I appreciate. "Sorry, Jen. I'm here for a tour for my little Rose." At the mention of her name, she squeezes his throat and clings to him.

I walk around the desk and over to the little girl clutching his side. "Morning, Rose. Would you like to come see all the toys we have here? We have so many. I'm sure you'll find one you love." Unfortunately, she doesn't move an inch.

The smell of Thomas's spicy vanilla scent wafts in my nose, causing my nostrils to flare. I ignore it to focus on Rose.

"Why are your cheeks turning red?" Lily questions me. "Did you hurt them too?"

Shit. Really, Lily?

Why does this keep happening to me?

"Ah, well... no, Lily. It's just a little warm here." When the words leave my lips, I want to kick myself. *How awkward.*

Rose lifts her head out of the crook of Thomas' neck and takes a glance at me before diving back, burying her face back into the safety of her dad.

"Rose." He chuckles at her response.

"How about we walk around and I'll give you the tour of our center? When we get to the toys, she may want to hop down and play," I suggest.

"Good idea."

Spinning on my heel, I grab my folder and pen and show him around. Lily walks next to me. She seems extra confident for her age, and I wonder about her mom. I bet she's confident, intelligent, and beautiful. A pang of envy hits, and I want to slap myself for being jealous of the mother of these girls.

I lead them into the toddler room where Emma is shaping playdough with the kids.

"Emma, this is Thomas and his girls, Lily and Rose. Rose is going to be in the toddler room."

She smiles. "Hi and welcome."

He barely glances back in her direction, his eyes finding mine again, just as quick as he left them. "Thanks."

Emma is a beautiful redhead with crystal-blue eyes; most guys are instantly drooling over her. Thomas, though, doesn't give her a second glance, which I won't lie, makes me feel good. I hide a grin and watch as Thomas rubs Rose's back, crouching in front of a barbie house. She still clutches on to him, not wanting to let go.

"Rose, darling. There are some fun toys here. Turn around and just have a look. I won't put you down. I just want you to see the toys they have here," he says gently.

She peels her head out of his neck and peers around. Her eyes light up and she smiles at the fluffy teddies on the table—clearly her weakness.

"Teddies," she says in the sweetest honey voice.

I walk over, pick a cream-colored teddy up, and bring it over to her. Her head leans back into Thomas, so I pause and stretch my hand out so she can grab it. She studies it and then reaches out to snatches it. A small win.

"What time does she nap?" I ask. "We like to stick to home schedules."

"Around eleven but can be up to one."

I nod and write it down.

"Any food allergies?"

"No."

I scribble that down too.

"Okay, it's almost the end of the tour. I just need to finish the rest of the questions at the desk."

He dips his chin, and I lead the way, with Thomas and the girls trailing behind me. I sit at the desk, and he stands with Rose still in his arms and Lily beside him.

"Are you wanting to enroll her in the centre?"

"Yes. Definitely. Can I do that now?"

I nod, "Of course."

I open the directory for families and with my pen ready, I ask, "In an emergency, if we can't contact you, who can we write down for permission to pick up Rose? And there are times other people may pick up Rose. We need to write down those contacts too." I grip my pen to the point my knuckles turn white and hold my breath, afraid to meet his brown eyes, waiting for his wife's name.

"It would be my mom and dad, Margaret and Geoff."

My brow furrows, but I quickly scribble down the details he calls out. I'm so curious why he makes no mention of their mother. I wish I hadn't kissed him. I would never kiss a married man. The thought makes me want to vomit. Even though I want to know about her, it would be rude and unprofessional to ask now, so I push the thought from my mind and lean forward, sliding my chair closer to the desk.

Lifting my gaze to meet his, I say in my most professional voice, "Thank you for the information. We are all set for Rose. When you are ready, we can book her in for a few hours for a trial. Let me know a date and I'll put her name down."

He rubs his clean-shaven jaw. "I'm due to start work next week, so could I do one later this week?"

I scan the intake book. "What day works best for you? We normally suggest an hour or two for the first day and gradually build her time up. That's if you can?"

"Makes sense and I'll work around it. How about Thursday for a trial?"

I check the book before confirming. "Yes, Thursday will work. Bring Rose in at nine, and we can see how she settles in and go from there." I glance back to look at his face.

He nods. "Okay, thanks, Jen. We better get Lily to school, but thanks for your patience. Girls, say bye to Jen, please."

"Bye, Jen." Lily waves so fast at me.

I wave back at her with the same excitement, which makes her beam.

"Bye, Lily," I call out before gazing at Rose, who has turned to stare at me but hasn't said a word. "Bye, Rose." She studies me, but never utters a word as she assesses me.

"Sorry. She's shy with new people," Thomas mumbles from behind her head.

I wave it off. "It's fine, really. I'm sure she will warm up to us in no time," I say, trying to appease the guilt etched on his face. "It's normal for her age, when they go to a new place,"

"Bye, Jen." His lip rises in a sensual smile, instantly sending tingles down my spine.

"Bye," I croak out, watching him leave.

Taking a deep breath, I get up out of the office chair and trek back to the room to give Emma a hand with the toddlers.

"My God, Jen, who was that delicious man? He was watching you like a hawk. You two know each other? I need all the details. Spill the tea right now," Emma insists.

CHAPTER 6

JENNIFER

EMMA STANDS IN FRONT of me, hands on hips, eyebrows raised, waiting for an answer. She's been a sweet friend and a great co-worker for the last year, but I don't feel comfortable going into too much detail. And there isn't much to tell. I kissed him on a drunken night out and now I find out he has a family. Not something I want to shout from the rooftop. The interaction with Thomas will be kept for Olivia and Katie only. I know Emma saw little of the interaction between Thomas and me because we were not in the room with her long enough.

"He was not, and I don't know him personally." I preoccupy myself with packing toys away, avoiding eye contact with her.

"Are you sure about that? He looked like a love-struck puppy."

I turn toward her at that comment, my mouth hanging open, as she mimics a sad puppy dog face. I roll my eyes at her actions and return to packing more toys away, but the corner of my lip rises.

"You, Emma, are seeing things," I say.

"If you say so..."

The door swings open and we turn our heads at the movement.

"Jen, Emma, I'm so sorry. What a nightmare," Helen puffs, saving me from further questions.

Helen's short brunette hair is ruffled and unkempt, as if she's ran her hands through it a lot. It's so carefree and unlike Helen. Her lipstick is completely worn off, which is rare. It's a testament to how bad her morning has been, I guess.

"It's fine. Helen. We have it handled here. I'll turn the kettle on and make you some tea," I say.

Helen's shoulders slump and she exhales a large breath. "That would be amazing, Jen. I'll be in my office. Could you please bring it to me there? Would you mind?"

I smile. "Not at all."

"You're a star."

Ten minutes later, I knock on Helen's door.

"Come in, Jen. You don't need to knock."

I step in and move some papers on her desk to lower the cup of tea, then take a seat across from Helen.

"Did I miss much when I was out? Give me a quick rundown." She picks up the tea and takes a sip.

I draw in a breath before talking. "Only one tour so far. A two-year-old girl named Rose. I booked her for a trial this Thursday, and she officially starts next week. I wrote it in the appointment book. And there is another tour this afternoon. Did you want me to do it for you?" I glance at the mess scattered over her desk.

She takes another sip. "No, thanks. I'll welcome the distraction after this morning. I got all the emails sorted while I waited for help."

I nod and stand. "I better get back and help Emma with the lunch and nap round."

"Good idea," Helen mumbles as I spin and exit her office.

I still have a few hours of my shift to go. All I want to do when I get home is watch Netflix in bed. I sigh. I should really go for a run tonight. I've avoided it since my embarrassing encounter with Thomas on Saturday. Although apart from today, I haven't seen my new neighbors around, so maybe it's safe to fit a quick one in.

When I arrive home, no one else in my family is home yet. Taking advantage of having the place to myself, I flop on the couch with a bag of chips. Before I know it, half an hour has slipped by, and I need to get moving before I ditch the exercise altogether. I quickly change into shorts and an oversized black t-shirt. I shove my headphones in, phone in hand, and go outside. I lock the door before I pull it closed.

I run in the opposite direction of Thomas's house and do a small run of the block in twenty minutes. It's slower than I usually do, but my legs keep giving out on me and I have to use the bathroom. I hold the left side of my stomach, panting, as I make it back to the front door. The driveway is still empty of my family's cars, so I stuff my hand into the pocket of my shorts and grab the—*Shit*. I frantically pat down my body, anywhere that could hide a key, but... nothing.

I'm busting for the toilet and an idiot for not going before I took a run. Standing at the door, I shuffle from side to side and look around to take my mind off the urge, but it is not helping ease my need.

I ball my hands into tight fists as I glance around the front yard for a spot, but there are no trees around and only a few small bushes along the path. The rest is grass, and I would be visible to cars that drive past. I can't hold it much longer. My parents will still be working so I call my sister—no answer. I try another few times. No luck.

I let out an audible sigh.

My parents should have listened to me when I mentioned leaving a key around the house for emergencies. Like today.

Desperate times call for desperate measures. I hustle to the entry of the house next door. *His door.* I scan the door for a bell but don't find one. I frown. With no doorbell to press, I raise my fist and knock on the door.

Minutes feel like hours, as I wait for someone to answer. But no one comes. His white Range Rover is parked in the drive, so I know they are home. I let out a deep breath and bang harder, shuffling from foot to foot. My bladder is spasming, reminding me why I'm standing at *his* door.

I hear the running and high-pitched squeals of the girls, which calms my heartbeat a tad until I hear heavy footsteps. The wooden door opens.

"Jen?"

"Hello," Lily speaks from lower down.

"Lily, could you stand back a moment, please? I just want to open the door properly."

His whole face comes into view. His brows are furrowed. His hand has not left the metal door handle. My heart skips at the sight of him. I feel a rise in my body temperature and perspiration running down my back, making the t-shirt grip like a second skin. He is in casual clothes—a white t-shirt, a pair of sweatpants, and bare feet. *Shit, he is hot.*

I clear my throat. "Hi, Tom. Hi, girls! I'm so sorry to bother you... I, er, need to use your bathroom." I lower my eyes to meet Lily's, avoiding her dad's.

"Why? Don't you have one at your house?" Lily squeaks, her head tilting up in my direction.

"Good question, Lily. I accidentally locked myself out, and I cannot get back inside." I twist my hands together, trying to shift the pain away from the bladder.

"Where are your keys?" Lily's questions continue.

"Inside my house."

Her face scrunches up at my answer.

My lips perk at her confusion.

"Lily, please, that's enough questions. How about we let Jen in to go to the bathroom?" Thomas steps aside so I can enter his home.

"Thank you so much. Again, I'm so sorry for interrupting." I step forward and onto the glossy white tiles.

My skin prickles as I pass him in the entry. He closes the door, locking it behind me, and I stand to the side of the large hallway.

"It's fine. The bathroom is down this way. Follow me."

The girls sprint past me in pretty matching white dresses. Rose trails behind Lily, and I smile as thoughts of growing up with my sister Megan filter in my mind. Megan was my shadow. She'd play any game I wanted to, and we were very close. The girls remind me of us.

As I follow him, I catch a glimpse of a dark bedroom with heavy drapes that are pulled closed. *His* bedroom. I wondered what it would look like. I would love to take a peek. Would it be a wood bed or a more modern style? My bladder twinges, reminding me I need to go and how inappropriate my thoughts are. Why does he have this effect on me?

We walk past a stunning white and marble kitchen with modern appliances, and he stops. "The bathroom is just through that hall." He points to the right. "Lily and Rose, can you leave Jen alone and help me in the kitchen?"

I laugh under my breath at his warning, but right now, I don't care if the girls follow. I'm busting at the seams. I hurry off to the bathroom and when I finish, I walk back to the kitchen where he has two white cups on the counter.

"Do you want a drink?" he offers as I wander closer to stand behind the island.

"Thanks for the offer, but I wouldn't want to take up more of your time. I'm sure you're busy." My gaze finds the girls in the family room, and I realize it's probably their dinnertime. "Thank you for letting me in. I don't even want to think about what I—" I pause as heat rises to my cheeks, not wanting to finish that sentence.

"What about the other neighbor?" he questions.

My gaze returns to him. "He isn't home much, because he travels a lot for work."

"Ah, okay. It's still early. I'm sure tea or coffee won't kill us." He winks and heat rises from my neck, leaving me speechless. At my lack of response, his eyebrow perks up, waiting for my answer to his question.

"Right, ah, I would love tea."

I pull out a bar stool that is tucked under the island and sit, trying to keep my balance so I don't fall over since I seem to make an idiot of myself in front of him. He probably thinks of me as some juvenile girl.

Without warning, the *Bluey* theme song blares through the kitchen, and I jump at the sudden increase in volume.

"Lily. Turn the television down, now. Do not be rude." His voice is stern.

I smirk as I turn my head to follow the sound. Lily and Rose are in the family room dancing and singing the words to the intro song. They are too cute. Just like their father. It's just a shame he is married.

They ask me to join them dancing and I can't say no to their adorable pleading faces. Lily walks over to me and grabs my hand, unexpectedly dragging me in and swinging her hips. I move mine and dance to the theme song, which doesn't last long. And I beam down at her at how easily she has taken to me.

After the song ends, I turn back around to face him, walking and watch him move around the kitchen. The muscles he keeps hidden are clearer through his tight white t-shirt. And I curse to myself at these thoughts that don't turn off.

I pull out the stool and sit. He stirs his coffee with his right hand with his left laid on the countertop and I notice the ring finger—empty.

Has he forgotten to put it on? I can't recall ever noticing one. I could kick myself for never paying attention.

Divorced? Widowed?

"Do you take sugar or milk?"

My gaze flies back to him. "No sugar and just a splash of milk, please."

He peers down at his finger and balls his fist before dragging it from the counter and dropping it beside him as he walks over to the refrigerator. A pang of guilt hits my stomach. With the hand still clenched beside his thigh, he grabs the milk before closing the door and walking back to the drinks. When he arrives at the counter, his fist unclenches, and I glance up into a pair of empty brown eyes. The spark is no longer there as he stares back at me with a blank look.

He slides the tea across the marble counter, and I take a sip of the hot drink, welcoming the burn on my tongue.

"Thanks for this. I'll head out as soon as I finish," I mumble, keeping my focus on the mug between my hands, ready to escape the tension I created.

I should leave, but I can't quite bring myself to get up and go. I can't help but wonder what happened, but it's none of my business. I'm ready to bolt when Thomas stops me in my tracks.

"She died."

Chapter 7

THOMAS

I SWALLOW THE LUMP that's formed in my throat. "It's just me and the girls," I say matter-of-factly.

Jennifer's wide brown eyes gaze back at me. Her bottom lip drops open, but no words leave her lips.

Those words slipping out allow my body to sigh in relief, giving me the courage to continue. I know she deserves more than those few words, but I don't know how much I am willing to give right now. I start slow, hoping it will be enough for Jennifer to understand me.

"I'm a widower," I say in a broken whisper, only loud enough for her to hear.

My gaze darts to the other room, to check if the girls heard anything, but they're distracted as they sit and watch television. Jennifer's warm, accepting, pity-free look makes me feel instantly relieved. Unshed tears sit on her lashes, but the way she turns her head and peers at my girls, I know it's raw sadness for them. How will two little girls who have lost their mother to death handle growing up without her? It's the same question I keep asking myself. Why couldn't it have been me?

My throat constricts, so I grab the drink and sip. My heart isn't ready to say anything else right now, at risk of falling apart or exposing myself. I don't want to do that in front of the girls. I don't want to upset them or cause confusion. They're too little to understand adult emotions.

"I'm sorry." Her voice is small and cracks.

I nod. "Thanks. I..."

The girls run over, interrupting.

"Cookie," Lily sings softly.

"Me some," Rose coos beside her.

Lily grips the counter, jumping up and down. Rose is too small to reach, so she bounces on the spot.

A small smile cracks as I peek down at their excited faces, the feelings of sorrow zapped at the sight of my girls. "It's almost dinnertime, but you can have one each. No more before dinner."

"Okay, Daddy."

I hand them over and they run back to the family room.

"Well, I better let you make dinner and start preparing mine." Jennifer slips off the stool and tucks it back to where it belongs.

I lower my head as a heaviness hits the center of my chest. "You can stay for dinner with us. I'm making lasagna and there will be plenty."

A soft gasp escapes her, and she glances down before meeting my gaze. "I would love to, but I really have to get going. I need to prepare dinner for the family." Something in the tone of her voice tells me she doesn't want to leave either, but she must.

I grin at her. "Maybe next time."

Heat rises to her cheeks, and she bites down on her lip. I stare at her mouth, my own lips parting, and force my thoughts from drifting in a sexual direction.

Why is it every time I'm near her, my common sense disappears? In any other circumstance, in another life, I wouldn't think twice about kissing her. But now, with the girls, I can't afford to. I swallow hard and stare at her.

"Definitely, next time. But I'm so sorry, I wish I could stay." she repeats huskily, then pivots to take her cup to the sink.

Not wanting her to feel bad I shake my head, "Don't be sorry."

She glances down before meeting my gaze again.

"Thanks again for letting me come over and use your bathroom. I promise to take the keys with me next time." She laughs, then calls out "Bye, Lily and Rose. I will see you soon." She waves as she passes the family room on her way to the entryway.

The girls wave back, and Lily calls out, "Bye."

I follow her through the house. "I'll see you out."

Nodding, she steps to my front door. "This house is gorgeous. Are the girls settled here yet?"

"Isn't it? As soon as I saw it, I knew it was ours. The space and the interior, plus the pool is a bonus. The girls have taken the move to this house really well. I think they love the space, but also it's not that far from where we were, so it wasn't a big change."

Her head whips to me. "And where were you before this?" she says, surprise in her tone.

"Just on the other side of town. My parents are still there, but it's only an hour drive, so it's not that bad, even if my mother thinks I moved to the country." I chuckle at the thought of my mom. I love her, but her dramatics are comedic.

"Oh, I can only imagine." Her soft laugh warms me.

"My parents are protective too, so I can understand your pain."

We reach my door, so she stands aside as I lean forward to grab the door handle. My face is just inches from hers, and my body trembles with familiarity. Holding my breath, I yank the wooden door and pull it open.

"Thanks, I'll see you soon." She pushes the metal door open before I can do it for her, and steps down, turning to face me.

"You're welcome to come here anytime." Without thinking, I reach out and brush my fingers over her cheek.

She leans into my hand, startling me. I breathe out shakily and retract my hand when I realize what I have done. I take a small step back, needing the distance between us.

"Bye, Tom," she says with a wry smile.

I watch her every step back to her house. When she's out of my line of sight, I release the breath I was holding.

"Bye," I whisper, knowing she won't hear.

As I step back inside my house, my head is spinning, my heart pounding. Feeling like I'm in a daze, I walk into the kitchen and cook dinner. I bathe the girls before we eat, and then finally tuck them in bed.

Once they are fast asleep, I sit in the family room, my feet resting on the coffee table, and pick up my phone to dial James. My head is still trying to figure out what to do with Jennifer. I know he will listen. Even if his advice regarding women is not to my taste, I just need to talk.

It only rings a few times before he answers. "Tom, what's up?" I can tell by his relaxed attitude he's in the office alone.

"Still working?"

"Yeah, bud. Are you okay? You sound... off?"

I chuckle. "How do you know?"

"How long have we known each other, Tom? The only sound I don't know is when you come, but I like a little mystery," he teases.

"I'm happy you don't know those finer details. I think you know enough, by the sounds of it."

"How about I come over for a beer? I can drive over now. I just gotta pack up here." I can hear his fingers typing away on his keyboard a million miles an hour. He's probably behind on work from helping me out with the move.

"No, I'll be fine. It's just, my head is spinning... Women are confusing." I sigh.

I hear a few taps and his keys jingle. "You and women in one sentence definitely requires a beer in person. I'm heading over. Do I need to grab some on my way?"

I roll my eyes at his urgency. "No, I have beer here."

"See you soon."

We disconnect and I shake my head. He may be a billionaire, but it doesn't stop him from dropping his life for me in an instant.

His office is in the city, which means he won't take long to get here, so I open Safari on my phone and google a local pizza place. The least I can do is order two large pizzas for delivery.

I don't want the girls woken up by anyone, so I watch for lights to flash in the drive for either James or the pizza delivery.

The pizza arrives first, so I bound from the couch and rush toward the door. As I'm taking the pizza boxes from the delivery guy and handing over money, James' sleek black Bugatti pulls up in my driveway. It totally screams money and sex, which is fitting for James. He doesn't have any issues with the ladies because he doesn't keep the same woman twice.

The car door swings open, and his tall frame, wearing a black suit and a crisp white shirt and black tie, exits with his brown hair still swept to the side in perfect arrangement. He is intimidating as hell, even to me, one of his oldest friends.

I whistle a sexy tune and he chuckles, shaking his head with a wicked grin on his face.

"Fuck off." His shit-eating grin lights up his face as he struts toward my house, holding his briefcase in one hand and phone in the other, pure power and sex.

He stalks up to me and pats my back.

"Thanks for coming," I say, balancing the pizza boxes as we step inside. "You really didn't have to. You could have stayed in the office and chatted on the phone."

I close the door, and we walk to the kitchen.

"I know, but when do you ever call me with women troubles?" His eyebrow rises in question.

I sigh. "Right, well, it's not like I have much experience."

"So, you called the expert." He winks and places his briefcase on the counter, setting his phone on top.

I roll my eyes and grab beers from the fridge, handing him one cold bottle.

He follows me to the den so we don't wake the girls. "If that's what you want to be known as, then sure."

I turn on the television, which is larger than the family room, perfect for sports with the boys and movies with the girls. I set my beer down on the glass coffee table and the pizza boxes next to it. I flick the television to football and take a long pull of my beer, then I take a piece of cheesy pizza and bite into it, groaning at the delicious taste hitting my tongue.

"That's the sound you should be making eating pussy, not pizza." I cough, trying to dislodge the pizza that's now caught in my throat. James is unfazed and chugs his beer and grabs a slice before sitting back in the black recliner. "Now, are you going to tell me what's going on?" he asks, between chews. "You know you are killing me."

After I finish coughing, I take a pull of my beer to wash the pizza away and then hold it, to pick at the label. "I met a girl."

James twists in his chair to face me, causing me to tilt my head. "And who is she?" His eyebrow quirks.

I glance back down at my beer because I know I won't hear the end of it.

"Well, you know the night at the Three Dots bar?"

"Yeah..."

"She's the same person who fell outside my house and is now my new neighbor." I rush out.

James thrusts upright in his chair. "No fucking way?" he questions.

"I know. I'm not going to pursue her. She is young. What would she want with me? I'm a single, old dad. I need to focus on the girls."

I wish I wasn't so damn attracted to her. And it doesn't help that her dad is over all the time checking on me and the girls. And here I want his daughter. I don't want to be causing issues with my new neighbors.

"I think that's her choice. You shouldn't decide for her. I'm sure if she were to pursue you back, she would understand your situation."

I let his words sink in, knowing he's right, but the other part of me feels guilty. I don't deserve to be happy. Victoria doesn't get that same opportunity. And I should focus solely on the girls, not fantasize about Jennifer.

"Yeah, I guess... I've seen her twice since the accident."

"When? Come on, spit it out, bud. I can't help with these shitty details."

"I'm due to start with Josh on Monday, so I need a new childcare center for Rose. I booked a tour of the one just around the corner. When I arrived, guess who conducted the tour?" I wait for a beat before saying, "Jennifer."

"Hot name."

I side-eye him at his comment. He ignores me and reaches for another piece of pizza while I continue with the story.

"During the tour, Rose hid in my neck the whole time, but Jen got her to open up with a teddy."

"Jen? Nicknames already," he says with a knowing smirk, his eyebrows raised.

"You're a dick." I roll my eyes.

He says nothing else, just keeps eating while I continue.

"Anyway, this afternoon she knocked on my door because she locked herself out of her house, so she came in to use the bathroom and then stayed for a drink. I was making them when I caught her looking at my ring finger, but she said nothing."

I took the ring off a few months ago when people would ask about my wife all the time. It was too hard to explain. At first it was strange, and I didn't like not having it on but now I'm adjusting.

"Did you tell her about Victoria?" he asks.

"No, I freaked the fuck out. I told her she's dead."

"Oh, shit. And how did she take that?"

"Great. She felt sad for the girls but there was no pity. You know how much I hate it when people pity me."

He nods, his fingers tapping the leather, waiting for me to finish the story.

"And then she left, but when I said goodbye at the door, I touched her face. I have no idea why I did it. But I feel so fucking stupid. What is wrong with me? I need my head checked." I shake my head, trying to remove my embarrassment, my inability to resist my urges.

Deep laughter leaves his lips. "You got it bad."

I groan and take the rest of the beer in one long pull. "What the hell do I do? I have never dated anyone other than Victoria, and we both know Victoria was a spitfire... Jen is shy. I don't know what to do. They are totally opposite." I look over at him. "Help me. I need to turn these feelings off."

"I don't understand feelings. You called the wrong person for that. I really don't see why you can't get with her. I'm sorry, I just don't... Just hook up with her."

I pinch the bridge of my nose, before sneering. "Are you serious? I don't just fuck around, Jay. I'm not you. I can't do one night of no strings attached."

He shrugs his shoulders, unfazed. "Your loss... It's actually fun. You should try it."

"No chance, and you're not helping at all." I scoff, shaking my head. "But in all seriousness, I need to be the adult and resist the urges."

"Yes, but you still deserve to be happy."

I stand, unable to answer him, and take the empty pizza boxes and beers to the trashcan. Do I deserve to be happy? People keep telling me I do, but why don't I believe them? I snag two more beers before I return and hand James a cold one.

"Thanks for coming here and listening to my shit when you could have been working or out."

"I'm here for you, anytime. You always get me whenever you need me. You're my family."

I leaned forward and clink my bottleneck against his before settling back into my leather chair, laying my head back, thinking about the previous year and how numb I was. And how Jennifer has ignited a spark, causing me to feel again.

CHAPTER 8

JENNIFER

I HEAR THE CREAK of the floors as I sense someone behind me. I turn around from the sink. Megan is standing at the counter, her eyes running over my outfit.

"You tried calling me earlier. I tried calling you back, but I guess you were running?" she questions.

I don't want to mention Thomas or the locked-out incident. I'm still recovering from the ordeal.

"Yeah, I just wanted to know if you would be home for dinner. But here you are. And how was school?" I say, trying to keep my tone as neutral as possible so she can't pick up on my nerves.

She shrugs. "Same as always—shit. Did you need a hand with the washing up?"

I nod. "Actually, could you? There aren't many left. I want to call Olivia and Katie for a minute."

I hold out the sponge, and she steps toward me, grabbing it from me. "Yeah, go. I got it."

"Thanks," I respond before dashing out of the kitchen without glancing back.

Finding the TV remote in my bedroom, I switch it on. I need noise to drown out the conversation I'm about to have with the girls. I don't want Megan to hear anything until I'm ready to tell her.

I scroll through my contacts until I come to 'Olivia' and tap on her name. The phone rings in my ear and my heartbeat rapidly climbs in my chest as I wait for her to answer.

"Hey. What are you doing?"

I trail over to my bed and collapse flat on my back on the double bed, staring at my ceiling as I answer. "I went for a run earlier..." I pause. "Can you talk right now? Are you around anyone?" I whisper.

"Just hanging out in my room. Why?" Curiosity laces her tone.

"Let me add Katie to the call. I don't want to explain this twice. Once for me will be enough."

"Okayyy," she says, drawing the word out.

I pull the phone away and hit the add button and return the phone to my ear. It rings, and my palms sweat as I wait for her to pick up.

"Hello?" Katie answers.

"Hey, are you free to chat? I have Olivia on the line. I want to do a three-way call."

I can hear footsteps and it sounds like she is outside. "Yeah, I'm going for a walk by myself, so go for it," she puffs.

I hit the button, so we're all on the call together. "Are you both there?" I ask.

"Yep," they say in unison.

The phone is silent. They are waiting for me. My nerves begin to pick up. But I push past and reveal.

"So, I, uh, kind of like someone."

Olivia's unmistakeable high-pitched squeal comes through the phone. I can't hear Katie's response. I pull the phone away from my ear for a second before putting it back. A smile tugs at my lip at her dramatic tone. "Calm down. I don't need anyone in your family knowing."

"Just tell us who this guy is. Tell me everything right now," she demands.

"And leave nothing out," Katie puffs out.

I chuckle. "Okay, well, there have been a few instances..."

"*What?* And I'm only finding out about this now?" Olivia screams at me through the phone. "Jen. How could you do this to us?"

I cover my face with my spare hand, groaning. "Don't Jen me. I didn't know if it was serious or not. And it's not that exciting. Just let me talk, will you?" Olivia and her dramatics.

"Alright, alright." I hear her exhale.

I lift my hand off my face and sit up, leaning back on my pillows, trying to figure out how to explain it all. How do I explain everything that is Thomas? The emotions swimming in my gut tell me I need them to know everything. I need help with these new feelings.

"The night of your birthday, Olivia, at the Three Dots bar, well, I chatted with a guy, and we had a drink together at the bar, then I ended up dancing with him and kissing him." I decide to keep the orgasm to myself. "I was admittedly tipsy. After I went to check on you, I went back to meet up with him again. But he was gone. I never thought I would see him again... But a few days ago, I fell outside my new neighbor's house while on a run. Guess who my new neighbor is?"

"It's him... No way," Olivia says.

"Yep. Then today, I locked myself out of the house. I forgot my keys inside when I went on my run, and I needed the bathroom. I had to knock on his door. I was that desperate." I laugh at how ridiculous it sounds.

"It's fate, like some fairy tale." Olivia's tone is giddy.

"Not all fairy tales. I haven't told you the biggest twist yet..." I sigh, remembering the two important people in this story.

"Oh, I don't like the way you're saying that," Katie huffs.

"He, uh, is a widower. His wife died."

Katie's voice whispers, "Wow."

"And I'm not finished," I say. "He has two little girls."

"Oh, *shit*," Katie says.

"That's, ah, not what I was expecting you to say," Olivia adds.

I exhale and continue. "I didn't know the night I met him. I knew he was older, but I'm still trying to wrap my head around it. He has his little one signed up at work, so I will see him there too. He is literally everywhere. I can't avoid him."

"Okay, I get that, but he lives next door, and then the youngest daughter signed up at your work? I'm telling you that's some fate intervention," Olivia says.

Katie cuts in, "But you said you kind of like him? Do the kids change that?" I'm about to answer, but she continues. "Are you really ready to be a stepmom? You're still young, so just be careful. Obviously, for you to be calling us, there is something there you want. I don't want you getting hurt."

I close my eyes, trying to process my thoughts, trying to figure out the best way to articulate the words to describe the emotional turmoil going on inside me.

"I love kids, so that's not an issue. I would happily date a guy with kids, but I don't know him or the girls well enough. The feelings I have when I am around him though..." I touch my face where he stroked not long ago, stirring feelings of desire, remembering how his hands felt on my body in the club.

"I can't explain it. It's intense... I need to figure this out, my head is all over the place." I sigh.

"I don't see a problem," Olivia says. "Why are you worried? You're into him, so go for it."

I wish I wasn't so reserved and just dove straight into things like Olivia, but it's not me. And there are two little girls in the mix now and I need to tread carefully so as not to hurt their feelings.

"Hmm. I don't know. Just because I'm attracted to him doesn't mean I can't have issues. He has serious baggage. I don't even know everything about his wife or how she actually died." I release a heavy breath.

"I agree, but get to know him, Jen. Sitting here talking to us will not get to know him," Katie says. "But just be careful."

A loud knock on my bedroom door interrupts our conversation, making me jump. Megan calls through the door above the blaring television.

"I better go. Meg is calling me."

"Okay, but make sure you let us know what happens," Katie says.

"I want updates and every detail. You never talk like this about a guy, like ever," Olivia coos.

I laugh. "Okay, okay. Bye, girls."

"Bye," they both say.

I hang up and toss the phone on the bed. Once I thank Megan for doing the dishes, I climb back in bed, closing my eyes, I cover my face with both arms, mentally wiped. Exhaustion hits my body, and I let sleep take me under.

I'm a stalker. I'm lying back on my bed, scrolling through social media on my phone, looking for Thomas with the television on in the background.

I'm not really paying attention to the show, but as I type his name on my phone, a loud bang makes me jump. My heart is frantically beating in my chest. I close the app on my phone and toss it beside me before glancing at the now black television screen.

I throw myself up off the bed and push the TV around, looking at the cords. I fiddle around with them. With no luck in fixing it, I step over to the bed, scoop the remote up, and press buttons on it. No luck with that either. I huff loudly. *Shit.* I really hope Dad can fix this, because I can't afford another one. This must be my punishment for searching for Thomas online.

"Dad," I call out from my room. Even though the door is closed, he can usually hear me. After a minute, I still get nothing. I shout louder this time. "Daaaad."

Again, I get no response. Throwing the remote down on the bed, I rip open my bedroom door and frown. The house is empty. Mom and Dad are nowhere to be found. They must have gone out, but just to be sure, I walk outside to the backyard. Nothing. Where are they?

I wander back inside and move toward the front door to check the cars parked in the drive. Both Megan and Mom's cars are gone. Dad's is parked next to mine. I wander out and stand frozen on the path. My flat gaze lands on Thomas changing his tire. I lick my lips at the sight of him in a black t-shirt, tight blue jeans and his tanned arm muscles bulging with every movement.

I linger and watch him move effortlessly to change the tire. Picking up tools and getting his hands dirty, the opposite of the other versions I have seen. He looks sexy in anything, but this dirty mechanic look is making my nerve endings stir and wetness pool between my thighs. I'm wishing I was that tire right now, getting touched by his expert fingers again, giving me the greatest orgasm of my life.

He moves and I can't see him. I'm too far away. So, I take a step forward and cause a loud snap. *Shit. Busted.* I glance down at the twig I snapped in half with my foot. I glance back up, hoping I would get away with it. But I can see him staring at me. Thomas's head is tilted with a look of surprise. He's probably trying to figure out what I'm doing out here.

Shit. What am I doing out here?

That's right. My television is broken. I carefully walk over, taking a few breaths to slow my heartbeat down. It's not working. The closer I get to him, the more it accelerates. He stands up. Now that I am closer, I see Thomas has a glisten of sweat across his forehead and a red flush on his cheeks. He's obviously working hard, and his appearance causes my sex to clench, and my body temperature rises. Being this close reminds me of his hands on me.

I pinch my lips together to stop myself from smiling too hard. Thomas's eyes bore into mine as he swipes his hand across his forehead. He smudges grease on his skin, and I have to restrain myself from leaning forward and rubbing it off.

"Hi." A mischievous grin forms on his face.

"Hi, Tom,"

"Are you okay?"

"I came looking for my dad. My TV made a loud noise, and it's all black." I stumble, feeling every bit stupid.

"He left with your mom. I can come look at it?"

Fidgeting with my fingers, I debate whether I say yes or no. But he busted me, perving on him, so looking at my TV is no big deal.

"Only if you're finished with your tire."

His eyes dance with humor, "I'm done. I just need to pack up. The TV will take me five minutes."

"Okay." I turn to walk into the house, knowing he is behind me. The hairs on my neck prickle as I feel him there. And most likely checking me out in my boring black sweats.

Entering my house and down to my room, I run my hand through my hair, hoping to calm some nerves down.

I enter and stand to the side, allowing him to pass, and I once again watch him use his damn good hands on something other than me. *What is wrong with me? First, I'm jealous of the tire and now the TV?*

But I just haven't had enough of his hands or mouth. I run my eyes downwards over his body at a much closer distance and it's even better. I'm biting down onto my lip to prevent panting. Not knowing what to do with my hands, I cross them over my chest and concentrate on slowing my breathing down. The air in the room feels thick with his manly sweat, and it's intoxicating. If I wasn't standing inside my parents' house, I would try to kiss him. It's taking everything I have not to give in.

Thomas backs away, and the TV is on.

"All fixed."

"Thanks so much. I owe you."

A rush of blood hits my cheeks as his eyes darken, knowing where his thoughts are going.

I need out of my parents' house. I feel like my breaths are quicker and my head is spinning with how much I want to touch him. Needing the fresh air from outside, I walk out of my room and he follows. I walk back beside the car and pause.

I know I should go back inside, but my body doesn't want to move. My feet are glued to the spot. He looks over my body seductively, and I feel a flush rising from my chest from his scrutiny.

"What happened?" My voice comes out strained.

He swivels his head to the flat tire. "Looks like I drove over a screw."

I gasp.

"A bad choice of word?" he teases.

I tug on my sweater neck. Needing to cool myself down.

"No." I shake my head. "You and screw in the same sentence..."

He tips his head back and a roar of laughter leaves his chest, but as he lowers his gaze back to mine there is a fire burning there and I suddenly feel unsteady on my legs.

"You are the devil."

"Am I tempting you?" I taunt.

He hisses, and bites down on his bottom lip. Tempting me himself. I must not be the only one fighting the sexual tension between us.

He takes a step forward and I take another one, inching closer into his personal space.

I stare at his mouth as my tongue darts out to moisten my lips. Urging him to kiss me. With a sharp intake of breath, he leans down, bringing his lips closer to mine. I can't wait to taste him again. I close my eyes in preparation, his hot breath tickling my lips. My body vibrates with desire.

The loud sound of my door slamming open has us freezing on the spot, and I step back, putting some distance between us.

"Sorry. I shouldn't have done that," Thomas mutters.

My mouth opens and closes, but words can't seem to escape. Mom and Dad are approaching, so I clear my throat and rush out, "I'm not. I want you."

They reach us, stopping our conversation. *Goddammit.*

I wanted him to kiss me so badly.

And he growls his frustration, which has me losing my mind.

"Jennifer, what are you doing out here? Your mother and me went to the shops."

I shake my head. "I came looking for you. I wanted you to look at my TV. A loud noise came out of it and the screen went black."

"Doesn't sound good. I don't think you're meant to watch that many Disney movies in a row." He winks at me. "I will look at it."

My mouth pops open. *How embarrassing.* "No. Thomas just did and fixed it." Thomas is going to think I really am a young woman and not take me seriously.

"I'm kidding. I'm just joking around," my dad offers, reading my icy glare.

"Not funny," I spit crankily because I am breathless and achy for Thomas. And furious they came home just as I was so close to having Thomas in my arms again.

With no other reason to be out here anymore and knowing I won't be alone with Thomas any longer now that Dad's back out here, I say good-bye and trek back inside and into my bedroom.

CHAPTER 9

THOMAS

THE FIRST DAY OF a new job is always nerve-racking. I barely slept. I would be lucky if I got a solid three hours. My mind raced with thoughts of new colleagues, new responsibilities, if I will perform well... Then *she* entered my dreams. My thoughts always seem to come back to her. I toss and turn in bed until my alarm chimes. I groan, not bothering to lift my head off the pillow until the tune is off.

I don't have the luxury of sleeping in with children. I have three people to organize in the mornings, not just me. Slowly peeling my eyes open, I reach for my phone on my bedside table. Still groggy, I scroll through my social media and do a quick read of some emails, which I will respond to when I'm in the new office.

Now that I am half-awake, I throw off the covers and climb out of bed. I wander into my bathroom and step into the large shower, turning the tap to hot. I have yet to use the oversized tub that sits off to the side because the shower is the quicker option. I strip my briefs and step into the open shower and straight under the hot water, letting the spray coat my back, instantly waking me up.

As I stand in the shower washing, visions of Jennifer hit me. My cock is instantly hard and my balls are heavy and full. I brace myself against the shower wall in front of me, letting the warm spray of the shower hit my back. I grip the base of my cock and slam my eyes shut so I can see her face. I imagine it's her hands on me and I groan. I move my hand up and down from base to tip in a fluid rhythm. My hand glides roughly over my length repeatedly, and with each stroke, my cock grows and my release builds. I spread my legs wider and feel my balls tighten and I imagine her on her knees begging to taste me. And that's enough for me to explode. I throw my head back and grit through my teeth. "Fuck. Ah. Jennifer."

As my seed spills out of me and into the shower, I grunt through the last few pulls until my balls are empty and light. Letting go of my cock, I lean both my arms on the shower walls and suck some deep breaths in. When I'm recovered, I push up and clean myself.

Turning the shower off, I wrap a towel around my waist and step into the walk-in closet and scan my suits, settling on my favorite charcoal suit, gray tie, and a white shirt. Nothing like my best outfit to give me the confidence I don't feel.

After dressing, I pick up the gym bag lying on the floor so I can pack it full of workout clothes and shoes. The new office has a gym on the ground floor, so Joshua has informed me. This is perfect. I can continue keeping fit without taking up time after work that I keep strictly for the girls, since Victoria is not here to assist. Her family is overseas, and Mom isn't living around the corner anymore, so I need to be available to pick up the girls on time from after-school care and day care. They are my world and prevent me from falling off the rails. I didn't have time to feel sorry or to grieve after Victoria's death, having to pick up the pieces and become the mother and father to the girls. I couldn't sit in my bed all day, screaming about *me,* while drinking a sickening amount of alcohol. I had to man up and plod forward.

Like now. I collect my gym bag and trek out to the kitchen to make myself a cup of coffee. While the espresso machine works its magic, I wake the girls. Stepping into Lily's room first, I sit down on the side of her bed. Her disheveled blond hair is the only part of her peeking out of the cover.

I rub her back, leaning down near her head to whisper, "Lily, it's time to wake up for school."

Lily's new school is around the corner from Rose's childcare, so it's convenient. Thankfully, she has adjusted well and doesn't ask about her old friends or her old *life*.

Lily shuffles her slender frame under the covers, and once I'm sure she's awake, I stand and head out to wake Rose. Peering over her white crib, I chuckle at the sight of Rose flat on her back with her arms flung wide and mouth hanging open. Lifting her up, I carry her in my arms out into the kitchen. As I gently pull her away from my chest to lower her into the highchair so I can make breakfast, she screams a high-pitched squeal. Her arms tighten around my neck, clinging to me, not ready to let go. She cuddles into my chest, resting her head into the crook of my neck.

"Shh, it's okay. Daddy's here," I murmur as I stroke her back with the palm of my hand.

Some days are harder than others and today is a hard day. Rose doesn't understand exactly what happened with her mom, but she sensed the change and hasn't adjusted well. Her screams are loud and inconsistent, happening without a pattern. All I can figure out is that she wants to be held close, holding me as tight as her little arms can squeeze for a long period. My heart splinters into a million pieces. Why? Why not me? And why did they have to lose their mother? *Will I be enough?*

I bob her up and down and enter Lily's room. Her sister's screaming must have helped wake her up because she's sitting on her bed waiting for me. In times like these, I really miss Victoria. I need to comfort Rose and help Lily dress. And if I don't get breakfast started soon, we will be a lot late instead of our usual a little.

"Lily, let's grab some breakfast first today, and then I'll help you get ready," I decide.

She nods, and I exit her room and stroll to the kitchen with the patter of tiny footsteps behind me. I turn on the television and scroll through the channels until I see a kids' morning show. Rose's head peeks out from my neck. My mouth curves in a small smile. *Victory.* Now that she seems preoccupied, I guide her down gently, with success this time.

Thinking back to over a year ago, I never appreciated how hard Victoria's role was. I never helped with the morning rush, and now I must do it all on my own. My chest tightens, so I take a deep breath and roll my shoulders back to focus on the task at hand. I serve breakfast and while the girls eat, I walk off to make their beds. After breakfast, I clean and dress the girls before we get out the door, only five minutes behind schedule. I drop Lily off at school first and then Rose. Over the last few weeks, Rose has settled into the center seamlessly and is staying longer every day this week, and by the end of the week, it will be a full day.

I don't see Jennifer when I drop Rose off, and I shake my head to clear it. Nothing seems to help me. Jennifer has been taking up a lot of my thoughts throughout the day and every time I pick up Rose, my heart speeds up at the thought of seeing her again. But a pang of disappointment has filled me at the last few drop-offs from not seeing Jennifer. *Why would she be interested in an older guy with two kids?*

When I arrive at work in the city, I park my Range Rover underground and make my way to the elevator. The doors open into the lobby, and I step out, glancing from left to right. The interior has a fresh look with large cream tiles and wooden panel accents.

It's quiet and there are no other people walking the corridors. A woman in her mid-fifties sits at a desk to my right, busy typing on her computer.

I stroll over and clear my throat to gain her attention.

She ceases typing and glances up at me from the computer. "Good morning. How may I help you?"

"Good morning. It's my first day here and I'm looking for Joshua Ward," I say.

"Okay, I can help you find him, but first I would like to welcome you to Ward Electrical and Infrastructure."

"Thank you." I offer a small smile.

"What is your name?" she questions.

"Thomas Dunn."

She gives me a friendly smile before picking up the phone and pressing a button.

"Good morning, Mr. Ward. I have Mr. Thomas Dunn here." Her eyes focus on mine again as she hangs up. "He will be down in a minute."

She peers down at her computer and carries on with her typing.

"Thank you," I say.

A few minutes later, the elevator pings open. "Hey, Tom. Welcome."

Joshua draws me into his arms and slaps my back.

I grin wide. "Thanks again. I can't believe I'll be working here." I gesture at the building with my hands.

"For me, you mean." He winks before we both crack up laughing.

Joshua is another part of our school pact. He recently took over the family business from his dad who retired, but he has expanded the business by purchasing and renovating the new building, turning it into this sleek establishment. "Yes, you hotshot." I push his shoulder with my hand.

"It's not all glamorous. Let's head upstairs. Thanks, Maria."

My brows draw together at his comment, but I don't question it as I walk alongside him.

Our dress shoes click on the tiles all the way to the elevator. Once inside, he presses the button for the eleventh floor. My mouth opens to speak, but he beats me to it.

"My office is on the twelfth floor. You're welcome anytime. I assigned your office on the eleventh floor. You have an assistant starting next week. Her name is Ava."

I frown. "I have an assistant?"

"Yes, with this business growing so much in such a short amount of time, you will need help. I want to set up the company right from the very beginning."

As I try to process that I have an assistant, the elevator dings and we step out into the lobby.

"No way," I mutter under my breath.

It is as big as a house, all the same tiles, and the same light-brown wood as the ground floor lobby. The desk in this open area with a computer set up and shelving lining the wall must be Ava's.

Joshua strides into an office that has glass walls and a glass door. My brows furrow as I follow him. No privacy? Weird concept. I take a few steps over to my desk and touch the back of the soft, white leather chair tucked neatly behind it. There's a plant on the desk and the computer is set up and ready.

Joshua stands at the floor-to-ceiling windows overlooking the city. I stroll over to stand beside him, looking at the view of the world below, the people, traffic, life happening outside.

"Amazing, right?" Joshua says next to me.

"You could say that. Are you sure this is my office, and that is my assistant's desk?" I ask in disbelief.

He chuckles at my slack mouth. "Yes, you deserve it."

I stand at the window for another minute before the sound of a ringtone cuts through the silence.

Joshua pulls his phone from his pocket, scanning the name. "I need to take this."

I nod. "Sure. I'll get started."

Joshua strides out of my office and walks over to the elevator, standing there chatting on his cell. I walk back over to the chair, tugging it away from the desk, and ease down on it. Ah, I love the cool leather against my burning hot skin.

When Joshua offered me the job opportunity, I was unsure. Working with friends isn't always a great idea, but he's a good persuader. And I wanted a management position.

I do well for myself, and so does my family, but this level of money is way above mine. Not as much as James, but a close second. Gazing around the luxurious office, I feel lighter about where my future is going.

Leaning forward, I switch on my computer and open the email account to answer the many emails from Joshua and future clients of new projects I will manage. I write a list of site visits I need to attend, frequency of visits, meetings with suppliers, builders, and inductions of new staff. I'm realizing the number of hours in a day I have don't add up with everything I need to do. A few meetings are scheduled for the late afternoon, which means it will be hard to pick the girls up on time from care. I need to condense them into one or two days, but even then, I don't know how it will work.

The rest of the day passes in a blur of meetings and learning the ropes until it's time to leave the office. I drive to pick up Lily from after-school care, weaving in and out of the traffic on the road. The music of the local radio station coming through the car speakers relaxes my tired muscles. My brain hurts from the long day. At a red light, I stare out my side window, watching as people walk the sidewalk. I don't realize the light changes until a horn honks behind me, causing my body to stiffen.

I inhale slow, uneven breaths as bile burns the back of my throat.

I grip the steering wheel, unable to move.

Chapter 10

THOMAS

One Year Ago

*I ENTWINE MY HAND with Victoria's, resting it on top
of my thigh as I drive us home from an appointment
in the city. Traffic is heavy, so it's taking a little
longer than expected.*

*My mind is still racing as I try to soak in the new
information we just received. We both sit silently in
our Audi, eager to get home to our girls.*

*I watch from the corner of my eye as Victoria leans
forward to reach the buttons on the center console.
She flicks stations before settling on Sam Smith's "To
Die For." The volume increases and the song blares
through the car speakers.*

*Her vibrant, angelic voice sings in tune with the
song on the radio. I take my eyes from the road to peek
over at her relaxed body settled into the leather seat.
Her eyelids close, absorbing the lyrics, and her pouty
lips moving as she sings to me in her soft tone. I smile.
She looks so at peace in this moment, the complete*

opposite of the fiery self she shows others. I'm the only person to get the whole Victoria.

An older, beat-up car approaches in the opposite direction, hugging the line that separates us. My jaw clenches as I watch the car weaving. I unlink my hand from Victoria's, grabbing the steering wheel in a tight grip before I slide it across the horn. There are only a few other cars on the road besides ours, so when the car speeds directly toward us, I slam the brake. The sound and the feel of the horn under my hand are the last things I remember before everything goes black.

When I wake, I blink my eyes rapidly, trying to focus on what caused intense shooting pain in my body. My back is sore and along my shoulders and chest there are small pinches on my skin. My head thumps in the same rhythm as my heartbeat. A cold, wet liquid drips along the side of my temple, down to my jaw. I gasp at the sight of the crumpled hood and the tree that has pushed the metal up.

I don't hesitate for a second before I twist my head to check on Victoria. The pain making me curse loudly. Victoria's head is slumped forward and blood trickles down her cheeks, sticking her hair to her face. I lift my hand to tuck the strand behind her ear, but I don't get too far before the pain slicing at my side makes me retract my arm and choke on a breath.

The image of Victoria and the gurgle of sounds coming from her chest are gut-wrenching. I just want to touch her, help her, but I'm stuck, unmoving, and riddled with excruciating pain in my torso. People in the distance people ask if I can hear them, but I struggle to answer. A flush of cool air hit my skin when the sound of a door screeches open next to me. My body hairs rise from the breeze and the shock of the event hitting my bones. My body shakes uncontrollably.

Without warning, there is a tugging of my upper body and red and blue flashing lights in my peripheral vision. I'm pulled out of the vehicle slowly, my feet dragging across the leather seat. I can still see Victoria slumped, unmoving, in the passenger seat. Blood seeps out of her open mouth. Watching her fade out of my vision, I feel as if my heart is being ripped out of my chest, leaving a shell of a man.

How do I stop them from taking me?

My throat closes, and I can barely breathe, let alone mutter an audible word. I close my eyes from the sight, wishing this was all a bad dream. Everything goes black again.

When I stir, I hear beeps behind me.

"He is waking up. Get the doctor quick."

I hear heavy footsteps and a door screech open and bang close. I open my eyes and squint, trying to adjust to the brightness. It's blinding.

"It's okay, sweetheart. You're safe."

A soft hand strokes my hair, and I recognize the voice—my mom.

My eyes slowly adjust to the light. I groan at the pain slicing through my skull.

Mom hovers beside me with tears staining her cheeks. I look around at my surroundings and I can see I'm in a room. My finger has a device attached to it and there is a needle in my arm. Stickers and wires are all over my chest. My brows crease; I'm in a hospital bed.

"Mom," I whisper. My throat feels full of razor blades.

Her eyes go wide, and she lets go of my hair and straightens up. "I'll get you some water."

I blink, unable to talk through the pain in my throat. I watch her hurry to the bed tray and pour a glass of water. She puts a straw in the glass and steps toward me. I open my mouth and wrap my dry lips around the straw and suck the cold liquid into my throat. At first, it burns, but then the cool liquid soothes, and I drain the glass.

"Do you want more?" Mom asks.

"Please." My throat is still dry and painful, but it's better than my first attempt to talk.

As I watch her refill my glass, I dare ask... "Victoria?"

New tears fill my mom's eyes as she walks toward me with a fresh glass of water. Her mouth moves, but the words don't register. "She is gone... I'm so sorry."

CHAPTER 11

JENNIFER

I NEVER THOUGHT I would have a compelling urge to see a man. But every time the bell above the door chimes at work, my gaze shoots toward the door, wishing *he* would walk through it. Every time it's not him, my gaze lowers, and a heaviness enters my heart.

I also never cared about my appearance. I always swept my hair in a messy ponytail for practicality. A bare face and bland clothing suited me. But since Thomas entered my life in a regular pattern recently, I started brushing my hair every day, careful to put it in a neater ponytail, applying a few decent coats of mascara on my lashes to show off my brown eyes, and choosing clothes from my wardrobe that fit and show off my curves.

But unfortunately, I have missed his drop-offs in the last few days. This new desire coursing through my veins is foreign. I haven't been able to shake my thoughts of how his soft pillowy lips felt against mine or how protected I felt in his arms.

The girls' words play in my mind. 'Get to know him, but just be careful.'

Am I ready to be with a man who has kids?

Do I want to be a stepmom?

It isn't something I have had to think about—until now. But I need to talk to him more, get to know him. Give myself a chance to find out the answers.

I have spent the morning playing tea parties with Rose and a few other children. She has her new favorite bear seated next to her and when she leans down, I pinch my lips together. Thomas's attempt at braiding her hair is adorable. It's totally crooked but the fact he tried to do such a cute style on Rose makes my heart swell. I get the vision of his large fingers trying to weave the hair over each other, fumbling his way through it. I leave them to play to attend to a little boy who has fallen.

While crouching down on the floor to tie a boy's shoe, Rose's high-pitched scream, almost cracks my eardrum. My heart beats frantically at the noise. I finish with the little boy's shoes and pop up, scanning the room, thinking she has hurt herself, but I find her searching around, looking for something. I raise my brows in surprise when her gaze lands on mine. Relief instantly fills her eyes, but tears still stain her cheeks, and loud sobs still heave from her little chest. The vision breaks my heart. I bend over and scoop her up in my arms and cuddle her into my chest.

She buries her little head into the crook of my neck like I am going to disappear or leave her. The closeness she seeks proves she needs more time to erase the pain of losing her mom.

"What happened, Rose? It's okay. I got you," I coo, trying to soothe her. I stroke her back up and down in gentle strokes. Her erratic breathing calms under my palm, and her shudders and sobs ease the longer I hold her and rub my hand along her spine.

Rose has settled into the center well, but at times, she is clingy. A normal two-year-old hangs on to your legs, seeking constant comfort and requesting all your attention. But Rose seeks extra cuddles and doesn't like to be alone at all or without visually seeing a trusted adult. When I'm on shift and scheduled in the toddler room, Rose seeks me out, staying by my side the whole time. She plays with other children but is often reserved.

The distress in Rose shatters me. I need to discuss my concerns with Thomas. I can only imagine this is about their mother. I want to know how to help her. I feel the energy of connection between us, and she must feel the same.

She knows I want to protect her. And she can trust me to keep her safe.

When Rose is ready, I take her into the toddler room and spend the rest of the day playing and checking in on her. It's getting close to the end of my shift and Rose is still here. What is keeping Thomas? I bite my lip with worry, pacing the now tidy room. Taking a seat on the couch with Rose cradled in my arms, I let her little body drape across my body, the back of her head lying heavily in the crook of my elbow. Rose's eyes are heavy-lidded and fighting to stay open. Her long dark lashes flutter and fan out on her cheeks. A warm glow flows through me as I watch her rest in peace.

The bell of the door startles me, and I jolt, jerking Rose in my arms, causing her little body to twitch and move.

"Shh," I coo at her as her breathing returns to a normal pace. The heaviness returns on my arm.

Footsteps stomp closer and my gaze lands on Thomas. As his eyes meet mine, his chest moves as he takes a quick intake of breath. The air swirling around us is warm and thick, and I feel my cheeks turning pink with him staring at me as I cradle his daughter. My breath catches in my lungs.

Lily is snuggled in Thomas's arms, but his face is pale and pinched in fatigue. I gently clutch Rose closer to my body and carefully stand, not wanting to wake her. Thomas pulls Lily from his embrace and guides her to the floor. Her eyes are heavy and her legs wobble as she attempts to stand. Thomas steps over as I run my eyes from his hair down to his shoes. He is a dream. The impeccable navy tailored suit shows off his lean, broad shoulders and his slim waist. I wonder what he looks like without the suit. I tuck the thought away just as quickly as it enters my mind, but my body is on fire, not letting me forget it.

He trails close to me, and I shift Rose's floppy body into his outstretched arms. As he takes her, his fingertips skim along my arms, and goosebumps fan across my skin.

"I'm so sorry I'm late," he whispers. "I got stuck in a meeting at work that went longer than planned." His voice is full of frustration.

"Tom, are you okay?" My voice is laced with concern.

He exhales loudly. "Yeah, I just didn't realize they would expect me to stay late at least one night a week, every week. The workload is a lot more than I expected." He stares down at Rose, then Lily who is clutching his leg. "I don't know how I will juggle this."

I nod, crossing my arms to hug myself to warm my body. I didn't realize it had gotten cold until Rose was out of my arms. A shiver runs through my body.

"My parents can't help. I just don't know. I really shouldn't be dumping this on you. I should let you go home. Again, I'm sorry, Jen. I will figure something out." He shakes his head and turns toward the exit with slumped shoulders.

My heart constricts with pain for him.

"I can help you."

He stops in his tracks. It's quiet for a few beats before he answers. "I couldn't do that to you. You work, and I'm sure you don't want to care for my two after hours. It's way too much. Thank you for offering." He smiles.

"No, seriously, Tom. It makes sense. I work here and you live next door. I could help you one night a week. I can talk to my boss, but I'm sure she won't mind."

I can see his mind ticking. It feels like forever waiting for his reply.

"How about you talk to her first? And then if she agrees, we can work on the day, times, and pay. It would definitely help, and the girls already feel comfortable with you." His lip turns up in a half smile.

"Okay, I will let you know on Monday after I talk to her. There was something else I, er," I stammer, trying to figure out the best way to ask without causing him pain or making the situation uncomfortable. "I noticed Rose is very cuddly, and if she can't see me, she can get quite distressed. Has she always been like this? Or is this just since their mother passed away?"

His jaw ticks at the mention of his wife's passing. I swallow past the lump that's now sitting in my throat.

"Yes, I have had some issues in the last few months. Rose requires lots of attention. I'm hoping once she settles into the new house and the center, it will pass in time."

I nod. "I just wanted to check and make sure it wasn't new. Nothing from starting at the center."

"Definitely nothing to do with you or the center. If it doesn't calm down soon, I will have to speak to a doctor." He peers down at Rose, who is sleeping peacefully, like he's trying to find the answers by staring at his daughter.

My eyes rake over his sober face. This vision is gut-wrenching. He is a beautiful dad to these girls.

"I think that's a great idea. But you're doing a wonderful job with the girls. Don't think you aren't." I stroke his arm, trying to appease his guilt.

His hand covers my own, and my pulse races. His eyes flick to mine and he offers me a soft smile.

We stand unmoving. The gentle touch of his hand over mine renders me immobile. I'm unable to move until he speaks.

"Well, I better let you go home. I don't want to take up any more of your time. I'll talk to you Monday."

I gently remove my hand, crossing it over my chest. "I look forward to it." I bite my lip to stifle a grin.

His lips part in surprise, then a smile spreads further across his face from my words.

"Me too."

I dart my eyes away to look at Rose and Lily, avoiding his heated gaze. Taking a step forward, I raise my hand and smooth my hand down her hair. "Good night, Rose," I whisper to her. Then I bend down and say, "Good night, Lily."

She whispers back, "Night."

I take a step back, putting some much-needed space between us before I raise my gaze to meet his. I falter. His eyes are firmly fixed on mine, and the air around us crackles.

"Good night, Thomas." My voice is deep and husky, filled with lust.

"Good night, Jen." A smirk appears on his face again before he swivels on his feet and leaves.

I stand there silently, my gaze burning into his back as I watch him disappear. Awestruck.

CHAPTER 12

JENNIFER

MONDAYS ARE THE BUSIEST days at Spring Side, so it's lunchtime before I get the chance to talk to Helen.

"Jen, come in. Is everything okay?" she says.

My lips twitch in an easy smile as I enter the office and sit in the chair that faces her. "Yes, this is nothing bad." I chuckle at her curious glare. "I wanted to talk to you about Thomas Dunn, Rose's father."

At the mention of Thomas, she sits up straighter in her chair, turning away from her monitor and releasing the mouse that her hand was just hugging, and her brows raise. "Yes, and what about them?"

"As you know, he is a single dad with limited support, and is new to the area. Well, on Friday night, he picked up Rose later than normal. He was frazzled and mentioned he needs a babysitter for one night a week for a few hours."

She leans back in her office chair as I continue. I sit up a little straighter, my hands gripped together like a vise, my palms sweating, afraid she might say no.

"I, uh, live next door to him, so I said I could help. But we agreed you would need to approve that. This is my number one priority, and I will always put this job first. Rose is just jumpy and clingy since her mother died, and I figured she feels comfortable with me, so it might help him out."

She nods and leans forward in her office chair, resting her forearms flat on the oak table, her hands clasped together.

"Yes, he certainly has had a tough year and poor Rose seems a little frightened of the world because of the event. But I'm hesitant to allow this. I don't know if it's a great idea. Professionally and then on a personal level. I will have to think about it."

My heart feels like it's shrinking. What will he do? He said he doesn't have any options. I will have to think of some way to help him, even if that help cannot be me.

I nod and let out a shaky breath. "I understand. He will pick up Rose tonight so I can let him know your answer then." I push myself up into a standing position.

"Okay, give me until your break, and I will think about it. But are you sure it's not too much? I don't want you to work a lot of hours. I don't want you burning out."

I shake my head vigorously. "It won't be a lot of hours."

Even if it was too much, I don't think I could pass up the opportunity. The bond I feel for Rose makes my throat ache and my eyes go glassy. I want to help her, offer her stability. And then there is Thomas. The raw desire I feel frightens me. But the opportunity to be around him is tempting and something I know I can't refuse. It would also give me the opportunity I need to get to know him.

"Go have your lunch and let me think about it. I'll get back to you this afternoon. Come back to me during your afternoon break, and I'll have an answer for you."

"Thanks, Helen. I'll see you then."

The next few hours pass by and before I know it, it's my second break. I trek to the office but find it empty. I stroll to the staff room and find Helen talking with Emma. Emma is in the baby room today while I work with Julie.

"I just went to your office," I say to Helen, "but it was empty so I thought I would have my break first and then come and talk with you."

"It's fine, Jen. I thought about it and you can help Thomas out."

Emma's brows rise. *Shit.* She's already curious about Thomas and me. Emma's mouth turns to a smug grin.

"Ah, thanks for letting me know." I walk over to the cups, avoiding Emma's curious gaze. I'm sure my face is etched with guilt.

"Just if it gets to be too much, be sure to let him know," Helen says on her way out.

I nod, not trusting myself to speak, and make myself tea before sitting at the table.

Emma moves in front of me, and I groan. Here we go. The interrogation starts.

I wish I could hide right now, but there is no way I can avoid the discussion Emma wants to have.

"Helping Thomas after work." She winks, amusement written clearly on her face.

I shrug. "He needs help one day a week for a few hours. You've seen Rose. She is a scared little girl. And she knows me, so I figured why not... but I had to ask first."

Her eyebrows rise. "Rose is the only reason you're helping Thomas out?"

"What else would it be?" I keep my tone neutral.

The smile on her face grows larger. "Because he is older and hot. Don't say you don't agree." She points at my face. "That flush proves you have the hots for him."

"Of course, I agree. He is attractive. I never once denied it. And I do not have the hots for him. You're delirious, Em. He is *way* too old for me."

"Sure, keep telling yourself that. You're the crazy one. If any of us had Thomas looking at us like a lovesick puppy, we would be on him like a rabbit."

Chuckling, I glance away. A warm feeling spreads in my stomach and it isn't just the tea. I haven't noticed him looking at me differently than the other girls. I can't ask her what she means because that would prove to Emma I care.

The day passes quickly and there are still five children to be picked up, including Rose. Every hour has dragged so slowly. I keep waiting for Thomas to enter. As I put on a clean sweater for another child who soiled his clothes, my back tingles and I jerk at the sound of his deep voice.

"Rose, baby," he calls.

His voice is like butter, so smooth. My heart picks up speed and I concentrate on my task, trying to not get rattled by him.

Rose squeals in delight and runs to him. "Daddy."

After changing the child's clothes into dry ones, I rise and swivel to face him.

He watches me with a flicker of warmth in his eyes as his mouth curves with tenderness. "Hi, Jen."

"Hi, Tom." My voice is higher than it usually is.

"Bye," Rose says, her little arms locked around his neck, holding on.

His gaze moves between us. "Just a sec, sweetheart. Daddy needs to talk to Jen for a minute. Then we can go home, okay?" She lays her head on his shoulder and he kisses her cheek before gazing back at me.

"Where is Lily?" I ask.

"Mom is here tonight, so she took her home to get started on dinner."

I smile back at him. "That's nice of her. I bet Lily was happy to see her."

"Oh, she certainly was." He snickers. "And so will this one when we get home. How did it go with your boss?"

"She was fine about it. She just doesn't want me overworked." I rub my neck that's gone stiff while I explain what happened.

His eyes darken at the comment, and I realize how that came out. And I cringe at the thoughts he must have running through his mind.

"I won't do that. We can just do one night, and then if I have a late meeting, I will ask you if you're free. If not, there is no pressure. But I will just try to stick to one a week. I want to spend time with my girls and not work late every night."

"One night works well. Maybe we could stick to the same day? It would make it easier for our schedules. And not a Friday. No one wants to work every Friday night. Here, we rotate it for fairness."

"How about Wednesday? Would this Wednesday suit?" he asks.

My eyes widen at his suggestion. "Um, I don't see why not."

"Are you able to pick up Lily from after-school care and take them home? I will have the house stocked with food for you and the girls."

The urgency in his voice shocks me. I really didn't think it would be this week. But I did offer to help, so I can't back out now.

"Of course. You'll need to make sure I'm on the list to sign her out of the school."

Knowing how strict our rules are here, I'm sure schools would work similarly.

"I'll do that tomorrow, and I'll get a set of keys cut for you. I also need your bank details to pay you." He juggles Rose onto one arm as his other retrieves his wallet from his suit pocket. He pulls a card out from his wallet and thrusts it in my direction. "My number is on here. In case you need it."

"Thanks," I whisper, taking the business card from him and glancing down at it.

I stuff the card into my pocket, the phone number already memorized.

A tug on my pants has me tearing my gaze from Thomas. A little boy peeks up at me, and

I bend down to pick him up and balance him on my hip.

"Sorry. I better get back to work. I'll see you soon."

He grins. "Yes, I can see that. Sorry to take you away from work. Thanks for helping me. I appreciate it."

"No problem." I bite my lip and turn with the little boy and wander over to the play area.

Now I have to figure out how to make my parents think this is okay.

***

Wish me luck. After work, as I'm cutting up chicken for dinner with Mom, and I fill her in. "I'm doing a babysitting job for Thomas next door. He was looking for someone one night a week to pick the girls up and care for them until he gets home, so I offered, figuring it would be extra money and good experience."

Mom continues chopping a pepper. "That's a great idea, love. Dad's been over helping him out. It must be hard being a single dad to two little ones."

"Exactly. When he came in tired and stressed about babysitters, I couldn't help but offer. It won't be hard and the girls are so sweet." I smile.

"Did you talk to the boss about helping Thomas? I don't want you getting in trouble with work."

I finish cutting the chicken, then wash my hands. "I did. I ran it past Helen."

"Okay, that's great. Dad will be happy you're helping too."

We finish preparing dinner and then I head to my room to shower.

I pull out the card Thomas gave me and save his number in my phone contacts.

After overthinking about how to write the text with my bank details, I hit send. A second later, it's been read, and I wait for a reply.

Shit, he replied.

Thomas: *Hi, Jen. Thank you. Is $50 an hour okay?*

My eyes bulge out of their sockets because that's double the amount I earn at the center.

Jennifer: *More than okay. Seems a bit much. You don't need to pay me that amount.*

Thomas: *No! You are helping me out, so that's settled then.*

An idea comes to mind, and I twitch in my seat as I type out.

Jennifer: *You can pay me in other ways. ;)*

After hitting send, I rub my lips with my finger as I wait for his response, wishing I could see what he's doing as he opens this. Would he glance up and quirk his brow? And ask if I was serious? Or would he pick me up, kiss me breathless, and take me to his room and ravish me.

My body tingles at the thought of him not having enough of me and pleasuring me until I'm boneless. My message tone interrupts my dream. I quickly open it and read.

Thomas: *Naughty girl... What are you offering?*

I don't want the conversation to end, so I keep up the taunting.

Jennifer: *Hmmm, what do you want?*

Thomas: *You.*

I'm about to respond when a second text pops in.

Thomas: *On your knees.*

I run my hand up my neck and stroke just under my ear, contemplating what I should write back. But again, he texts me before I have time to type.

Thomas: *Taking me in your mouth and you swallowing what I give you.*

My lips part. *Holy fuck!* This man is insatiable. And if I'm being true to myself, I would love to be doing that right now. The thought of me bringing him pleasure and swallowing his release makes me wet.

When no other message comes, I quickly type a response.

Jennifer: *I would love to be there with you, on my knees, licking you, sucking you and swallowing your cum.*

Thomas: *This is torture. I'm going to go now and stroke myself, but I wish it was your mouth wrapped around me. You better touch yourself and think of me.*

There is no question there. I will touch myself as soon as this conversation ends. I'm too wound up and I need to shower.

Jennifer: *Don't you worry I will be touching myself and pretending it's your fingers fucking me.*

Thomas: *Fuck! I wish it was me there. I would lick your sweet pussy clean from all your cum.*

Jennifer: *You are killing me.*

Thomas: *But you love it, Princess.*

Yes, I do. He and his dirty mouth do things to me, and as long as I keep my heart out of it, I'll be fine.

CHAPTER 13

JENNIFER

I'M FAILING ALREADY. WANDERING through the grounds of the local primary school to pick up Lily with Rose sitting on my left hip, the cool air whips us, and Rose grips my neck tighter. I follow a concrete sidewalk that splits down the middle, separating the brown weatherboard classrooms. Seeing a small sign stuck on a building, I squint to read, *Administration Office*, and move in the sign's direction.

As I hurry along, I admire the well-manicured school. The gardens are neat, no rubbish littered around, and the buildings are kept clean. A bird chirps above on the nearby building, breaking the silent air. I reach a pair of doors and pull one open to step inside the office. The brown theme continues inside with mocha carpets and beige walls. No one is at the reception desk, but there's a sheet of paper on it that explains the desk is... only manned during school hours.

I frown. What do I do? Spinning around, I trail the hall.

Rose lifts her head out of my neck, and says, "Lily."

I beam at the beautiful little girl gazing at her and lean down to peck her cheek. "That's right, Rose. Lily is just in here. Let's pick her up and go home to play."

Her legs swing and kick my sides. Her grin is wide. I love her soft mannerisms and sweet baby face.

The corridor has multiple doors lining either side, and I read the black signs hanging above each door until I arrive at the one that reads After-school Care. Through the window in the door, I spot Lily in the drawing nook. I knock and take a small step back. A staff member arrives a moment later, pulling the door ajar.

"Hi, my name is Jennifer, and I'm here to pick up Lily," I say.

"Hi, Jennifer. Yes, we were expecting you. Come on in, and I'll collect her bag for you." I step into the classroom. "Could you sign her out too, please?" She points to a table with an open book.

After I sign my name, I turn and Lily's face lights up when she spots me. She pushes out her chair and starts running. I squat down with Rose in my arms, thinking she is excited for Rose. But when she arrives, she grabs me by the side unoccupied by Rose and squeezes me in a tight, warm hug. Blown away by the sudden outburst, my heart freezes, then pounds again.

I rub my hand up her back. "Hi, Lily. Are you ready to go home?" I ask.

She peels her head back to gaze into my eyes. "Yes. I'm so excited you're here." She bounces.

The twist of my stomach forms a vise-like knot. "I'm excited too. Let's grab your bag and go home."

She nods on my shoulder before stepping back. I stand and Lily returns to my side after saying goodbye to the staff. She slips her tiny hand in mine, and I wrap my hand around hers, gently squeezing it. She beams up at me as I gaze down at her with a soft smile. Nudging my chin in the exit's direction, we leave and head back to the house.

Helen and I agreed on a Wednesday day shift to allow me to get the girls home from care, so Thomas dropped the spare keys off this morning, and I left work to pick up the car seats and install them before driving back to collect Rose. Lucky for me, the daycare center, school, and our houses are all ten minutes away because the car seat proved to be a challenge. I had to pull up a YouTube video to figure out how to secure them in my car. Lily's booster seat was much easier than Rose's car seat—the way the belts went in was a maze.

I'm a little later than I originally planned because of the car seat issues, but I still get home just before five. The girls run straight for their toys, and I bring their bags to the kitchen to unpack and get a start on dinner. Tugging open the fridge, I scan the contents. There is an array of meat, fish, and vegetables. I trail to the pantry and pull open the door to find a hidden walk-in pantry. *Wow, this is massive.* It's another big room. I grab some noodles for a fast and simple recipe.

I quickly prepare dinner by chopping up vegetables and chicken I found in the fridge, then I search the cupboards until I find a bowl and soak the noodles. While cooking, I decide to clean their bags, so Thomas doesn't have to do it tonight.

Once I'm done, I walk to their rooms to tidy up, but to my surprise they are already clean. I can tell I'm in Lily's room because of a bed instead of a crib. It's a simple room with a white bed with pink covers and dressed in a soft pale-pink wallpaper. I step farther in to move closer to the dressers, passing a small desk to the right and a bookshelf sitting above it. I pick out a pair of pajamas from the wardrobe before walking down the hall into Rose's room.

Rose has flowered wallpaper and a white crib in the left-hand corner with a canopy draped over the top. There is a changing station that matches the crib. I step to the wardrobe and pull out her sleepwear.

With all the girls' sleepwear, I move into the bathroom and place the clothes on the counter and head back to the kitchen to serve dinner.

"Girls, dinner is ready," I call out.

They rush out and when Rose is close enough, her arms thrust out in front of her toward me. I scoop her up and guide her into the highchair, clipping her securely. Lily takes a seat in a chair, which must be her chair. I set them up with the noodles and forks before taking my seat in between them and eating the meal I prepared. I enjoy cooking, so preparing the girls a meal is easy. I kept some aside in a bowl for Thomas, and I wonder if anyone has cooked him a meal since his wife died? That thought makes me feel a bit off. My stomach hardens at the thought. *Why am I jealous?* I have never been jealous in my life.

Staring down, I twirl my fork into my noodles, and a bang of cutlery wakes me from my daze. I glance up at Rose, covered in noodles and sauce, laughing at the noodle hanging from her baby hair. I reach out and grab the noodles with my fingers and put them down on my plate.

"Are you saving this for later?" I say, grinning at her.

Seeing the girls now playing with their food, I know they've finished their dinner.

"Let me run the bath for you girls." I peer over at Lily, who is almost finished with her dish.

"Bath time," Rose repeats.

I stand up and leave the kitchen, walking over to the bathroom and turn the bath taps on. In the cabinet under the sink, I find bubbles and pour some in. The bubblegum scent reminds me of my childhood baths with Megan. The memory brings a warm smile to my face.

When I return to the kitchen, I collect the dishes from the table and walk to the sink to stack them in the dishwasher after the bath.

"Lily, could you meet me in the bathroom, please?" I ask, walking back to Rose in her chair.

Unclipping the straps, I lift Rose and carry her into the bathroom. The girls get into the bath without a fight. I toss their clothes into the dirty laundry and watch them play with their toys. They have behaved so well tonight. I feel bad that Thomas will pay me for this. This doesn't feel like work. It's enjoyable.

After I finish washing them, I help them out of the bath, dry them both, and as they dress, Lily asks, "Can you sing 'Twinkle Twinkle Little Star'?"

"Twinkle star," Rose mumbles.

My lips part in surprise. "You like that nursery rhyme? I used to love it when I was a little girl too."

"My mommy used to sing it to us in the bath."

My eyes widen at the comment. Lily clearly does not realize the information she is sharing.

"That's beautiful. Well, I can sing it to you. I'm sure I won't be as good as your mommy," I say.

"She died."

My body stiffens. The honesty of this girl never stops shocking me.

I nod, staring into her sad little eyes. "I know and I am very sorry," I whisper.

"It's okay. Will you sing now?" she encourages me.

I smile. "Sure."

I sing the girls the nursery rhyme as I dress them. Lily joins in and once they are both dressed, I guide them to Lily's room and read them a bedtime story before tucking Lily in, kissing her cheek. "Good night, Lily."

"Good night."

I walk out and carry Rose to bed. Lowering her into the crib, I whisper, "Good night, Rose, baby."

She rolls over and I wander out.

When the girls are settled, I clean the bathroom and tidy the mess in the kitchen. After everything is loaded in the dishwasher, I mosey over to the couch and flick on the television.

Yawning, I lie down on the soft gray couch that is twice the size of a normal couch. It feels like a cloud underneath my head, so soft, and it doesn't help my heavy lids. They seem to close on their own accord, heaviness hitting my body. Until I wake to his voice.

CHAPTER 14

THOMAS

I'M LOOKING FOR JENNIFER. It's eight thirty when I arrive home. Everything seems quiet except the soft mumbles of the television. When I step into the family room, my gaze lands on the sleeping beauty on my sofa.

Her relaxed face compels me forward. She's curled up on her side, wearing those black work pants that hug her hips. Her white top has ridden up on her stomach, exposing creamy white skin. I squat next to her.

She is sleeping peacefully, her breathing faint, barely making a sound. I reach out with my hand and touch her cheek softly, brushing it with just my knuckles.

"Jen," I whisper, trying not to startle her.

Her eyelids snap open, and her stunning eyes stare back at me with horror, her cheeks turning pink.

"I'm sorry I kept you so late," I say.

She pushes herself up into a seated position, blinking rapidly and gazing around before her gaze returns to me.

My lips twitch in fascination. "Did you want something to drink or do you need to get home?"

Rubbing the back of her neck, she croaks, "Tea, please."

My stomach growls. I haven't eaten dinner yet. Rising from the couch, I walk to the kitchen. I immediately notice how tidy everything is. When I open the fridge, there is a bowl of stir-fry noodles wrapped in cling. A surge of happiness fills me, she keeps astonishing me.

Peering around the fridge door. I watch her rise from the couch and stroll over, eyes glassy.

"You didn't have to come over. You could have relaxed on the couch," I say.

She rubs her eyes with her hands.

"Is this for me?" I question, touching the bowl.

"Yes, eat. I'll make some tea. Do you want anything?" She walks into the kitchen and scans the cupboards for a cup, placing it on the counter before stepping into the pantry.

I watch her ass move in those tight pants, and can't help but groan inwardly. This girl has me twisted. *How can one person turn you inside out? I was fine without her... but now?*

Now I want her.

I shake my head. "No, thank you." I refocus on my food, taking the bowl over to the microwave.

Once it's warm, I sit at the counter to eat. Jennifer sits on a stool next to me, hugging her cup of tea.

I twist the fork in the bowl and scoop a large portion into my mouth, moaning out loud. "Mmm, this is delicious. Thanks for cooking for me. I didn't expect it. It's a nice surprise."

She twists her face in my direction and her cheeks have a cute flush of pink.

"How did it go with the girls?" I ask between bites.

"They were a dream. I feel bad you're paying me for this."

I snort. "It's a lot of work and you could relax at home tonight instead of working a double shift."

She shrugs. "I don't do much after work. I kind of hang out with the family or in my bedroom."

"Still, you don't have to be helping me, so thank you."

She nods but says nothing, just brings the cup to her mouth and sips.

I scrape the bowl before sliding off the stool and stacking the bowl and fork in the dishwasher. Grabbing a bottle of water from the fridge, I twist the cap and pull half in one go. I wipe my mouth before spinning on my heel. My gaze hits hers. Her eyes are a shade darker, and her lips part. Clamping my lips together, I try not to embarrass her too much for staring at me. I can't stop looking at her either. I want to touch her so badly. It's torturous fearing she may want to leave and I don't want her to just yet. It's strange... To want someone to stay.

But I want her to.

"Did you want to hang out for a minute before you head home?" I ask.

My gaze doesn't leave hers. She swallows hard and I can see her trying to work out what she should do. The air is thick, and I know she feels the electricity between us. I'm a package deal, though. It's a lot to handle.

She lifts her cup and drains it. "Sure, why not."

Speechless, I amble to the sofa and grab the remote to scroll through Netflix to find a show or movie. I sit and she joins me, leaving a gap between us.

"See anything that interests you?" I ask.

She shrieks with laughter. "I don't think you would be into what I have been watching," she answers honestly.

"*Ha*. Try me. You do realize I get kids' channels and reruns of *Bluey*, right? Is the show girlie?"

She moves her head up and down. "Yeah, you wouldn't like it."

"You'll be surprised. Just don't tell my friends. I wouldn't hear the end of it."

Her mouth curves into the biggest grin, showing off her beautiful smile. She is so pretty. I wish I could reach over and kiss her.

Would she let me?

"Firefly. Don't say I didn't warn you," she answers, cutting off my thoughts.

"What is it about?" I ask.

"These two best friends, Tully and Kate, go through some good and bad times from their teens to their forties... Cheesy but addictive."

I scroll through to find it. "What episode are you up to?"

"Four."

"It doesn't sound that bad. I've seen worse things."

I kick my shoes off, then remove my suit jacket and tie. I feel her eyes on me, burning a hole through my skin. The pull of attraction is getting harder to resist. Fuck, I wish she was undressing me.

"Don't be complaining to me if it's shit. Remember I warned you," she jokes.

I laugh. She is so easy to be around. I lean back and prop my legs on the coffee table, sinking into the plush material. She follows and tucks her legs under her and relaxes back too.

I try not to move during the episode, but after a while I keep taking small glances her way and lock eyes with her. My hand tingles to touch her so I reach over and rest my palm on her thigh. It twitches beneath my palm. But I don't move, needing just to touch her even if it's utter torture, because it makes me feel calm.

Her body shivers, and I peer over at her and notice her tight pink nipples taunting me through her top. "Are you cold?" I ask.

Fuck. I am so fucked.

She hugs herself, covering her nipples but pushing up her tits, and I practically bounce off the couch to grab her a blanket. Otherwise, I will devour her here right on my couch.

I come back carrying a blanket and cover her legs and tuck it in at her sides. My face hovers in front of hers, and I inhale her sweet vanilla scent. Making my mouth water. Her brow pops, but her face softens.

And I laugh, reading her mind, mocking me for tucking in the blanket.

"Sorry. Habit with the girls."

I settle back down beside her for the rest of the show. My hand returns to her blanket-covered leg, unable to keep my hands to myself.

When the credits roll, she slides her legs off the couch and stands. "I better go."

Even though I don't want her to go, and would rather toss her back on the couch and lick her from head to toe, I stand too.

"Yeah, you have work tomorrow, so you need to sleep. Thanks for tonight. It's going to help me so much."

"Of course, they are angels." She crosses to the front door, and I follow her to let her out.

"Not always." I chuckle.

"That's normal. They're kids." She smiles.

She reaches out for the handle, but I take a giant step forward. "Let me grab that."

My face is near hers, and the scent of her hair consumes me. Her breath hitches, and I turn my head, gazing down at her bottom lip.

My restraint snaps. And I seal my lips onto hers.

She lets out a little gasp and crushes her lips back to mine. Our lips move in perfect tune, and I dip my tongue inside, massaging it along with hers in a drugging kiss. I groan from her taste and the desire running through my veins. I tug her flush against me, the need to be near cutting off any sensible thought. Her hands roam my neck and face in exploration and when she slides her hands down across my chest to my torso, I tear my lips from hers, staring down at her beneath heavy lids, taking deep shaky breaths, trying to slow my rapid pulse.

I want more of her. But I don't know how much she wants me in return.

CHAPTER 15

JENNIFER

MY LIPS BURN WITH fire as I stare up at him with longing from under my lashes, shocked at my eager response to his touch. His brown eyes are almost black.

Our faces are inches apart, our heavy pants the only noise that can be heard. My body is aching for his touch. With lust urging me on, my hands glide along his chest, feeling his ripples of muscle. The heat pouring through my palms is scorching, causing my breath to quicken.

I have an achy need for more... I want to surrender and see what happens.

Pressing my open lips to his, I skim my tongue across his bottom lip.

A groan leaves his throat as he raises his mouth just an inch and stares into my eyes. "Are you sure?"

A shiver of want runs through me. "Yes."

He pauses before he takes my hand and leads me to his bedroom. When we enter, he flicks a switch to turn a lamp on, then shuts the door. My palms sweat as the lock clicks. Adrenaline pumps through me.

I blink and glance around at the light-gray walls and heavy drapes that are closed. I take in his modern black and white bed. I haven't moved, feeling his body slide up behind me, his closeness intoxicating.

His buttery soft lips sear a path down my neck and a shiver runs down my spine from the touch. I clench my thighs to ease the ache, but it doesn't work. His hands find my hips and he spins around to face him. Standing on tiptoes, my lips connect briefly with his before I pull back and bite down on the corner of my lip.

His lips turn to a smirk. "Here I thought you were shy."

"I am. I just..." I search for the right words to tell him I haven't felt like this toward a guy, without sounding desperate or ruining the moment.

"It's okay. We'll take this slow. I don't want to rush."

I try again. "I just..." But the words don't come, so I just nod.

His head dips, his mouth covering mine hungrily. We kiss until the ache is so intense I need more relief.

He must read my body language because he takes a few steps toward the bed and eases my body back to lie down. I sink into the most comfortable mattress in the world. He pecks a thousand kisses on my lips and down my neck.

He pulls back, hovering over me, before sliding down onto his knees. My heart almost comes out of my chest. His gaze doesn't leave mine as he stares back at me and slowly skims the band of my pants until he reaches the button. He quickly undoes it. As he tugs down the zipper, I suck in a sharp breath and watch him remove my pants and shoes. The ache sparked by one kiss is now bordering on painful when his hands skim my thighs. Still wearing black panties, I lean up on my elbows to stare directly down at Thomas, not wanting to miss out on a single thing.

His hands caress the skin of my thighs. The touch is painfully teasing, causing wetness to pool between my thighs. His eyes meet mine in a heated gaze, and I watch as he lowers his mouth to my center and kisses me through my panties. And then takes a large inhale. I moan, my eyes closing for a second before I tear them open to continue watching his mouth worshipping me.

"I have been dying to taste you again."

Thomas rips my panties down my legs and tosses them on the floor.

"I have missed your pussy, and now it's about to be all mine." A growl leaves his chest.

I whimper.

He is a dream come true, and here he is on his knees for *me*, about to bring me to orgasm. His cock straining through his pants, and I can tell he is big. I pant with anticipation. Bare and aching for physical touch, I instinctively arch my body toward him.

His hands stroke my quivering thighs.

"Please," I beg.

His lips break into a sexy grin, and I squirm. His face flickers with an unreadable expression before leaning forward and taking my clit into his mouth.

He pulls away just an inch to rasp, "Is that what you want, Princess?"

An involuntary shudder vibrates through my body from the feel of his breath on my needy, wet pussy.

"Yes. Please," I whimper.

His chest rumbles a chuckle, knowing I'm so achy and so close to the edge. But I need him.

I need his mouth and fingers on me. Now.

And just as I'm about to beg again, he runs his fingers through my wetness, rubbing my clit in teasing circles. I let out a deep groan through clenched teeth.

He stops the hard circling of my clit and moves to rub my slit. Moving slowly up and down, spreading my slickness with his fingers.

My body quakes with need when he enters one finger deep inside me.

I moan from his hungry licks on my clit as he enters a second finger, stretching me. I thrust my hips up, and his mouth covers my bud, grazing his teeth on it.

Sinking back onto the bed and closing my eyes, I cry out, "Thomas..." Gripping his hair roughly through my hands. Not wanting him to move. "More," I stumble out through heavy panting.

I open my legs wider, allowing him to get deeper with his fingers. His tongue adds more pressure to my clit, causing me to get wetter and I know I'm going to shatter into a million pieces on his hand.

Feeling the pressure building, his pace picks up, and he hits my magic spot repeatedly. He groans, and I tremble as the climax slams into me and I come hard. Eventually I stop trembling, so he slowly removes his fingers and I shiver with pleasure as he licks me clean.

My chest heaves from his expert touch, and I try to calm my sensitive body. When my pulse calms and my heart isn't trying to beat out of my chest, I peel my eyes open and perch up on one elbow. My mouth twitches at the sight of Thomas sitting back on his heels in a state of his bliss, his mouth split in a grin that reaches his eyes. He crawls over me, and pecks me in the softest of kisses, before pulling away. Grabbing his head, I lower it and kiss him passionately. He kisses me back harder and I taste myself on his tongue.

When he pulls back, hovering, a ragged breath leaves his lips. "I wish you could stay, but it's best we don't." It's barely a whisper but I catch it.

I sigh. "Me too." I can't help but speak the truth. I don't want him to think it's just him who feels this way. I would love nothing more than to climb into this bed and have Thomas wrap me with his body.

He grabs my panties off the floor and slides them up my legs. I take over and stand to pull them all the way up. Thomas picks up my pants and holds them out as if I'm one of the girls.

Tugging it out of his grip, laughing, I say, "I'm a big girl. I can do it myself."

He chuckles as I dress. "Sorry, it's out of habit, I guess."

"It's okay. I'm happy to remind you," I tease as I slide my shoes back on.

CHAPTER 16

THOMAS

I'M SLUMPED OVER MY desk, which is littered with paperwork. There are a few projects I'm currently working on but today's designs have involved frequent changes between the builder and myself. I rub my brow with the hand that's holding my head up and blow out a breath as I finish the edits of the new layout for the wiring.

I send off a new invoice for the additional changes. The building is local to the city, so they can do it today. I'm a little tired from the amount of work since I started, but having Jennifer watch the girls on a Wednesday allows me to be more productive and get extra work in, keeping my weekends free. My assistant helps me so much. When Joshua first mentioned an assistant, I didn't realize how much help she would be. She is young, with an extremely fiery attitude, but her organization skills are something beyond what I have seen for someone her age.

I'm finishing the edits and stacking the paperwork when my desk phone rings. I snatch up the receiver.

"Good evening, Ward Electrical and Infrastructure, Thomas speaking."

"So professional. Look out world," James' smooth voice blares through the receiver.

I chuckle, leaning back in my chair. "If I had known it was you, I wouldn't have bothered."

"Oh, unfair." James groans.

"Shut up. You're so full of it. I'm almost done with some notes. Can I call you back in the car?" I ask.

"Well, I'm just about to see you in your office so I'll see you in five." He hangs up, not bothering to wait for my answer.

I pull the phone away from my ear and hang up. Standing up, I stalk over to the doorframe. "Ava, you can head out as soon as you're done."

"Sure thing, boss," Ava replies.

Just then Joshua prowls in, and his eyes widen at the sight of Ava.

"What are you still doing here? I won't be paying you overtime," he spits.

She raises her eyebrows with a smug grin on her face. "I don't work for you." She returns to her work, clearly brushing him off.

My eyes bounce between them. *What have I missed?*

"Ha, technically you do, Ava." A smirk takes over his face.

"Whatever," I hear her mumble under her breath, but she never lifts her head again. I'm sure Joshua heard it too, as his face has turned to stone. I press my lips together to prevent a laugh from escaping.

He hasn't moved.

Ava closes down the computer, stands, rips open her drawer, and grabs her bag before slamming it shut. "See you tomorrow, boss." Her lip turns up in a genuine smile.

"Good night, Ava," I respond.

She storms past Joshua without another word, her chest high and proud. She really doesn't give a shit about anyone. I'm rendered speechless over what just occurred. I haven't seen Joshua riled up like that over a woman before.

"Hey, Vixen," I hear James say in the corridor.

Ava doesn't respond, as I knew she wouldn't.

"Fuck, who was that? I don't do emo, but if I did, I would fuck her in the elevator." James comes prowling through the door in a black three-piece suit, hands stuffed deep inside his pockets. He stops beside Joshua.

"Ava is my assistant," I say.

"Lucky son of a bitch." James winks at me.

I peer over at Joshua, who has said nothing. His jaw is clenched, and his eyes are slightly narrowed. "You okay, Josh? You and Ava?" I point to the door she just exited from and back to him.

"I don't want to discuss it. She's a pain in my ass," Joshua spits.

"Well, okay then. What's with the lovely surprise from both of you?"

"James said he was coming by to check out your office, so I figured I'd come down to see you both," Joshua says, calmer than a few minutes earlier.

"Sure you weren't checking out the vixen?" James taunts.

The vein in Joshua's neck pops. "No. I can't fucking stand her."

I clear my throat. "If you two don't mind, I have kids to get home to."

"Aren't they being looked after?" James checks his watch. "It's only just after seven."

I shake my head. "Yes, I know, but it's an extra night for Jen, and she has work tomorrow."

"Jen?" Joshua and James say in unison. I piqued their interest. *Shit.*

"Jennifer, the girl that works at Rose's center and lives next door." I try to say it as if it's not a big deal.

"Oh, so that's the real reason you want to hurry this up?" James asks, mocking me.

"You're reading too much into this," I tug at the collar of my shirt, feeling it too tight around my throat.

Joshua laughs. "You can't even look us straight in the face."

My gaze shoots to Joshua. "You are reading way too much into this. Just remember, I'm a single dad with two kids and she is far too young for me. I need to focus on the girls."

"Doesn't mean you don't have needs." James quirks an eyebrow.

"I can't be fucking around like you playboys. I can't have anybody over, and leaving the house is impossible—and before you say it, no, you will not look after them."

Joshua slaps his chest with his hand and lifts his chin into the air as if I have wounded him. "The audacity."

Rolling my eyes at the fake dramatics, I spin around and stroll to my computer and shut it down.

"Alright, I'm off," I say.

"How about the game on Sunday? Are you are free to watch it?" James questions.

"If we can do it at my place, then yes," I say.

"Done. We'll bring the beers and order food when we get there," Joshua says.

When we finish our chat, I pack up and walk to the elevator and drive home, cursing the boys for holding me back. I told Jennifer I would be back early so she could go meet her own friends. I hope we can kiss and make up.

We need a date. I burst through the door, huffing. "I'm so sorry Jen. The boys held me up. I got here as fast as I could."

"Shhh." She scorns, "Dinners in the fridge."

And I jerk my head back with a playful beam, loving her warning and her bossy attitude. I lower my gaze slowly over her delectable body, memorizing every inch for later when I'm alone.

The electricity in the room zaps and I step closer to her, moving my lips to her ear. "I'm only hungry for you."

She gasps and I capture it with my lips. My hands grab the sides of her head, tilting it up for a better angle. She slams her body flush up against me, gripping the lapels of my jacket into her fists. Kissing me back harder. Feeling my cock growing hard just from our rough kiss.

I deepen it when a whimper escapes her mouth, massaging my tongue with hers. I want to fuck her so badly in this moment. I can't get enough.

Will I ever get enough of her?

I don't think so.

When she pulls back from our kiss, I groan, not wanting it to end. When our lips separate, I see her swollen wet lips. I have to restrain myself from capturing them again.

"I wish I wasn't leaving right now," she chokes out, trying to catch her breath.

Standing here with my hands cupping her cheeks, I wonder what the fuck I'm going to do. Wishing her eyes had the answer. I'm in too deep. So, before my brain can catch up with my lips, I blurt, "Would you be free to have lunch or even a coffee on Friday?"

"That sounds nice. How about at one?" she says brightly.

I can't help but smile back at her happy face.

"Perfect. I better let you go home."

"Wish I didn't have to," she mumbles cutely.

Me too. But I don't say anything, knowing she needs the rest of the night off to hang out with her friends.

Holding hands, we creep to the front door and step outside.

I let go of her hand reluctantly and she turns to me. "Good night, Tom."

"Good night, Jen."

I wave and watch her walk to her house next door, excited to see her on Friday.

CHAPTER 17

JENNIFER

IT'S FINALLY FRIDAY. I have been singing and humming lullabies to the babies in the baby room today with pre-date jitters. Assuming it's a date, I don't really know. *Surely?* All I know is I want to spend more time getting to know him. He makes me feel calm... and sexy. Who knew one person could make you feel both at the same time?

I send off a quick text to Thomas.

Jennifer: *I finished work. Meet you at The Social?*

The bubbles move straightaway, and I can't help but grin.

Thomas: *I'm here. See you soon.*

Hurrying into the car, I drive around to the café, park, and rush out.

As I walk closer, I see him sitting outside. Slowing my steps, I take in the vision. He is seated with his ankle crossed opposite his thigh, a frown on his face as he speaks on the phone and points to his laptop. His soft blue shirt, open at the top, is paired with soft cream suit pants. Smoothing down my work top, I take a deep breath to calm my thumping heart, then proceed. He looks up, tilting his head with a cheeky grin forming on his lips. As I approach, he hangs up the phone, twisting his body before standing to greet me.

I thrust my hand out, and I never handshake. I don't even know why I did it, but now I can't take it back. My hand just hangs between us awkwardly. What is it with me and this man? I can't stop myself from being embarrassing. His face softens, and a deep chuckle slips out as he clasps my sweaty palm. But then he kisses my cheek. Of course, he is always a gentleman. He gestures to the chair opposite him, and I slip into the seat.

"Hi," I choke out.

"Hi." His eyes shimmer with humor. "How was work?"

Having him ask me about work is strange. No one really cares other than my family. And even then, I don't think they care to hear it. They ask to be polite.

"It was good. I was with babies today. So, nothing too exciting, just the usual, changing diapers and feeding bottles... And you, looks like you have been here working while waiting."

I nudge my chin to the computer. He closes it and tucks it into a bag.

"Yes, I didn't know if you would run late so I figured I could get a few emails done."

I nod as a waitress interrupts to take our order.

"Hello, can I grab you two some coffee?"

Thomas raises his hand, offering me to go first. "Hi, yes, can I order a hot chocolate? And can I have one of your blueberry muffins?"

"Sure, and you, sir?"

"A latte with no sugar and I'll take a blueberry muffin too, please."

"Will that be all?"

He nods. "Yes, thanks."

She walks away and I raise a brow. "Copying me?" I tease.

"Well, I would have shared, but I don't know if you would be someone who shares her food. I have never asked you."

I ease back into the chair, moving my finger. "No, I don't share. I love food."

An easy smile plays on his lips. "I like that. So, I made the right decision. Is the muffin that good?"

"You haven't tried it?" I say, offended.

"No, I'm new to the area, remember?"

"Oh." *Duh, idiot.* "Yeah, you will crave it after today."

His eyes go dark, and as he looks at me, I feel it in my core.

"Here we are," our waitress says. "Latte for you, a hot chocolate for you, and here are two blueberry muffins. Will there be anything else?"

I shake my head, while Thomas answers, "No, thanks."

She hurries back inside.

The aroma of warm muffins enters my nose, and I moan. "So good."

I cut it open and apply a thick layer of butter.

"Is this the trick to why it's so good?" Thomas asks.

"Yep."

I take a bite of the muffin. The flavors are so good. I watch him layer the butter on and take a huge bite. His mouth and lips remind me of the vision from the other night. I need to get away from these thoughts before I'm achy for him again.

"Do you have any siblings?" I ask when I finish my mouthful.

"No, unfortunately just me."

"Come on, you get spoiled. Don't tell me you weren't." I sip my drink, watching him over my cup, feeling happy just hanging out with him in a normal way. It's an excellent test to see if

I'm just attracted to Thomas the dad or Thomas himself, away from the girls.

I'm certain it's him. He is different.

"Spoiled is an understatement. And it still hasn't ended."

I laugh at his honesty as he takes a sip of his coffee.

"I know you have your sister Megan, because your dad talks about you two all the time. Have you got any pets or had any?"

"No, my parents haven't let us have a pet in years since our last dog passed. It was too hard. What about you?"

He shakes his head. "I had one growing up. But no, the girls would love one, but it's a lot of work. I don't have time, which you now see."

"Fair enough, but you have a house cleaner? The place is tidy. Maybe they can help with the animal?"

Sipping the last of his coffee, he lowers it, then answers. "Oh no, I don't have one. But I have thought about it this last week... the house, the girls, and the job are becoming a lot."

His cell phone rings, and he pulls it from his pocket. "Dammit. Sorry. I have to take this. I'll only be a minute."

"Of course, go for it."

"Hello?" he answers.

I can't hear the other person on the line, but I sit back, stunned in silence. This guy really does everything.

I eat more of the muffin as he talks, chewing slowly and thinking of what I want to know about him next.

"Okay, leave the design on my desk and I'll be back shortly to sort it out."

My shoulders sag because he needs to leave now. I don't want this to end. When will I see him again?

He hangs up and stuffs the phone back in his pocket. "Sorry, work. I need to leave, which sucks. I was having such a good time."

"Me too." I smile back.

"How about next Saturday night? Do you have plans?"

My eyebrows rise. "What did you have in mind?"

"I have the girls, so dinner at my place, and then we can watch a movie when the girls go to bed?" He just stares at me, waiting for me to answer.

"I'd love to. Do you want me to bring anything?"

Shaking his head vigorously, he says, "No, just yourself." He picks up the check. "Let me take care of this and I'll walk you to your car."

"Okay, but I can pay," I say as I grab for my wallet.

"It's fine, I got it." He takes off inside before I can argue.

I finish the muffin and drink, and when he returns, he picks up his laptop and thrusts his chin toward our cars. "You ready?"

"Yep."

We walk side by side slowly until we arrive at my car.

"Thanks for everything. I really enjoyed myself," I say.

"Same. I will see you next week?" He leans in and kisses my cheek. My eyes flutter closed and my heart beats faster.

He pulls back with a sexy grin, and I nod, moving to open my car and climb in. As he steps away to his car, I pull out my phone to text Olivia and Katie.

Jennifer: *Dinner tomorrow night? Are you girls free?*

Katie: *I'm free. Sounds good.*

Olivia: *I'm in... I cannot wait!*

I love catching up with the girls for dinner. It's one of my favorite activities.

Tonight we're meeting at our regular Mexican restaurant. The waitress ushers me to an empty table in the middle of the place. I'm here first, so I take a seat and scan the menu.

Katie arrives next, which is good because I want to ask more about Jackson. I wave at her as she comes over to the table, shrugging her jacket off, then pulling out her chair and taking a seat.

"Hi," I say.

"Hey, have you been waiting long?"

"No, only a couple of minutes. Before Olivia gets here, I want to ask about Jackson," I whisper.

She rolls her eyes and softly shakes her head, leaning back into the chair. "There isn't anything to tell." She shrugs.

"But the two of you have... I don't know. A spark or something."

I remember the night at the bar and the way Jackson leaned in close and whispered something in Katie's ear, a lazy grin on his face. Katie giggled, a blush spreading over her cheeks. There was definitely something there.

She lets out an audible breath. "Don't say anything to Olivia, but I think he's hot—really hot. I just think he's a player. There is a connection on my side, but it's definitely one-sided."

"Are you su—"

"Hi, girls," Olivia cuts in.

Damn it!

My lips turn up in a smile, and I stand to welcome the oncoming affection I know is coming. She hugs Katie and then dances toward me, hugging the shit out of me. Her floral scent wafts up my nose, and I have to stop myself from coughing with the amount she sprayed.

A waitress comes over and we order some drinks and dinner.

"What did I miss?" Olivia asks, and my eyes flick to Katie's.

"Not much. I had only just arrived. Just told her how work has been quiet. Not many customers," Katie says.

"Well, I matched with someone online today, so after dinner with you girls, I'm meeting up with him," Olivia gushes.

"Oh, so that's why you're dressed up? I thought it was strange you were in a hot red dress, and here we are in jeans and sweaters," I say.

Olivia's face brightens. "You think I look hot?" She rubs her hands together, then skims them over her outfit.

"You know you are," Katie replies quickly.

I giggle and nod in agreement.

The waitress interrupts to bring our drinks and entrees over, setting them down in front of us before leaving us alone.

I pick up a tortilla chip and eat it before reaching for another one.

"What about you? What's new with that... what's his name...?" Katie asks, clicking her fingers, trying to think of his name... "Thomas."

"Yes, Thomas." Picking up my glass of wine, I take a large sip, needing the liquid courage to explain what happened Wednesday night and yesterday.

"Have you listened to my advice?" Olivia asks.

"Well..." I whisper and lean forward so no one can hear. "I'm helping him on Wednesday nights to pick his girls up from care and take them home. I offered, and he is paying me good money for it."

"What do you do with the girls? Are they nice?" Katie sounds unsure.

"Yeah, beautiful. I already care for Rose at work, and Lily is a lot like you, Olivia. Honest and loud." I chuckle. "I pick Lily up from school and cook them dinner, bathe them, and put them to bed. They are so easy, it's ridiculous."

"Who cares? Bonus money. What you need to tell us is where Thomas fits into all this." Olivia takes a bite of her taco.

"So, I fell asleep on his couch, and he woke me up by stroking my face, and then, uh, as I was leaving, we kissed. It was hot; he was hot." I fan my blazing cheeks.

"Whoa," Olivia says.

"Jen, you definitely got to know him then." Katie laughs.

I shake my head, waving my hands out in front of me. "No, no, no, not all the way."

I'm fully aware that I now represent a tomato—from my head to my toes.

Olivia jerks forward, eyebrows raised. "Not all the way? What does that mean? How far are we talking?"

I need more wine for this conversation, but I'm out, so I take the glass of water and drink. Feeling the cold water calm my body down, I then inhale a deep breath.

I lean as close to them as I can, and they lean in, understanding I'm not wanting to inform the restaurant. "We made out for ages in his bedroom, and, uh, he went down." I look down, pretending to pick off lint on my jeans, hiding my embarrassment.

"On you?" Olivia asks enthusiastically.

I nod, not wanting to say the words or look up.

"By the way you're hiding your face, it was good," Katie mocks.

"You can say that." I raise my chin and smirk. "But he then asked me for coffee yesterday. We met at the local café. It was nice to talk to him without the girls. His work called, so he had to leave, which sucked. I wanted to stay and chat with him more. But as I was getting in my car, he asked me to come over Saturday night, have dinner, and then watch a movie with him and the girls."

Olivia bounces in her seat. "And how do you feel about it? Because I'm excited over here."

"I can tell. It's like this is happening to you." I laugh.

"I'm just excited because you haven't dated for a while, so he must be something, even though he has two kids." Her voice turns serious.

"Yeah, he sure is something," I gush, "and the kids are so easy to love. I have this special connection to them, especially with baby Rose. She has my heart," I coo.

"You have always been great with kids. I'm happy you're getting to know him. Just don't get swept up. Be sure stepmom is something you are ready for. It's an enormous responsibility, and you just applied for a promotion," Katie states.

"Speaking of, when do you find out about your promotion?" Olivia asks.

I shrug. "No idea, hopefully soon."

And hopefully, it won't interfere with helping Thomas.

CHAPTER 18

THOMAS

I'VE SPENT THE DAY with the girls cleaning the house. Now, I'm about to step out with them to get food for tonight. I want to have snacks for the movie or if we watch another episode of the show we started. But things don't always go as planned.

The house door creaks open, and when I glance down the hall, I see my mother walking toward me.

My mouth curves into an unconscious smile. "Hi, Mom. What are you doing here? It's a lovely surprise."

She comes closer and I hug her before I kiss her cheek.

"Nana," Lily screams so high-pitched it nearly bursts my eardrums.

She runs into Mom's open arms. As she lifts Lily into her arms, she squeezes her in a tight hug. Rose's feet patter across the tiles and she hangs on Mom's leg, wanting a cuddle too.

Mom gently lowers Lily to the floor and lifts Rose to hug her.

"Nana," Rose sings.

Mom finally addresses my question. "I just came to say hi to my favorite girls."

"And not your favorite son?" I tease, my mouth curving in the corner.

"Of course, you too."

"I'm just teasing, Mom. The girls and I are happy you stopped by."

She nods at the keys in my hand. "Where were you off to?"

"Just to the store to pick up a few snacks."

I open my mouth to continue talking, but Lily cuts in. "Jen is coming to our house." *Fuck.*

Mom peers up at me with amusement and her eyebrow perks. "And who is Jen?"

"Daddy's friend," Lily speaks.

"Just a friend. She works at the center Rose goes to and the girls love her." I try to sound casual and imply it's all about the girls. I really didn't want to be having this conversation right now with Mom. It is way too early.

"And you? Are you dating her?" she asks.

My mouth drops open. "Mom, jeez... Just friends. You realize men and women can be just friends?"

Feelings are starting, but I don't want to confuse the girls after losing their mother. And I need to protect my heart from further pain.

And reminding myself that Jennifer is in a different phase of her life will prevent me from falling in love. Love isn't in the cards for me. That chapter closed for me when I lost Victoria.

"I'm just checking. I don't want my boy hurt. And you need to focus on my precious grandbabies." She winks, still cradling Rose in her arms.

I shake my head. "It's fine. You will know if I ever meet anyone."

She beams at my answer. "How about you run to the store, dear, and I'll stay and play with the girls?"

"That would be great, thanks. I won't be long."

"Take your time."

I swipe my wallet from the kitchen counter and kiss Lily and Rose. "Bye, girls. Have fun with Nana. I'll be back soon."

I wave and they wave back. "Bye."

After shopping, I arrive back home carrying bags of food. I unpack the bags and I prep dinner. I never mentioned to Jennifer a specific time to come over, so I want to be prepared for the girls' usual dinner time.

Mom is playing with the girls while I get ready for Jennifer's arrival. She keeps giving me side-glances and sneaky grins. I roll my eyes, knowing she is excited to meet Jennifer. I promised she would be welcome to say hello, but I would prefer her not to stay. Mom agreed. She has to get home for dinner herself.

My mind keeps drifting to last week and how she snapped my restraint. Her intoxicating kiss made me crazy. My mind burns with the memory of her sweet taste on my tongue and her moans as she came undone. She does not know her beauty and just how addictive she is. If she didn't leave and go when she did, I don't know how far we would have gone. But I know if it was up to me, I would have stripped her bare and sank myself deep into her.

"What time is she coming?" Mom's question cuts through my daydream.

I glance over to her drawing with the girls. "We didn't arrange a set time."

I check the time. It's only five, and I wish the time would hurry. I can't focus. The knock at the door sets my heart racing.

Both girls look up at my face and Lily squeals, "Jen's here."

Clapping, Rose says, "Jen."

Lily drops her pencil and climbs down from the chair. She takes off into a sprint to the front door. My lips perk up and Mom stares at me with wide eyes, clearly surprised by the girls' reaction.

"Come on, you can say hi, but you're leaving," I say firmly, reminding her of our agreement.

"Unfair." But she steps to the counter and scoops up her handbag and throws it on her shoulder.

Rose bounces in her highchair, so I unbuckle her and carry her on my hip to the door where Lily is patiently waiting by the locked door. I can see Lily talking to Jennifer through the door. My mouth twitches, thinking of what she could be talking to her about. The closer I get to the door, the more my heartbeat increases, and my palms sweat.

Reaching the door, I unlock it and push it open. Her shy smile and sparkling eyes peer back at me as she reaches out and holds it open. My breath hitches at the sight of her in tight, ripped gray jeans and a gray slouchy sweater that's tucked into her jeans at the front. She has on tan boots and her hair is curled. The obvious effort makes me grin.

"Hi, Jen."

"Hi, Tom," Her gaze drops from mine down to Lily's.

Lily takes a sudden step into the open arms of Jennifer. The exchange sends warm tingles over my body. Rose kicks in my arms, and I know she wants a cuddle too. Heck, I want one too.

Mom elbows my rib, shoving me out of the way, reminding me she is there, awaiting a formal introduction.

"Jen, this is my mom, Margaret. Mom, this is Jen." I wave between them.

Jennifer tucks a piece of hair behind her ear and smiles as she takes in my mom. Leaning forward, she offers my mom a handshake. "Hi, Margaret. It's lovely to meet you."

"Come here, love," Mom says. "It's wonderful to meet my son's young friend." Mom yanks her forward and hugs her, but her eyes are on me, surprise on her face.

I wince at the way she says 'young friend' in a mocking tone, reminding me of facts that I already know. I'm trying to remember our different paths every time she is around me. I just wish my heart followed my damn head. I hope Jennifer doesn't notice. She hugs my mom back before they separate.

"Thanks for coming, Mom," I say. "It was lovely to see you. Jen, you better come in. It's chilly."

Mom's face drops, and I hide my grin. There is no chance she is asking Jennifer a million questions tonight.

"Good idea." Jennifer turns to my mom. "It was nice to meet you."

"You too, dear." Mom kisses my cheek before walking to her car.

"Drive safe, Mom," I call out.

"Will do." She throws her hand in the air as she continues to walk.

"That's my nana," Lily tells Jennifer.

"Oh, you're a lucky girl." Jennifer carries Lily into the house.

"Jen, she's way too heavy for you," I say.

"No, it's fine. She's light."

I don't believe her, but she walks on through the house. I listen to Lily continue the conversation.

"Yeah, she wanted to stay but Daddy said no." Jennifer peers back at me and I bite the inside of my cheek and quickly avert my gaze.

"Oh, did she? Maybe next time." Her voice sounds like she is questioning me.

My stomach twists in knots. My mother will assume she is my girlfriend, and it's just too quick. The thought makes me dizzy. I'm just taking one step at a time, enjoying my time with her.

"Would you like a glass of wine?" I ask, putting Rose on the ground near the toys. "Dinner won't be much longer,"

"Oh, you cooked?" Her eyes widen and her brows shoot up.

A deep chuckle vibrates through my chest. "Um, yeah? I figured it was healthier for the girls. I have snacks for us for later."

Her eyes flash with a sudden darkness. *Dirty mind.* I tug at the collar of my black t-shirt, trying to get some much-needed air around my throat.

"I would love a glass of wine," she says, as she lowers Lily down and joins the girls.

Nodding, I swivel on my heel and grab the wine from the door of the fridge, then grab two glasses from the cupboard and fill them halfway. Wandering over to the girls, I hand over a glass of wine to Jennifer.

"Thanks, Tom." She takes the glass from my hand.

I smile down at her before easing onto the couch to watch the girls play, sneaking lust-filled glances at her. Her face is lit up like a Christmas tree, genuine interest and happiness written across it. She sips her wine as she talks with the girls. Both seem infatuated with her and Lily asks her a billion questions about what she has been doing these last few days, to which she throws her head back and laughs.

"Lily, my love, you are a very inquisitive soul."

"What does that mean?"

I chuckle at Lily's comment. The oven timer goes off, so I excuse myself and mosey to the kitchen to serve dinner. I'm carving the roast chicken when I feel the buzz of energy shift. Lifting my chin, my gaze lands on a pair of chocolates.

She stands at the other side of the island, clutching her wineglass. "Do you need a hand to set the table?"

"You're our guest. You relax and enjoy your wine and tell me about your day."

"My day. Well, I wish it was more exciting now that you asked... I just went for a run, slept in, and watched Netflix. Nothing really."

"That is still something. It's the weekend. You're allowed to chill."

"So, your mom came to visit. She seems nice."

"Yeah, she just came unannounced because she missed the girls. It was great. I was able to leave them here so I could run to the store."

"I could have gone."

I shake my head. "Guest, remember?"

She laughs at my authority. This fun side is refreshing. I always feel lighter when I'm around her, less empty and lonely.

"Okay, if I can't help here, then I can go play with the girls until dinner is ready." Spinning on her heel, she doesn't wait for an answer before going back to the girls.

I finish plating dinner before serving them on the table. When it's ready, we sit and enjoy the meal. The casual nature of us all talking and laughing sends heat radiating through my chest. It only intensifies when dinner is finished.

Jennifer and I put away the dishes together before bathing the girls and putting them down for bed. Jennifer puts Rose down in her crib while I put Lily to bed. The help tonight gets me choked up. It's easier with help. The girls won't take long to fall asleep because of my mom wearing them out today.

As we step out of the opposite girl's room, we pause and stare. How is this beautiful young woman wanting to spend her Saturday night with me and my daughters? I feel undeserving, but I push it to the side as she wanders closer and I follow her down the hall. When we are alone, my skin prickles and the heat inside my chest intensifies.

I need a drink to cool me down.

"Would you like another glass of wine?" I whisper as I walk to the kitchen to grab some snacks.

"Mmm, that sounds great."

"I'll set up the den, so we're more comfortable and don't wake the girls." I head into the other room and her light footsteps follow behind me. She takes a seat on the couch, and I hand her the remote. "Scroll through and I'll be right back. I'll grab our drinks."

"Thanks." She points to the screen and begins scrolling.

Minutes later, I return with a bag of chips and two glasses of wine. I hand over a glass before taking a seat beside her, giving her enough room but still sitting close to her. I feel like the tension from before is still there and my body is buzzing from having her near.

"What did you want to watch tonight?" I ask when I notice she hasn't chosen anything. "The show we watched the other night or a movie?"

"A movie sounds great."

"I'll flick over the movie channels and let me know if anything stands out."

It doesn't take long before she says, "*Jurassic World*. Let's settle on a movie we both would like, not too girly."

"I've wanted to watch this," I say honestly.

I press play and we watch the movie. She finishes her glass of wine a while after I finish mine. I want her close to me, to wrap my arms around her. I enjoy her sitting so close, yet she feels so far away.

"Did you want to come closer?" My eyebrow rises in question.

A small smirk appears on her face before she bites her lip and nods, then she scoots over to sit beside me. When she is close, I grab her shoulder and lie her beside me so I can have her head in the crook of my arm, and her hand resting on my stomach.

My heart is beating noisily under her ear, but she doesn't comment.

My cock also remembers her from the other night, so it stands for attention. Because I don't want to scare her too much, I readjust by shifting down so it's not poking her stomach. I'm sure she felt my desire for her, but she doesn't utter a word. She sinks into my side, and I sigh. This feels so natural and comfortable, having her beside me, watching movies on a Saturday night.

The movie plays for two hours, and we devour the chips and drinks. When it's over, I'm not ready for Jennifer to leave yet.

"Will you stay?" I say as I stroke her hair.

The question hangs in the quiet air. I swallow hard, waiting for her answer. It feels like forever. We haven't moved positions, but now that I asked that question, she sits up and swivels around to face me.

"I don't know… the girls?" Her face scrunches.

I know what she means, but I can't bring myself to stop and send her home. I want her too much.

Reaching out, I stroke my thumb over her cheek, cupping her face. I lean forward, as if drawn in like a magnet. Her eyes flutter and my eyelids become heavy as I tilt my head and whisper against her lips, "I want you to stay, please."

The slight movement in her head gives me the confirmation I was looking for. I reclaim her lips. The kiss is passionate and harder than our last kiss. My hands land on her head, moving her in the direction I want her, and I claim her mouth with my tongue. When I break the kiss, her swollen pink lips let out sexy little pants, making my dick twitch. I grab her hands and help her stand. I lead her back to my room. She follows with no hesitation.

Inside my bedroom, I close the door and spin her around. I return my lips to hers and she gives herself freely to the passion of my kiss. I skim my hands down her sweater to the bottom and pull my lips from hers to glance down at my hands. I lift it up over her head and remove the simple white cami underneath too. Her perky breasts tantalize me inside the cups of her bra. Her skin is taut and flawless, so different from my scarred body.

My hands slide across the silken skin on her stomach to her jeans, popping the button. Her sharp intake of breath spurs me on as I grasp the top of her jeans in one hand and tug the zipper down with the other. I skim my hands featherlike across the top of her pants, and she shivers underneath my touch. I take the edges of her jeans and guide them over her plush curves to the floor. Her hourglass shape is magnificent. My heart hammers inside my chest at the sight of her standing before me in a red lace set.

Her hand reaches out to the bottom of my black t-shirt. Cool air hits my skin, setting goosebumps alight across my body. I hold my breath as she removes my t-shirt, knowing what she is staring at—my scars and tattoos.

I don't comment and neither does she. Her hands are shaky, but she doesn't hesitate as she pops open the button of my pants and my black briefs come into vision. She pulls down my pants until they pool at my feet, and I kick them aside. Reaching out, I trace my finger across her plump bottom lip, and her mouth opens. I drop my hand and step closer, leaning down and peppering her with hungry kisses. Her moan sets me off. I toss her down on the bed, climbing over her to shower her lips and neck in breathy kisses.

Her back arches, so I reach around her back and remove her bra, letting my fingers brush her heated skin. My hands roam intimately over her breasts, and I trail kisses down her neck to her nipple, my tongue caressing the swollen bud.

She moans and wriggles underneath my touch. My lips move across to the other nipple, giving it the same attention. Her skin is smooth and soft under my large hands. I lean off her, balancing on one elbow, watching her eyes peel slowly open. Her eyes are glassy and heavy.

If I think she looks magnificent now, I can't wait to have her completely.

Tracing my fingertips over her stomach, I slide my hand under her red panties. "You're so wet."

I run my finger up and down over her clit to her entrance. Her soft whimpers send thrills through my spine. My cock twitches, reminding me he wants attention. I pull my hand out and her soft groan makes me chuckle.

"Soon, baby," I grunt out.

I drag her panties down, tossing them to the side. Her pussy is shining with her slickness, and I need to feel her wrapped around me soon.

Peering up, I find her gaze following my every move. I grab my briefs and guide them down my thighs, freeing my cock. Her eyes bulge and she swallows hard.

"You know how to make a man feel wanted. I will take it slow and make you feel good," I whisper.

"Okay." She lets out a shaky breath.

Reaching over to my bedside table, I pull open the drawer, feeling my way for condoms.

I sheath myself and line up at her soaking, hot entrance. I push forward and let the tip slip in. Her eyes slam shut, and her mouth forms an *O*. Pushing further, it's like a vise, she is so tight. I let out a grunt and wait for her to adjust to my size before I push completely in, filling her to the brim. It feels like home. She welcomes me into her body, and I watch her come undone in front of my eyes. Moving slowly at first, but soon as she is adjusted, I pick up the pace and thrust harder and faster. I groan as I chase my own orgasm, feeling her trembling thigh muscles around me.

"Fuck, Princess." I growl out.

She feels so fucking perfect. Her moaning is getting louder so I know she is close, so I drive the last few thrusts harder, making sure I come at the same time.

"Thomas... I'm coming." She moans.

She comes hard, her walls tightening and after a few deep strokes my body surrenders to the sensations. I groan, my balls drawing up to my body, and empty inside her.

I collapse beside her, and she drapes half her body over me and snuggles in. It's bliss having her tiny hands on my abs, her head lying in the crook of my arm and chest, her leg thrown over mine. I run my hands through her hair, relaxing her, feeling her breathing slow and steady. We lie like that until sleep takes over.

CHAPTER 19

JENNIFER

MY MUSCLES ACHE IN the best way. A smile forms on my face at the memory of last night, when I wake in darkness, feeling his scorching body beside me.

I don't have a clue what time it is, but I know it's early morning from the lack of light. I tilt my head back to gaze at him and my heart rips open. I knew I already had feelings for him. But the man I had last night was the most caring lover I've had. Not to say I have a lot to compare with, but Thomas makes it feel different. I feel different when I am around him.

His eyes are closed, soft breaths leaving his parted full lips. "Good morning, baby," he says, surprising me with his husky morning voice. He lifts his head so he can peer down at me, a grin appearing on his face.

"Good morning," I say. "I should get up and put some clothes on before the girls wake." The pitch in my voice is going up a level.

He reaches to hit his phone to check the time. Smiling back at me, he says, "We have another hour at least, so come here and get closer."

Loving this affection he shows me, I don't question him. I just shimmy up and wrap around him tightly. His hand strokes my back in a soft rhythm that has me falling back asleep.

The next time I wake, I'm alone in his enormous bed. The space next to me is stone cold.

My brow creases with worry, and I throw the covers off and swing my legs over the side of the bed. He's not in the bathroom when I check, so I go back to the bedroom to get dressed. As I gather my clothes strewn about the room, I hear the slight giggles of the girls and soft murmurs of a television playing.

The girls are up.

What am I going to do? I dress and pace the room, trying to figure out how to handle going out there. After a deep breath, I open the door and tiptoe into the hall down to the kitchen. I spot the girls playing together, and Thomas is at the stove cooking.

"Smells good in here," I say, keeping my shaky exterior at bay.

Thomas's head whips in my direction and his mouth curves into a smile. "Pancake Sunday."

I step closer to check out the pancakes and his hand wraps around my waist. My eyes bulge and I suck in a sharp breath, glancing at the kids dancing.

Oblivious to my reaction, he drops his hand and whispers into my ear, his breath tickling my ear, "It's okay... They can't see."

Needing to do something, I offer to make coffee and tea.

"That would be great." His expression is amused.

Thomas serves breakfast and I finish making our hot drinks, placing them on the table in the spots I know we'll sit. I stand next to the table, waiting for directions.

"Girls, pancakes are ready," Thomas shouts.

The squeal that fills the room makes my lips roll, and I hide my smile.

My heartbeat picks up. What will Lily say about the fact I'm here for breakfast?

The squeals stop when they come into my view.

Lily's face beams, but then her nose scrunches. "What are you doing here?"

"She's here for Pancake Sunday," Thomas answers matter-of-factly.

I wince, tilting my chin down. "Right. Here for the pancakes."

Lily doesn't ask any further questions, just shrugs and heads over to her chair. Thomas dishes her pancake onto a plate. She spreads her own thick layer of chocolate spread.

Rose runs over to me, and I pick her up as she hugs me. "Jen."

"That's right, Rose. Let's sit down and you can have some pancakes."

I place her into the highchair and serve her a pancake with a thin layer of spread.

I sit, cutting off a chunk of my pancake. "Mmm. So good, Tom." Thomas's brown eyes bore into mine, and I flush at the sudden inspection, feeling stupid for the sexual groan over a pancake, no matter how delicious.

Cutting another piece and popping it into my mouth, I take a sneaky peek from under my lashes and glance at his chest, remembering the scars tattoos displayed on his lean body. They were rather large—a lion, a sketch of a rose, footprints and writing. I wonder what they all mean and what he had been through to get them. I never asked him last night because I was too caught up in the moment, then cuddled up with him afterward. He was asleep before I got a chance.

The whole morning goes without a hitch, but I stay quiet, lost in my own thoughts.

I help Thomas get the girls ready for the day, and then decide it's time to leave.

"Girls, it's time for me to go home now. Thanks for breakfast."

"Oh, okay. But will you be back for the next Pancake Sunday?" Lily asks.

I bite my lip and lift my gaze to an amused Thomas. Clearly, he is not going to help me.

"Maybe. I will try. They were delicious."

Lily likes my answer and runs off to play. I walk to the door with Thomas. His hand finds mine, spinning me just before the door. He stares at my mouth, then glances back at my eyes.

"I'm going to miss you."

I lean forward to capture his lips, answering him with a seductive kiss. It probably wasn't the smartest idea because I now need to leave in a fluster.

"I better go. I will speak to you soon."

He nods, pecks my lips, and pulls open the door. I rush down the path to my house and gently open the door. When I tiptoe into the kitchen, I roll my shoulders, then look to see if anyone else is home. Relief washes over me and I continue taking light steps until I hear, "Where were you?" from behind me.

I jump on the spot, and my heart accelerates inside my chest. My hand dives to clutch my chest. "Shit, you scared me, Dad."

I let out a shaky breath and spin around to find dad leaning back on the couch, his head facing me with his arm draped over the back of the couch, his eyebrows raised in question.

Opening and closing my mouth, nothing comes out quick enough before he repeats the question, but with a firmer tone. "Where did you go last night?"

No matter how old I am, my parents will always want to know where I go and who I visit and what I do. Sometimes, it really bothers me, and I wonder if I need to move out to get some independence.

"I just stayed at Olivia's after we went out," I lie.

I don't want to lie to my father, but I don't know what Thomas and I are yet. Are we friends with benefits? Are we dating? If I don't know, how can I explain that to my dad? I want to ask but it's too soon. *Isn't it?*

"And where is out?" he asks.

I inwardly roll my eyes. The twenty questions begin...

"To a bar in the city," I answer nonchalantly.

His brows crease. "You were safe and didn't drink too much?"

"I was safe," I answer.

If only he knew how safe. I wish I could go back next door and be back in Thomas's warm embrace, just relaxing with him and the girls. It feels so natural. We don't need to be doing anything in particular. Just being together is enough.

He nods. "Good. You want to come hang out with your old man?" He drops his hand and swivels his head back to the television, telling me the discussion is over.

"Yeah, of course. I'll just shower and come back. Give me five."

He nods. I hurry down the hall and collect fresh clothes from my room before hitting the shower. As I close my eyes to let the hot water spray my back, memories of Thomas rush through my mind... his mouth on mine, his fingers on me, and the sex. The shower takes longer than the five minutes I planned, and when I finish and go back to the family room, I pause, taking a step back.

What the fuck is he doing here?

I stare at Nathan sitting opposite my dad, relaxing on the couch like it's a normal day. "What are you doing here?" I question in a disbelieving voice.

"Jennifer, don't be so rude to your friend." My dad's voice is stern.

I'm not his friend, I want to say. He is actually an acquaintance who I hooked up with once, but I refrain.

"Sorry, but I am confused."

Why is he here?

What does he want?

Why did my dad just let him in?

All these questions circle in my head as I try to understand why Nathan is here.

"It's fine," Nathan says. "I'm sure this is a bit of a shock. Do you want to talk for a moment?"

No, I would rather not. I'm still buzzing from Thomas, and now Nathan is ruining it. "Sure," I mutter. I don't want to give him the wrong idea.

He stands and walks toward me dressed in blue jeans, a navy sweater, and dress shoes, his blond hair swept in a neat man bun on top of his head. His aftershave hits me—he must have sprayed on a whole bottle. I swallow down the bile that is threatening to come up.

I take a peek at my dad, who is smiling at the two of us. My stomach twists. I wish I could tell him I'm seeing Thomas, but it's way too early for that bomb.

I need to find out what Nathan wants, so I lead him out the front door. I want him to leave as soon as our conversation is over. "How did you get my address?" I ask.

"Jackson gave it to me. Are you okay?"

"I'm fine. It's just I'm trying to understand why you are here, talking to my dad."

Shaking his head, he says, "Oh no, wrong idea. I wanted to talk to you, so your dad let me come in and wait for you."

Of course, my dad did. He needs to tone down his niceness. Nathan could have been lying, and he just welcomed him inside.

"Okay, so what did you want to talk to me about?" I stand with my arms crossed in front of me.

He glances down at the path, kicking his foot around, dusting the ground. His hands are in his pockets, and when he looks back up, there is a sparkle there.

"I wanted to see if you wanted to go on a date with me."

Well, shit.

I take a deep breath, my stomach in knots. "Thanks for asking, but I can't. I'm seeing someone."

His eyes narrow. "Sorry. I didn't know that. Jackson didn't tell me."

I drop my arms and sigh. "It's kind of a very recent thing."

He nods. "I can understand. You're beautiful—shame for me." He lets out a laugh, but it's strained.

"Is that your car?" I ask, trying to distract him and also usher him to the car.

"Yeah, it's new. Got it with the job."

"What is it you do?"

I hear giggles, and I follow the sound.

"I'm a—"

I stop listening as I focus on Thomas from the corner of my eye. He is exiting his house to go somewhere. *I wonder where they are all going?*

I blink and stare flatly. He must feel the heat of my eyes burning into him, because his gaze flicks to mine as he saunters toward his car.

I turn back to Nathan, who hasn't realized I haven't heard a word he has said.

"Mm-hm," I answer, trying to listen to what he is saying.

"Hopefully that only takes a year to get."

"Yeah, hopefully," I reply.

"Well, I better let you go. If you ever want to go out, the offer stands."

Not knowing what else to say, and not wanting to lead him on, I say nothing more. I want Thomas, and that won't change. And I hope Thomas seeing me with Nathan doesn't give him the wrong idea.

CHAPTER 20

THOMAS

"LET'S GET INTO THE car, girls. We don't have much time before the boys are coming over."

I'm taking the girls to the park to play. As we leave the house, I look toward Jennifer's out of habit and do a double take. I notice her standing there looking towards a young guy walking to a car. At first glance, I was jealous, but with the way she is staring at me, I know I have nothing to worry about and smile to myself as I walk to the car.

An hour later, we arrive back home, and the boys show up individually. It has been quite a few weeks since we have caught up for a football game. Usually, we meet at a sports bar or restaurant. James gets here first, bringing beer, and we prep the den. The girls' table is set up for toys and drawing, and the coffee table is cleaned and ready for snacks.

"Hello."

"Come in," I call out to Joshua.

I leave the room to meet him in the hall-way. He's carrying a bottle of scotch, which he thrusts in my direction. I take it from him and laugh. "The hard stuff."

"Damn straight," he replies.

We move to the kitchen, and I put the scotch away for later and gather the snacks I bought.

"Let me help you," Joshua says.

"Thanks. Where is Ben?" I say.

We drop the snacks in the den where the girls are playing and talking to James.

"He has a game."

I nod. He may have told me, but I'm preoccupied with a few things on my plate at the moment.

"Let's go, boys. The game is about to start," James calls out.

I hand James and Joshua each a beer, and everyone takes a seat. As soon as the game starts, I remember that less than twenty-four hours ago, I was on this same couch with Jennifer cuddled up beside me. I had the best night, having her in my arms, wrapped around me in bed. The intimacy and sex were better than I could have ever expected. Her body is so responsive to me. I want to hear her moan and feel her writhe under me again. I can't wait to have another night with her.

"Come on, man. That was a shit pass!" James takes a seat on the edge of the couch, screaming at the television.

"Bullshit," Joshua spits.

"Little ears." I point down at the girls in front of us who are drawing on the table.

Joshua winces. "Sorry, girls."

I check the time, knowing it's close to the girls' dinnertime. "I'll order the pizza. Does anyone have any preferences?" I ask.

"I'm easy. I'll eat anything," James replies.

Joshua stares at the TV, not listening, so I order a few types of pizzas.

The pizzas arrive and we eat a lot, the girls picking at a slice each. After the game is over, I get the girls bathed and in bed, then join the boys back in the den. They are now watching a basketball game, but not as engrossed as football.

"They're asleep, so are you boys ready to play some cards?" I ask.

"Yeah, let's go. I'm ready to win some money." James rubs his hands together and grins.

Joshua rolls his eyes. "Sure, but you'll need to beat Tom first."

James raises his eyebrow, a smug grin on his face.

I grab the cards and another round of beers. James takes the deck because he's a control freak who needs to deal.

"Thanks. Poker?" He pops a brow.

I nod, watching as he shuffles the pack an even number of times. *Control freak—like I said.*

He deals out the cards and we begin.

"So, Jen stayed over last night."

Joshua spits out his beer in a cough. "Give some warning before you blurt that shit out."

I chuckle at Joshua's reaction. "It's not that exciting."

"You said Jen stayed over and I'm assuming you two slept in the same room and did more than talk all night?" James's smug grin and accusing eyes stare at me.

Actually, I can feel both sets of eyes staring at me.

"Yes, we slept in the same bed."

James whistles. "Good on you. You deserve to be happy."

"I agree," Joshua says.

"How did the girls take it?" James asks, thankfully steering the conversation away from sex.

It's my turn, and I put my cards down on the pack and sit back. "Lily was shocked but happy, and Rose was ecstatic. She was hugging Jen, and it was adorable. But they didn't know she stayed over. They thought she came for breakfast."

"They're good kids, Tom. I'm sure if you're happy, they are happy," James says.

I sit up and absorb what he said. I'm hopeful it wasn't a one-off. I know I couldn't keep going forward with the relationship if the girls didn't accept her.

"Speaking of women, I need help." Our eyes widen as we look across at Joshua.

"Calm down. It's not like that." He scoffs, turning his head. "I just need help dealing with Ava."

"You can't get rid of her. I like her. What's your issue?" I question.

Joshua sighs. "She has no respect, and her attitude is disgusting."

"Only to you." I wink.

He rolls his eyes. "Her outfits are highly inappropriate—"

"If I have an issue with her outfit, I will let her know," I cut him off.

"Guys, let's change the subject. Clearly, we are wasting our time talking about this woman. I can tell you who was under me last night if you all want," says James.

I shake my head. "Who isn't under you is more like it."

We all laugh. I have a grin on my face, but the boys know this is a slow progression between Jennifer and me, that I want to keep some aspects—like intimacy—private.

For the next hour, we play cards and drink way too much alcohol, and I win the money again, then I walk them out.

"We can't let it go so long next time. I missed this," I tell them.

They agree and I watch them drive away. I head inside to clean up our mess before I crawl into bed. As soon as my head hits the pillow, her scent hits me like a bus. The rich vanilla scent is becoming my favorite smell in the world.

CHAPTER 21

JENNIFER

THE NEXT DAY AT work, Helen opens the classroom door and peeks around the door. She smiles wide, a gleam in her eyes when she sees me. "Jennifer, come join me for a chat in my office, please."

My brows furrow in confusion. "Of course, Helen."

She closes the door again, and Emma looks at me with curiosity on her face. "What will *that* be about?"

I shrug. "I have no idea. I'll be back." I push off the carpeted floor and walk to the door.

"Good luck," Emma calls from behind me.

What could be the reason she wants to talk to me? My palms sweat as I walk down toward the office.

I roll my shoulders back and step into the doorway. "Knock, knock," I say as I step into her office.

She swivels from the filing cabinet, smiling at me, then crosses to her office chair. The grin on her face makes my shoulders sag in relief.

"I won't take up too much of your time. I just wanted to discuss your application for the assistant manager. You've proven to me you're more than capable, so I would like to offer you the job." She hands me a piece of paper with details. "I will still honor your duties to help Thomas Dunn on Wednesdays so we will keep your Wednesdays as a morning shift, but the other days will now be a set nine to five."

My mouth opens and closes, but no words come out. I really wasn't expecting this. I scan the contents of the assistant manager contract.

"Read it over and sign at the bottom," she says, "We can transition your role starting next week if that suits you."

I swallow hard, darting my eyes between the paper and Helen. "Thank you. This means so much to me. I'll read it now and sign it."

She laughs. "No, Jen. Take a minute, read it properly, and then give it back."

"Yes, right, thank you," I reply in a shaky voice.

"Alright, well, take it with you and hand it back when you're ready, but you deserve to be recognized for all the extra work you do around here."

I clutch the paper between my sweaty hands. "Thank you, Helen." I turn around, disoriented, and walk back to the room.

I push open the door and Emma spots me. "What happened?"

"I, uh, got the assistant manager position."

"Jen, that's wonderful! Congratulations. You deserve it," she squeals.

I smile. "Thanks, Emma." I place the paper down on a high counter, planning to read it after work.

After work, I sit down in the break room and read through the contract. I'm happy with the new role and all the responsibilities and the higher pay. I sign it and drop it back at Helen's office before heading home to tell my family.

It's finally Wednesday. I resisted text messaging Thomas. I didn't want to come across as too forward, so I didn't cave to the desire. This new addiction for him is strange to me. I can't put my finger on what it is about Thomas that draws me in, only that I know I crave more time with him, his arms wrapped around my body, keeping me safe.

Tonight, as I wait for Thomas to arrive home from work, my knee bounces as I watch the clock, eagerly waiting. When the door swings open, I feel a lightness in my chest. And when he comes into view, I almost faint. Will I ever get over his handsome face? My body has a mind of its own, and I'm pushing off the couch and wandering over to meet him near the kitchen.

His eyes are shimmering and his mouth grinning wide, which makes me smile. He dumps his keys and wallet on the counter before he steps right into my space. He stares intently into my eyes. I gaze back, unmoving. He reaches out and strokes my cheek with the soft pad of his thumb before he skims the skin all the way to behind my neck.

My body is alight with shivers as he pulls me forward, his breath tickling my lips. "Hi."

I open my mouth, but he doesn't wait, crushing his mouth to mine. I moan and sag into the passionate kiss. Our tongues massage one another for a few minutes before I pull away, gasping for air. My hands drop to rest on his chest, feeling his heart beating a million miles an hour under my palms.

He pecks my cheek and steps forward to wrap his arms around me in a warm embrace. The steam is floating thick in the surrounding air. I didn't realize I was missing a connection to a man until I met Thomas.

"Are you hungry?" I ask.

He pulls his head back and his eyes sparkle with a deep lust. I swallow hard at the meaning of his stare. His mouth twitches into a large smirk.

I smack his chest and whisper, "You know what I mean."

A deep chuckle leaves his chest, causing movement under my hands. "I know, and yes, dinner would be great." He pecks my lips and pulls away.

I shudder at the cool air hitting me from the sudden loss of his body. He trails into the kitchen to heat the bowl I prepared for him, and I follow, plopping down on a stool, watching his body move effortlessly in the kitchen.

"I wanted to talk to you about the other day," I say. "I was out front with Nathan, who is Olivia's brother's friend. I didn't want you to get the wrong impression. We were just talking. I'm not interested in anyone else."

His gaze flicks to mine, his face relaxed. "It's fine. You can talk to anyone. I trust you."

My shoulders relax. It's so different with him. Most guys are jealous. But Thomas trusts me, and it's refreshing.

Wanting to change the topic and get off the whole Nathan talk, I ask, "How was work today?"

He sighs. "Good, but just so busy. A few of the buildings are in early preparation, so lots of design planning."

"So, wait, you design the buildings?" I ask.

He laughs. "No, I manage the electrical design of the building, make electrical orders, and look after the electricians and on-site managers. There are lots of sketching and meetings with builders after the initial contract sign-up. Sorry, I'm probably boring you, so I'll shut up now." He swiftly takes his bowl from the microwave before strolling to the utensil drawer to pull out a fork, then he sits on the stool next to me.

"No, it's not at all boring. Please, continue," I plead, twisting to face him, resting my elbow on the white stone and propping my head up in my hand. I want to know every detail about Thomas. I find him utterly fascinating. The more our connection grows, the more I need to peel back his layers. "The buildings you are currently running are all in the city?"

"No, they can vary. I have two new apartment buildings in the city to design where the electrical will go. But I have established schools and mall parking lots in suburbs too."

He twirls his spaghetti, and I watch as he lifts the fork to his mouth and wraps his lips around it, feeling jealous of the noodles disappearing into his mouth. I want his lips and tongue on me.

I ask more questions to refocus.

"That sounds interesting. Did you always want to do this job?"

I can see his mind ticking, and I watch his throat bob before his stare meets mine. "I started as an electrician and then studied project management and then recently my friend Josh offered me a job in his business... But enough about me. How about you? Did you always want to work in childcare?"

I watch as the change of his face turns from curiosity to care, making me want to melt into a puddle. "Yes, I've always loved kids. I want a large family." I glance down and rub my legs with my hands.

I wouldn't have expected that, so I change the subject, blurting out, "I actually received a promotion to assistant manager. I've been waiting to see how my application went for weeks. And don't worry, we worked it out so I can still help you on Wednesdays."

His shoulders drop with relief. "Congratulations." He kisses me. "I don't want to hold you back if you need to work on a Wednesday for the promotion. I'm sure I can find someone else."

I shake my head vigorously. "You aren't. I love the girls. They are easy. You have great kids, Tom—really great kids. I just can't help you out on days other than Wednesday."

His smile is wide and there is a twinkle in his eye—is it pride? But his smile then turns to a seductive grin. "Are you staying tonight?"

With that one grin, my sex throbs and memories of our last sexual experience come flooding back. Goosebumps cover my skin.

I peer down at my lap where my fingers now tangle together before I glance back up, lifting my chin to meet his questioning eyes. "I shouldn't. We both have work tomorrow. But of course, I want to."

His hand snakes across my thigh, giving it a squeeze. "There is no difference other than you can't sleep in, but do you think your family will mind?"

I sigh loudly. "My family won't notice during the week. Weekends are another story."

I doubt my family would mind. Yes, my family is protective, but they would be happy for me. They have never not supported me. I need to tell them soon if we are to be serious. I just need a good way and time to tell them.

He shakes his head. "Deal." He reaches out to crush my soft body against his hard muscles. "Let's go to bed and put the TV on." He winks before pulling away from me to take his bowl and cutlery to the dishwasher.

"I can check on Rose if you want to check on Lily."

After checking on the kids, we enter his room and he finds a shirt for me to put on. Undressing, he calls out to me, "Did you want to come to the zoo on Saturday? It is supposed to be a sunny day, and I was planning to take the girls. We would love it if you could join."

His black shirt looks like a nightgown on me, but his eyes flare with heat as I come to bed wearing only that. "That sounds like fun. I would love to go."

I crawl on the bed and snuggle into him. Thomas reaches out and strokes my hair. I soak this up, because I know he's not going anywhere.

CHAPTER 22

JENNIFER

ON THE DRIVE INTO work, my smile brightens as I think about the night I spent with Thomas. As the sunbeams through the window hit my face, warming my skin, I feel at peace. There was no sex in any form... We just slept.

I decide to call Olivia in the car on the drive to work. "Hello..." she grumbles through the speaker.

"Good morning, sleepyhead," I singsong.

"What time is it?"

I laugh at her grumbling. "It's almost seven. Shouldn't you be getting up soon for class anyway?"

"Yeah, it feels like way earlier."

"I only have a few minutes before I'll be at work, but I wanted to talk about Thomas," I gush, like I am sixteen all over again.

"How is that sexy dad?" Her playful tone causes me to giggle.

"Amazing."

"Ugh, you sound loved up. It makes me sick but also, I'm excited for you. If it wasn't so early."

"I'm not complaining that I have kept my hearing from your squealing." I smile as I continue. "I just left his house to go to work."

"Weekday sleepovers? How are the parents taking that?" she asks.

"Well, I haven't exactly told them. Last night they wouldn't have noticed because they go to bed early and then leave before me. And weekends, I kinda have been saying I'm staying with you," I confess.

"You know I'll always back you up, but if you're getting serious, you need to tell your family."

I sigh. "I know. He invited me to the zoo with the girls this weekend. And I think I need to ask him what's going on."

"Aw, look at you hanging out as a family, being all cute and shit."

I grin. "He is just perfect. I didn't think I could feel like this about anyone, but Tom is different. He is sexy, driven, successful, and the best dad to the girls. I just need to know more about his late wife. He won't open up to me about her, and I don't want to ask in fear I'll hurt our new—"

"Relationship," she cuts me off. "Yeah, I get that, but you two are still getting to know each other. Just enjoy the ride. I'm sure he will tell you about her soon. Just give him time."

"You're right. I'm worrying myself for no reason. I'm sure he will tell me. I'm getting way ahead of myself."

There is still something in the pit of my stomach when I think about his past. I'm determined to think of a way to ask him about his late wife.

"Exactly. Just chill out."

I glance down at the dash to check the time. "I better run. I don't want to be late for work."

"Well, now that you woke me up, I'll get ready for school and talk to you soon."

"Okay, I'll speak to you later." I hang up, climb out of the car, and walk inside work.

Something isn't sitting right, but I push it aside.

———

The next few days pass easily. The girls are in bed by the time Thomas arrives home from work. I haven't been able to sit comfortably for the last hour, my gaze darting constantly to check the time on my phone. The sound of the front door opening and closing causes my heart to thrum in my chest. I nibble on my lip. When he comes into view, I smile and walk over to meet him in the kitchen. He dumps his keys and wallet on the counter before coming closer.

My lips part and I lean in, but he unexpectedly lifts me onto the counter and parts my legs.

A soft "Oh" leaves my lips.

He reaches out and grabs my neck, capturing my mouth in a hard kiss. I skim my tongue along his lips to gain entry, and he opens instantly, granting access. His skilful tongue meets mine in a violent kiss. I would happily be greeted like this daily. His groan spurs me on. I run my hands along his biceps and his toned shoulders, until I hold his neck in my hands, feeling the pulse in his neck beating wildly. My beats match his in the frenzy.

He pulls back just an inch away from my mouth, his breath tickling my lips, and my lust-filled eyes stare at his eyes, wondering why he had to stop.

"I think I need to eat before we go any further. I feel I will need the energy tonight." His smoldering stare telling me his thoughts, I feel a flush rising from my chest. *Unfair. I want it now.*

He leans to bite my earlobe, dragging it slowly between his teeth as he pulls back. A shudder runs through my spine from pent-up desire. I feel I'm about to explode as I hop down from the counter and onto a stool. I wriggle, trying to get comfortable.

I clear my throat. "How was your day?"

He heats up his dinner as we talk. "Busy, but I got more plans approved today, so I feel like I am catching up on my work. I don't know how long it will last though."

"I guess it's not a bad thing to be busy."

"Definitely not, especially because Josh has just taken it over, so he needs as much work as possible. I just don't want it to affect the kids... But enough about me. How did your day go today?"

I take a deep breath. "Helen pulled me aside at work today."

"Yeah?" he questions.

"Yeah... She asked if you had looked into any child psychologists for Rose." I slowly lift my gaze.

He pauses with his fork in midair, then he takes his bite and chews. It's quiet for a few seconds.

"No, I haven't, but you don't think she has improved either?" His disappointed tone has my shoulders dropping.

I reach for his hand. "At work, she consistently seeks me out and gets highly emotional if I'm not around. I think it would help her if she had the right person. It's not a reflection of you. You are a wonderful father, Tom—the best I have met. But I think you need help."

Saying that was hard, and I swallow and watch for his reaction.

His mouth flattens into a thin line. I feel my throat constricting, panic setting in. It's too late to take it back.

He rubs his forehead with his spare hand before covering our hands and glancing back at me.

"You're right. I have tried to help her for a while now and it doesn't seem to work... and I'm all out of options." He offers me a small smile.

"Helen has some contacts if you need some recommended ones."

"Thanks, that's great. I might need them."

He gently tugs his hands from mine and finishes his dinner. I watch in silence, giving him time to process everything, even though inside I feel uneasy.

He scrapes his dish clean and stacks it away before walking around the kitchen to my side and standing in front of me. "Let's check on the girls and get to bed. I need to finish what was started in this kitchen earlier."

I nod before clasping his outstretched hand and walking to Lily's room, because I sense Thomas wants to check on Rose tonight. When we make it into his room, he walks straight to the bathroom to shower and brush his teeth. He comes out ten minutes later, wearing a white towel wrapped around his hips, his chest glistening from the water.

He drops the towel on the floor before stalking over to the bed.

I lie down, and he hovers over me and captures my lips with his. This kiss is rougher and more urgent, which excites me. I love the multi-layered man Thomas is. My hands dive into his brown locks, and I pull his head closer to me, panting between kisses. He tastes minty and fresh. Feeling his hand trying to lift my top, I remove my hand from his hair and rip my shirt off so fast, throwing it across the room. I quickly unhook and toss the bra. Thomas breaks out into a laugh at my urgency. But he got me way too hot and bothered earlier, and I need release as soon as possible.

He smashes his lips back to mine as I reach out with my palms and feel his body. The hot, soft skin and all the ripples are sending me wild. Heat pools in my sex. I'm achy and needy.

"Tom, I need you," I whisper into the still air.

My pants and panties are off in a flash. The cool air hits my warm entrance. I shiver. "Hurry," I say.

He grabs a condom and rolls it on before he grabs my hip bones and quickly lines himself up. His eyes never leave mine, our gazes locked. I expect him to slam into me, but of course he inches in slowly on purpose, it's utter torture.

I palm his ass in my hands and squeeze, urging him to go faster and deeper.

"What's wrong, princess?" he teases.

I blow out my cheeks in frustration. "You need to go faster."

He chuckles in the crook of my neck. "I want to enjoy this."

I know he is playing with me, but the ache in between my thighs is throbbing and he is moving at a torturous pace. I let out a frustrated groan.

Moving his hand, he palms my breast, rubbing his coarse thumb over my nipples, causing me to shiver with pleasure. My eyes close. This feels incredible. He continues to play, squeeze and pinch them at the same time, thrusting his hips harder. *Yesss.*

Needing more, I trail my fingers between our bodies over my skin and find my clit, rubbing lazy circles over my bud. My eyes are closed, and my breathing picks up as I feel myself climb higher.

"Fuck," he grunts.

My eyes snap open to see his dark, hungry eyes staring down at me. I close my eyes and smirk to myself. And go back to stroking myself as he plunges into me harder now. His hand on my breast is more desperate, rough and it's exactly what I need.

"You like touching yourself, princess?'

"Yes," I moan and arch my back as I feel my thighs quiver with tension.

I'm so close. He leans forward, capturing my nipple into his mouth and sucking hard. And that's enough for me to buck underneath him, my thighs tightening around him as I come hard.

"Fuck," he rasps out, losing control.

A few ragged pumps of his hips later, I feel him pause and his cock jerking inside.

He continues at the pace he wants, and I just enjoy it. He slowly releases and my whole body shakes from the loss. Blinking my eyes open, a satisfied smile plays on my lips. He kisses me softly, lips lingering over mine, before he drops down beside me, breathing hard, trying to recover.

Knowing he is just as affected by our intimacy overwhelms me.

CHAPTER 23

JENNIFER

IT'S FAMILY DAY. I'M dressed in blue jeans, a white t-shirt, cardigan, and sneakers, ready for the day at the zoo with Thomas and the girls. I wander out of my room to the kitchen to eat some toast before heading next door. Thomas said we need to leave at nine, but I want to arrive a bit before to help him get the girls sorted and in the car.

I step to the pantry and grab the bread. When I turn around, Mom's there, frowning and assessing my outfit.

"Where are you going?"

How am I going to get away with this? I don't want to lie. Taking a deep breath, I lift my gaze to meet hers and answer confidently, even though I am silently shaking. "Going out on a day date."

My mom's brows shoot up and her lips form an *O*. Then she asks, "With who?"

Shit. I'm not ready to say Thomas. "It's still early, Mom. I'm still getting to know him."

"Well, when do we get to meet him?"

I put a slice of bread in the toaster. "I don't know. I'll ask him today."

She leans against the counter. "How about dinner? He could come here, and I could cook a nice dinner for all of us."

"Okay, Mom, I'll ask him."

I know if I don't agree, she won't stop asking. The toast pops so I grasp it, and layer peanut butter on, taking a bite.

"Okay, will you tell me anything else?" she asks.

I shake my head. "No. I have to leave now. I will see you tomorrow."

"Hang on, young lady." My dad's voice sends goosebumps running over my skin. "You're staying at a boy's house?" He obviously heard the last of the conversation between Mom and me.

My muscles tense and I clench my jaw. "A man's house, and yes. I'm not little anymore, you do realize?"

"Don't be smart with me. I'm allowed to ask questions under my roof," he curtly says.

I huff. "I get that, but I don't need a lecture. I've shown you how hard I work with my job promotion and now you discredit me."

He comes to a halt in the kitchen. "Not true. Your mother and I are very proud." Mom nods.

"It doesn't change the fact I want to know you're safe, young lady."

"I know, and I am grateful that both of you care. But you two need to trust me." I plead to my dad with my eyes. Growing up, Megan and I used to know all the tricks to get my dad to cave, like giving him our sad eyes, but now that we're older, it doesn't always work.

"I want to meet him," he replies.

I nod. "Okay, okay. I'll ask him today if he will come for dinner and I'll arrange it with Mom. But I'm safe and very happy. I have to go or else I'll be late." I take another bite of my toast and walk up to the door, talking around mouthfuls. "Bye."

"Bye," my dad grumbles.

Closing the door, I walk slowly next door, trying to figure out how I'll go about asking Thomas to meet my parents when I'm not even sure we are officially together. I will need to ask today. There is no way my parents will accept anything else if I don't arrange a meeting.

I knock loudly. The girls scream and squeal with excitement. The giddiness of the girls makes my heart constrict.

The door opens a moment later, and Thomas stands before me like a dark angel in a sexy black bomber jacket, black t-shirt, and black pants. He has finger-swept his hair back and his brown eyes shimmer in the morning light.

Flustered by how sexy he looks, I have to drag my eyes down to see the girls to recover.

"Hi, girls," I say.

They have each clutched a leg for cuddles and pull back to stare up at me when I address them. I smile down at their excitement.

"We're going to the zoo," Lily calls out.

"Yes, sweetheart. We sure are. Are you ready?" I ask.

They nod.

"Alright, girls, let's get into the car." Thomas bends down to pick up Rose, adjusting her on his hip.

Thomas steps out of the house, dragging the door shut behind him. He locks it and spins. Taking a step forward, he kisses my lips in an all-too-brief kiss that leaves me breathless. He stares back at me with a hint of humor, because he knows exactly what he did. But I'm not amused.

I help Lily get in the car, breaking the tension that is built around us when we are around each other.

The drive to the zoo is a little less than thirty minutes. We have the music going for the girls, and they dance in their seats as I relax in mine. Thomas doesn't talk much on the drive. His focus is on driving, which I don't mind because it allows me to work out the best way to approach my parents' dinner offer with him.

When we arrive, he pulls into an empty parking spot, and we get out and each grab a child.

"I'll get the stroller," Thomas says. "Lily, please stand next to Jen."

I juggle Rose on my hip and hold my hand out for Lily. She rushes over, placing her tiny hand in mine, and we step over to the sidewalk to wait. Thomas opens the stroller and pushes it over to us, taking Rose from my arms, then strapping her in. We set off.

Thomas pushes the stroller, and I follow with Lily, taking in Thomas from behind. A small smile forms on my lips. He's in his element of being a dad out in a social setting and watching him makes my heart race.

We arrive at the gates within a few minutes and Thomas pulls out his wallet. "Thomas, I can pay for myself."

He swings around with a glance that insinuates I have insulted him. "No, I pay." He faces the cashier to pay the bill. Before moving forward, he grabs a map from the display stand and moves to the side. "What animal would you like to see first?" Thomas pops the brake on the stroller before squatting down to show Lily and Rose the map.

"Um." She gazes around the map before pointing to the lion. "I want to see Mommy first."

Thomas freezes, no words leaving his mouth. My brow furrows, trying to understand what Lily means. He snaps out of his daze and clears his throat. "Okay, let's go." He releases the brake and strolls off, not waiting or explaining what is going on.

My mouth parts. *What is happening?* Lily tugs my arm, reminding me we are standing still as Thomas walks farther away, disappearing in the distance. I walk, Lily's hand in mine, and we try to close the distance at a quick pace.

We still trail behind, and I can see the tension rolling off Thomas's body. He stops outside of the lion enclosure, and we creep up next to him.

Lily bounces up and down. "I want to see them."

I bend down and lift her to let her see into the enclosure. I don't say a word, taking a side-glance at Thomas who is standing like stone, clenching his jaw, his eyes narrowly watching the lions pacing the enclosure. Returning my gaze to the lions, my heart beats faster in my chest. I want to ask Lily why the lions are her mom, but I don't want to upset Thomas further. There is a niggling feeling in my stomach, but I push it away.

"Let's see the next animal on the map." His voice is strained.

I lower Lily back down to the pavement. Clasping her hand, we follow Thomas and Rose around the bend to the giraffes. Thomas relaxes, and we wander around the zoo for another hour until Lily is hungry. We find a coffee stand with some benches and stand at the kiosk to browse the menu.

"What do you want me to get the girls to eat and drink?" I ask.

It's the first time I've spoken to him. He slides his hands around my waist and I freeze, then melt into the welcome surprise.

"I'll get it. You came on this date with us. I pay." The word date rolls off his tongue with ease, and it makes me giddy.

I peer down at Lily who is not fazed about it. She keeps her eyes ahead, and we shuffle up to the front of the line. While he orders, I take the girls to a table. Thomas joins us with burgers, and while we eat, I can't hold it in any longer.

"Are you okay?" I ask. "You seemed upset at the lions."

A flicker of hurt washes over his face before he glances away and answers. "It's all still raw, I guess," he whispers so only I can hear. "I'm okay, and then something the kids say rip open wounds I think I'm over."

Before I lose my nerve, I whisper, "How long has it been?"

The silence makes me feel like I shouldn't have asked, the question too deep. The shimmering sadness in his eyes pangs my gut.

"Over a year now." He sighs.

I'm elated he answered me, but I'm also riddled with worry. Is he ready for dating?

Or are we just having fun? Is it too soon? Am I a rebound? The side of my temple is throbbing from all these thoughts.

CHAPTER 24

THOMAS

I HATE I MADE my issues so obvious. I can't help having a reaction whenever the kids bring up their mother and my mind flashes with memories. It brings up feelings I thought I had buried.

I look at my kids. The vision in front of me hits me hard. Lily is speaking to Jennifer with a big, toothy smile. I inhale a deep breath and prepare for more hard questions.

Jennifer's gaze meets mine, and I give her a small smile.

"Lily, where should we go next?" Jennifer asks. She takes a sip of her drink.

I frown, expecting more questions, but none come. I'm elated that we don't have to have the conversation here. She is thoughtful with my girls. More than I realized. They know nothing other than their mom is an angel in the sky. But I can't avoid the questions forever.

"Ahhh, the butterflies, we haven't seen them," Lily says.

I sip my coffee. "Okay, let's finish our food and drinks, then hit the butterflies."

Sitting across from Jennifer, I can't help but stare, amazed at how effortlessly she fits in with my family. I never could have imagined being connected to another soul other than Victoria's. When it happened, I thought I could never move on and date, yet I sit here today, on a family date. No matter what we do, she never comments or complains if the girls come with us.

Finishing my coffee in silence, I let my brain ponder and can tell she has a lot on her mind as well.

"Are we ready?" I ask.

Lily jumps up. "Yes."

Rose kicks her legs in the stroller, and Jennifer drains her cup before getting up to put everything in the bin. We wander off and spend a few more hours in the zoo before finally walking back to the car and driving home. Rose has fallen asleep, and Lily looks ready for a nap. She passes out a few minutes down the road.

I want to reach out and hold Jennifer's hand, but I resist the urge. I still get sweaty hands, and I'm constantly scanning for cars. The first few months driving after the accident were the worst. I got anxious sitting in the driver's seat, but I had to drive to work or get the girls around. My symptoms settled to a lesser degree, and I have maintained control. But I will never be the same and I have accepted that. I'm grateful I can drive at all.

I glance in the rear-view mirror, double-checking the girls are asleep.

"Did you have a good day?" I don't take my eyes off the road, but I can sense Jennifer's eyes on my face, which makes me smile.

"Yes, the date was perfect." I can hear the happiness shine through.

"I'm glad. I do have to take you on a real dinner date... No girls."

"Today was great. You don't have to. The girls are a package deal and I love them."

I know the girls are easy to love but hearing her utter the words makes me feel lighter. "I know. They are awesome, but it's not the same."

"I'm happy with anything. So does this mean we are officially dating?" My lips twitch at the way her voice lowers like she was scared to ask.

I chuckle. "Well, I haven't dated in years, so I don't know how this works, but I don't plan on dating anyone else. I enjoy what we have going on. But how do you feel?"

I wish I could watch her face right now, but I will not remove my eyes from the road. We aren't far away from home now.

"I don't have much to compare. I have dated very little, but I agree. I love where this is going.

I feel comfortable and at home around you," she answers in a light voice.

Her answer makes heat radiate through my chest. Could she be any more perfect?

"So, while we are talking, uh, my parents know I'm dating someone, and I didn't tell them it's you. I didn't want to say anything until we were official, but I guess now we are, so I can tell them. But I would love to do it together. They want you to come for dinner."

Her family, especially her father, have been so kind to me and the girls, I don't see a reason why not.

"Of course, I would love that. I'll get Mom to come and mind the girls."

"Oh, don't be silly. They would be upset if you didn't bring the girls."

"Are you sure? It might be a lot for them."

"Yes, I'm sure. All three of you for dinner. Mom will be so excited."

I laugh at her comment. "I'm glad someone is. I'm not going to lie. I'm nervous. It's been a very long time since I met someone's parents."

The car is quiet, and I know she is thinking of how to ask or what to say about what happened at the zoo. I'm bound to get some questions soon.

"It won't be anything you can't handle," she says, surprising me because that was not what I thought she was going to say.

"Are we home yet?" Lily's voice comes out of nowhere, making my body jump in its seat.

"Soon, baby. We are around the corner. Are you hungry or thirsty?"

"Yeah, both." I check Rose and she is still asleep. "Just a few minutes and then I'll get you a snack."

"Okay," she mumbles.

I pull into the driveway and twist in my seat to face Jennifer. "Can you please bring in Lily? I want to carry Rose to her crib."

She nods, so I hand over my keys. She swiftly takes them and climbs out of the car before I have a chance to peck her. I climb out my side and step around to get Rose out of her car seat. She stirs a little when I reach for her but otherwise returns to sleep.

Jennifer opens the house and holds the door open for me. Lily has already gone inside. I peck her on the lips as I pass. Moving gently to Rose's room, I put her down in her crib to nap.

When I step into the hallway, I hear Jennifer in the kitchen making Lily a snack. Lily is plastered beside her and from the looks of it trying to assist in the preparation. I rub the back of my neck before rolling it on my shoulders, trying to relieve tension.

"What's going on over here?" I walk to the front of the counter, grabbing a blueberry and popping it straight into my mouth. The sweetness explodes in my mouth, and I want more so I reach over, but she smacks my hand gently, scolding me.

"Wait for a second. I'm making a plate."

I sit back on the stool and watch in utter fascination. After a few minutes, the plate of fruit is beautifully decorated and I smile at Jennifer.

"This looks so good," Lily says as she grabs fruit from the plate.

"Lily, I'll get you a plate and you can pile what you want on it," Jennifer says.

"Oh, yes." She has her hands on the counter and jumps up and down.

"Please," I correct Lily.

"Please, Jen." She still bounces.

Jennifer opens the cupboard to retrieve a plate and Lily pulls fruit onto her plate.

"I'll bring it to the table, and you can eat it there," I say.

"Okay, Daddy." She runs to the table.

I take her plate over and sit beside her.

"What do you feel like having for dinner?" Jennifer asks.

She looks right at home in my kitchen. Am I dreaming? She raises her brows as she waits for my answer.

I clear my throat. "I'll eat anything." My double meaning causes her to flush from her neck to her cheeks, and her eyes dart away from my intense stare.

I never thought about sex that much since Victoria. It was always something I just did for relief. But since Jennifer, I crave her body, her sounds, her taste. She is addictive.

"That's not helpful," she huffs, blowing out her cheeks.

It makes me chuckle out loud.

"What's funny, Daddy?" Lily asks.

"Nothing, sweetheart," I reply.

Lily shrugs her shoulders and continues to eat fruit. I glance over at Jennifer who is biting her lip between her teeth.

"I'll check out the pantry and see what I can pull together," she says.

"I'll give you a hand," I say, my chair scraping along the floor as I stand.

I enter the pantry, surprising Jennifer, and I know Lily can't see, so I grab her around the waist and spin her to face me.

"Oh," she squeals in surprise.

My hands are on her lower back, keeping her body against mine, her softness to my hard muscles; it's the perfect puzzle piece. I lean down and breathe her in, my skin sensitive to her. Every hair on my body stands for attention whenever I get this close.

Her eyes flutter closed and her mouth parts, soft pants leaving her lips. I close the distance between our lips, and her lips move with mine until I slide my tongue across her lower lip, seeking entry. I groan but pull away, not wanting to be caught by Lily. Jennifer whimpers from the loss, and my mouth twitches into a grin at her sedated state. I love how I can unravel her with just a simple kiss.

"Later," I whisper, my tone dark and seductive. I smack her butt and spin around to walk back out to the kitchen, and Lily is right there behind me, watching. "Shit, Lily. You scared the crap out of me."

A frown crosses her face. "Daddy, you just said a bad word."

"Oh, I'm sorry, sweetheart."

She crosses her arms over her chest. "Well, I think you can go into time-out."

I roll my lips inward to prevent laughing at her sass. I can hear Jennifer behind me struggling to hold it together, so I quickly push Lily out of the pantry.

"Why were you kissing Jen?"

This inquisitive age is really testing. "Because she's my girlfriend."

Lily's face scrunches up. "What? That's gross. Boys have germs."

A deep chuckle escapes this time.

"I know, really gross." Jennifer winks as she saunters out, passing me with the sauciest grin on her face.

Rose calls out from her crib, so I head to her room and pick her up and cuddle her. We walk out to the kitchen where she sees Jennifer and kicks and pushes off to get down.

"No, Jen," she mumbles.

When she gets down, she runs to her, and Jennifer squats to take Rose up in her arms, flying her through the air. Rose squeals in delight, lighting up the room. I never thought I would see this day. My daughter is falling for another woman other than my mom.

"Rose, come and play with Daddy and Lily," I say. "Jennifer is trying to cook us a surprise dinner."

Rose glances up at her, and Jennifer nods in acknowledgment. "I won't be long, sweetheart." Jennifer strokes Rose's face.

I walk over and scoop her up in my arms. The rest of the night is seamless, and Jennifer and I work as a team. When the girls are in bed, I pour us each a glass of wine and settle on the couch. She nestles beside me.

I bring the glass of Shiraz to my lips and take a large gulp, giving myself liquid courage.

"Lions remind us of Victoria, my late wife." My heart beats wildly in my chest. Beads of sweat form on my forehead, and I feel her flinch in my arms, so I stroke her arm in slow motions until her body is relaxed again. "Victoria was fierce like a lion and didn't take any shit from anyone. She was strong, independent, and stood up for what she wanted. No bullshit approach. When she passed away, I used to tell the girls their mom reminded me of a lion, so now they are obsessed with lions." My lips form into a thin line.

My stroking continues, but I take another pull of wine, my heart rate picking up in my chest after the mention of Victoria to Jennifer. I don't know why. I feel comfortable with her, but this topic is unnerving. It rattles me. I feel exposed. She hasn't said a word yet, but I can hear and feel her steady breaths.

"They are wonderful traits to have and it's good the girls can have a positive thought about her. I see Lily takes after her then, her strong-willed personality."

"Definitely, and the more she grows, the bigger the sass. But I love it." Talking about my girls warms my soul. Having kids will change you forever. It is one of the hardest yet most rewarding jobs of my life. They have taught me to be patient, to love, and to cherish. They are my world and without them, it wouldn't be worth living.

"The tattoo on your chest is about Victoria then?" Her voice is soft and kind.

"Yes. I got it in her memory after she died."

After I left the hospital, I was furious at the world for taking Victoria from me and the girls. Every day, I had painful memories flash behind my eyes, and the scars that marked my torso were a daily reminder I loathed.

Tiny fragments of glass from the shattered windshield seared into my torso. They only took a month to heal, but I can feel them under my fingertips every time I wash my body.

One night, I decided to get a tattoo. Many hours later, I ended up walking out of the tattoo parlor with more than one. The marks are now disguised by different tattoos, and when I remove my shirt, I see the colorful art that's displayed on my body.

A small bead of sweat trickles down my face. Not wanting to continue this conversation, I trace my fingers across her collarbone, down her neck. Her body shivers underneath them. My heated stare fixes on her hooded brown eyes.

I stand and hold out my hand. She gazes between my face and hand before she reaches out and clasps her hand in mine. Staring at her lips makes me want to do crazy things, and my tongue skims my lips in need.

"You're so beautiful."

I tug her to me in one swift motion. Her hands land on my pecs, and they tighten under her touch. Grabbing her face, I smash my lips to hers, and kiss her with urgency, thrusting my tongue inside her mouth, tangling with hers. Her hands on my neck bring me closer. I'm not sure how much closer we can get. But I need more.

I rip my mouth away from hers, heavy breathing racking my body, and tug her toward my room. She whimpers from the loss but follows.

I close the door and lock it. "You're staying tonight," I command in a growl.

"Yes," she husks.

Unable to hold back my restraint anymore, I step farther into my room and hastily remove her cardigan and shirt. Her plump breasts sit high in a navy bra, and I harden from the sight. *Magnificent.*

"Fuck you're perfect." My voice is shaky, and I lean forward and trail kisses up her to her ear.

She shivers, and her body melts underneath my lips.

"Are you wet for me?"

She answers, "Yes," on a moan.

"Good."

Snaking my hand around, I grip the bra, unclasping it, and my fingers guide the straps off her shoulders. I throw it across the room. She slips my jacket off my shoulders, and it lands with a thump on the floor. My shirt follows.

She sucks in a ragged breath, staring at my tattoos and scars. My heart thunders as she moves her hand to my chest, tracing my lion tattoo, her soft fingers bumping over the scars.

I haven't told her about the accident, but I need to... I just don't feel ready.

CHAPTER 25

JENNIFER

NOW I KNOW THE meaning of this lion... the late wife. I still don't know or understand what happened to her, other than she died over a year ago. My heart breaks for this man standing before me.

He is wounded in more than one way, and I really hope he is ready for *us*. I have fallen for him and his girls, and I don't want to be hurt in a game to get over his wife. I want him, and I'll give him my all.

I really should stop this going any further and ask hard questions. But I know he isn't ready for more right now, and I can't get my lips to move to ask them.

I skim my hands over the healed scars on his chest and upper abs to his black pants. He sucks in a sharp breath, and I pop open the button and unzip the fly, pushing them over his perfectly muscled ass and letting them fall into a pile on the floor. He stands in his black briefs and my core clenches at the sight of my boyfriend. I smile. *My boyfriend.*

"What are you smiling at, princess?" he asks.

"Nothing," I mumble. I'm too embarrassed to tell him I'm giddy over him being my boyfriend, but I guess his intelligent brain doesn't miss a thing.

"Tell me," he coaches.

I flush. "It's embarrassing and stupid," I huff.

"Nothing is embarrassing. Tell me." He strokes my hair.

"I can't believe you're my boyfriend or that I have a boyfriend... Told you it was silly and embarrassing." I slam my eyes shut and shake my head.

"Princess, don't be embarrassed. I'm happy you're my girlfriend. I didn't think... I could be happy ever again," he murmurs.

His fingers move from my hair to the curve of my waist, before lowering to my jeans. I shift from side to side to help him tug them down, and in swift perfect form, they are off. The steam in the room is thick, the lust real, and my heart feels like it wants to explode with happiness.

His hands trail along my ass down behind the backs of my thighs, and he lifts me up. I yelp, my hands quickly linking around his neck as he carries me to his bed and sits with me on top of him. He leans forward, licking my nipple and then sucking it into his mouth before releasing it with a pop. My core squeezes. He kisses a line to the other nipple and licks that bud and sucks it into his mouth, then draws out the nipple with a graze of his teeth.

As I shudder from the sensation, he worships my body like no one ever has. He runs his hand along my thighs before pulling back my panties to reach in and touch my core.

He groans. "Fuck, you're so wet."

He gets me so hot just by touching me. I can feel his cock straining in his briefs, the temptation to rub along or seek pleasure from it high. Before I have a chance to move, he slips one finger through my wetness, grazing my sex. I whimper as my walls clench down hard at the intrusion. I lift on my knees for him to gain better access, leaning on his shoulders with my hands for support and resting my forehead against his. We watch his hand move inside my panties. It's extremely sensual. The sound of my arousal should embarrass me, but Thomas makes me feel adored.

The build of exquisite pressure in my sex forces my eyes to close. I pant as his fingers move harder and faster, groaning with each stroke, climbing higher, seeking relief. When my orgasm slams into me suddenly, I fall apart on his hand. When I come down from the blissful state, breathing hard and fast, my pulse erratic, I peel my eyes open and raise my chin to meet his stare. The look in his eye tells me he's not finished with me.

Oh, shit.

He swivels us to lie down with my back on the bed.

His eyes bore into mine as he crawls over my body, hovering over me before claiming my mouth in a hard kiss. My panties are ripped away and he grabs a condom, rolling it on. He lines up his hard dick at my core and with one swift movement, he enters me. Throwing my head back, I moan from the building sensation. He moves in and out in a delicious rhythm, and I run my fingernails across his back. I'm building up fast again, and he groans in appreciation as my walls clench around him.

As I come, he joins me, growling loud as he empties deep inside me. His dick stills, and he slowly pulls out of me. When he looks down, his face drops in horror. Glancing down I take in the broken condom.

"I would get pregnant if I wasn't on the pill." I joke, twisting to face him.

His eyes grow wide, and he stands in a rush. "No, no more kids, ever."

I sit up, wincing at his words, and watch his stony face. *What did he just say? No more kids.*

I'm at a loss. Obviously, I would want my own kids one day. I love Rose and Lily so much, but I would want more and definitely one of my own. Surely, he isn't serious?

"Why?" I mumble under my breath, staring down at my hands running along my thighs. I'm not cold but I want the feeling of doing something, a distraction.

I wait for his answer. It feels like forever, even if it's only been a few minutes.

He thrusts his hand through his hair and blows out a breath. "Fuck. Because I have two already. I don't have enough time, and this new job is taking more time than I have." He walks to the bathroom and turns on the shower.

I'm utterly confused. Clearly, there is more to it than that. Why can't he be honest? He is frustrating. I rise from the bed, pick up my panties and shirt, and slip them back on. When I'm done, I slide under the covers and wait for him to come back.

CHAPTER 26

THOMAS

MY STOMACH IS KNOTTED with guilt for snapping at Jennifer as I pace the bathroom, rubbing my fingers across my pounding forehead. I step into the shower, hoping the tension evaporates like the steam surrounding me.

The thought of another child to raise is a lot to ask of me. The memory of Victoria flashes under my closed eyelids, and the hot spray feels like it turned to ice. Chills rake through my body. Reaching over, I quickly shut the water off and rip the towel off the hook, drying my body with rough motions, trying to warm myself up with the friction.

It doesn't help.

Stepping over to the vanity, I lean over the sink, staring at my reflection in the mirror. I'm only just relearning how to connect with a woman again—one whom I don't deserve—and now I'm expected to think about creating another child. I drop my chin to my chest. I don't even want another child. I'm content with my girls. Even if I consider it—

No. I don't think I could ever be ready, and maybe it's a difference neither of us can move past.

I lift my head and stare at my reflection. The sad, pale face is too much to bear, so I step into the wardrobe and grab a clean t-shirt and boxer briefs.

I'm ready and have no other reason to stall in here anymore. I inhale a deep breath and head into the bedroom. I pause. Jennifer's eyes are closed, her pretty face in a blissful state. I lean my shoulder against the doorframe and take her in.

The covers are draped over her legs, and the t-shirt has ridden up, showing me an inch of her milky skin on her stomach. Her breathing is a steady rhythm, and she looks perfect in my bed. My chest aches at the sight of her. Why do we have to want different things and why can't things just stay as they are? It was comfortable. I was comfortable. And then her joke is messing with my thoughts. *Ruining us.*

I sigh and push off the frame, creeping quietly to the bed, lifting the covers with care so as not to wake her, and slide in beside her. I watch her for any movement, but she doesn't stir. Lowering my head on the pillow, facing her, I close my eyes and drift off to sleep.

In the morning my body feels hot and clammy. I try to wriggle, but something is on me. I peel my eyes open, blinking a few times, and peer down to see Jennifer's brown hair spread over my torso and her arm thrown across my body. My lips raise upward from the vision.

She stirs under me, and I stare down at her. "Princess," I whisper.

"Mm," she murmurs back, still in a sleepy haze. She tightens her grip on my side, making me chuckle.

"I need to get up before the girls."

The girls have adjusted well to Jennifer and me dating, but it's not a good idea for them to see so much too soon. And I don't know how to answer their questions. I've been closing the door in case Lily has a nightmare and comes in. I'll hear the doorknob rattle and have time to reach her and take her to her bed and resettle her.

Pain travels through my temple. I need to talk to Jennifer about *our* future. The whole subject doesn't sit well with me. I untangle myself from her and slide out of bed. She resettles in the bed, and I move to the wardrobe quietly and get dressed before I leave the room, closing the door behind me.

Rose calls out and I go to her. We sit in the family room and wait for Lily and Jennifer to wake up. Jennifer comes out next, all dressed, looking fresh and pretty.

Rose's face lights up when she sees Jennifer, and she pushes out of my arms, running for her, screaming, "Jen." As she reaches her, Jennifer scoops her up and throws her in the air, and Rose squeals in delight.

When Jennifer mentioned the thoughts on a therapist, I felt like someone punched me in the gut, but I also agree. The more I pay attention to Rose and her actions, the more I see zero improvement. It's unfair to Rose if I don't seek help. She can only benefit from it, so I plan to call and book an appointment this week.

Lily comes out of her room, notices Jennifer. "You're here?"

Jennifer answers, "Yes, is that okay?"

Lily just shrugs. "Yeah."

A deep chuckle leaves my chest. She is not bothered by anything. But I also don't think Lily has registered that Jennifer stayed the night.

We eat breakfast before Jennifer leaves us to go home.

When I walk her out, she asks, "Can you do dinner with my family on Wednesday? They won't stop pestering me until you do."

I pause. "I don—"

"Can we go to your house for dinner?" Lily sneaks up and cuts me off. "What does your house look like? Can we go now?"

I sigh, offering a short perk of the corner of my lip. "Sure, but not now."

"Great. I'll wait for you to arrive home, and then we can all walk over together," Jennifer says. "You might have to give me a specific time. Otherwise, Mom will call me constantly on Wednesday."

I rub my brow. "How about six?"

"Perfect." She leans in and kisses my lips before hurrying across the drive.

Somehow, I don't think the dinner is going to be as perfect as she had imagined.

I scheduled an appointment for Rose. First, I made a call to Helen, asking for recommendations. Then I researched them all before deciding on one and booking Rose. I spent the last hour sorting it out, and now I need to work.

I refocus on an email I need to send out to the supplier. The number of errors with lighting supplies is impacting productivity. I've stayed behind as much as time would allow every day. But it's Wednesday and I type away in a hurry, finally hitting send before I power down the computer.

Ava stands in my doorway. "Boss, do you need something done before I go? You look frazzled as shit."

I laugh and prop myself back in my chair to talk to her. "No, thanks. I'm almost done and I'm out of here too. I'm meeting the parents." I sigh.

She pushes off the door and ambles in to pull out a chair in front of my desk. Sitting down, she crosses her ankles. "You're meeting the parents. That's a big deal." Her eyes roam my face, searching for something.

"Yeah," I blow out a breath, "I'm taking the girls and we're having dinner at Jen's."

Her brows rise and her head tilts. "Nice. I'm sure she is perfect. Where did you meet?"

I don't speak about my life to anyone other than the boys, but I need a girl's opinion sometimes and my mother is way too close to offer any sound advice.

"At a bar."

"No way. You?" she shouts and covers her mouth with her hand.

I nod. "Yes, I know I don't go out, but it was to celebrate my promotion here."

"Ah."

"But I don't know if we are suited. She wants different things in the future." And I want to add that my ex-wife died because of me, that I don't deserve to be happy, but I don't need to burden another person with my shit.

"That's a lot. If I didn't know you, I would say end it, but you are careful. She must be special to get to you."

I run my hand through my hair and stand. "Yeah, I guess. I'll have to fill you in later. I don't want to be late, so I gotta run." I pick up my keys.

"Me too, I'll catch you tomorrow."

She trails behind me and I nod, lost in my own thoughts. Stalking to the elevator, I enter, then hit the button to go down.

I park in the drive at home, pausing at the wheel as my heartbeat accelerates and my throat constricts. Not allowing my thoughts to wander, I shove open the door and march inside.

"Made it. Are you ready?" I call out as I enter the house.

I don't bother changing out of my suit. The girls run up to me and latch on to my legs. I hug them tight. Jennifer moves in front of me, so I bend over to peck her on the lips.

"Yes," she answers breathlessly.

"We're going to Jen's house," Lily singsongs.

I smile as I peer down at Lily. "Yes, we are, sweetheart. Let's walk there now, okay?"

She nods. "Okay."

Scooping up Rose, I carry her on my hip as we exit the house, then I turn and lock the house before we venture next door. For a second, I wish she lived farther away just to give myself time to calm my erratic heart. We arrive next door much too soon. Jennifer opens the front door, and I'm hit with the smell of food as we enter.

My stomach growls, remembering that I hardly had time to eat at work today.

Rose clings harder around me as I walk farther inside her family home.

As we trail down the house into the kitchen, her mom's eyes nearly bug out of her head. She looks at the girls and me, not stopping, just circling her eyes.

"Oh, hi," she says, her voice laced with surprise.

"Hi, Mary. These are my girls, Lily and Rose." I point to Lily, who is standing beside Jennifer, and a shy Rose, who is in my arms, her head buried in my neck.

"Hi, I'm Lily."

Mary smiles and crouches down. "Hi, Lily. It's lovely to meet you. Are you hungry?" she asks.

"Mm-hm," Lily responds.

"Great. I'm almost done cooking."

"Let's go in the family room for a bit," Jennifer suggests.

I nod in acknowledgment.

Her dad is waiting and watching from the family room, his body stiff and his eyes glaring directly at me. Moving toward her dad, I hold out my free hand to shake his. He glances down, and for a second, I think he isn't going to shake my hand. But he slowly extends his hand, and his firm, rough hand lands in mine in a hard shake. The glare is still written on his face.

"Hi, Paul," I firmly say.

He grunts and nods his head before returning his gaze to the television. This is not the same easy-going man I know. That guy has vanished, and a stern father is sitting in his place. Not that I blame him. I would be the same way meeting one of my girls' boyfriends. But I'm not some stranger either.

"Take a seat, Tom. Would you like a drink?" Jennifer asks.

"Water, please." Looking over at Lily who has already taken a seat on the couch, I join her, swiveling Rose to sit on the couch beside me. She is shy and unhappy I'm not holding her, so I wrap an arm tightly around her, keeping her close.

"I'll bring you girls' water, okay?" Jennifer spins and saunters off to grab our drinks. She has a cute smile on her face and hasn't noticed her dad's unimpressed glare toward me.

"Did you watch the game on the weekend?" I ask Paul, trying to break the ice that is circling us.

His eyes flick to mine and then back to the television. My body is tight and unmoving, waiting for his answer. I gaze around the family home. It has more color than mine. The kitchen is wood and white with lots of pictures on the wall and potted plants in each room.

I haven't gone through photos since I packed them. They're still sitting in a box in the garage. I like the idea of them in the family rooms.

"Yes, I caught it. It wasn't the best game to watch."

My shoulders sag with relief that his tone is slightly less cold and I have found something we can talk about that might help him calm down. Otherwise, it will be an awfully long night.

"I'll put the drinks on the table. Dinner is ready," Jennifer calls.

I bound to my feet, just to put some distance between her father and me, and grab each of the girls' hands. We walk over to the table and my mouth drops open. Before me is a delicious Italian spread unlike anything I have seen in a while. I understand now where Jennifer learned to cook.

A sharp punch to the gut hits me. My girls won't have Victoria laughing and having fun teaching them how to bake and cook.

"Oh, yummy pasta and garlic bread," Lily coos, bringing me back to earth and out of the nightmare that memories bring me.

Mary giggles aloud at Lily, while Paul comes and takes his seat at the table. I wait for directions on where we may sit.

"Please take a seat anywhere." Her mom gestures.

I nod and take the closest seat to where I'm standing and lift Lily onto one and Rose can sit on my lap.

"Sorry, I don't have highchairs. I didn't realize the guest would have kids. Jennifer didn't mention it. Sorry. I would have been more prepared if she had told me." Her mom gives Jennifer a hard glance.

"Yeah, she is full of surprises tonight," her dad spits, anger still vibrating off his body.

"I didn't think anyone would mind," Jennifer says. "They are the cutest little surprise guests."

Jennifer helps me dish up some food for the girls before she takes a seat next to Lily and her dad. I chose to sit directly opposite him, hoping we can chat like we always do the longer we are near each other.

The front door opens and closes. My brows crease as my head tilts to see who has arrived. I didn't know we were expecting someone else. A tall dark-haired girl enters, wearing a navy school uniform.

"Perfect timing." She dumps her bag on the kitchen counter before dragging out a chair next to Jennifer and slumping into it. The smirk on her face aimed at Jennifer seems like they are having some kind of conversation between each other.

"Tom, Lily, and Rose, this is my sister Megan," Jennifer says. "Megan, this is Tom and his girls, Lily and Rose."

I smile and greet her. "Hi, Megan. Nice to meet you."

"Nice to meet you. I would say I know about you, but then I would be lying." Her face is aimed at Jennifer with a smirk and a pop of a brow.

Jennifer smacks her arm, whispering, "Calm down. He lives next door with his girls."

Of course, she wants to know all about Jennifer and me. They are sister's. But it all seems too much. I need some time to sort my head out, yet Jennifer is all in. We have only just worked out that we're not seeing other people. And I'm still unsure if we should date, the other night still playing on my mind. Seeing that condom broken still causes a tightness in my chest. Making me think... are we destined to be together if our futures want different things? I'm not certain anymore.

I peer over at her dad, who has already begun to eat, so I dish my plate.

As I am eating, Paul asks between mouthfuls, "How long has this been going on?" I glance up at him as he points with the end of his fork between Jennifer and me.

"Not long, Dad. Calm down." She rolls her eyes with a little shift of her head.

"Jennifer, stop telling me how to feel. You, young lady, are not a parent. You're twenty-two and have your whole life ahead of you. This—I'm sorry I disagree with; you should be living your life, not playing house. You need to travel, go out, and to be frank, *live* like people your own age do."

Fuck. It feels like he just slapped me. My eyes bulge out of their sockets, and I rub the back of my neck, trying to relieve the tension that is forming there. I process what he is saying as I continue to chop the girls' food and Lily eats.

I'm not angry with what he is saying. *He is right.* I'm holding her back from living like a young woman should. I can't ruin another woman's life.

I think I got so swept up in how good she is with my girls and how much they love her I never once stopped to think about what this would mean to her. How much she's giving up just to be a part of my life. She doesn't know what she's missing out on because she is now tied to me.

Another major concern is that she wants her own child, an issue I can't get over.

My head feels like it's in a windstorm and I can't hear the surrounding conversation. Just mumbles and raised voices around me letting me know they're fighting. I need to get out of here. I need space to process this, and I don't want the girls hearing or listening to this type of behavior. I drop the fork I had been feeding Rose with and clutch her in my arms and push the chair out and stand up.

Clearing my throat, I stare between Paul and Mary. "Thanks for welcoming me into your home, but I think it's best if we leave now." My voice is stern.

I tug on Lily's arm, and her eyes meet mine as her head tilts. "Dad, I'm not finished," she pouts.

"Oh, please, don't leave," Mary pleads, joining me while I stand, her hands clenched together at her chest.

I softly shake my head, and my lip lifts slightly at the corner of my mouth. "It's fine, really. I actually agree with Paul."

Jennifer gasps. I take a glance at her. Her face is carved in tortured pain.

"Can we talk outside for a moment, Jen?" I say in a controlled voice.

CHAPTER 27

JENNIFER

MY FEET FEEL LIKE they are moving through concrete as I follow Thomas and the girls outside, feeling a drop in my stomach. The delicious pasta dish Mom served up evaporated, replaced with a sour tang.

"Can we talk outside my house so I can let the girls inside to play with their toys? I don't want Lily to hear this conversation. I think she heard enough." The last few words come out harsh, like he's angry at me.

"Sure." I nod.

He opens his door. "Lily, take Rose inside and play. I want to talk to Jen for a minute."

"Okay, Daddy." She grabs Rose's hand. "Come, Rose, let's play," Lily calls.

They amble off together, and I stand frozen, clutching my elbows with my opposite hands to hug myself, preparing for the next minute. He spins and looks at me with a sadness that matches my own eyes.

He puffs out a breath before starting. "I'm so disappointed with what went down. I don't want arguments in front of my children. They have been through so much, especially Rose. I really wish it didn't happen."

His words hit me, and I wince. "Sorry," I speak flatly. I don't really know what else to say, wishing I could turn back time and tell my parents I had been seeing Thomas. It's my fault that my dad acted the way he did. But I can't undo anything.

I know I shouldn't speak to my dad like that, but it's a knee-jerk reaction to him rejecting the relationship. I didn't think my dad would be angry. He is always helping Thomas. If I had known, this meeting wouldn't have occurred.

My dad is aware how smart, sensible, and mature I am. I'm not like the average young woman. I wish he would see it from my point of view. But now he is about to cost me a relationship with the person I want.

My chest constricts as I stand here, and I slowly bring my gaze up to meet his stormy eyes. As they meet, he glances away. I watch his tight jaw tick before he drags his eyes to meet mine again, a new determination written in them.

"Your dad is right. I'm making you settle down when you should be working toward your goals, traveling, partying, meeting a guy to start a family with... not settle with me and my family."

I don't move.

His eyes dart around my face as he says the final blow, "You and I cannot be together. We want different things."

I listen to the words leave his mouth, but I'm too slow to reply, and I'm sure I haven't heard him correctly. My throat is dry and constricting, preventing me from talking. I simply stare blankly into his sad eyes.

Don't I get a say in what I want? Why won't anyone listen to me? I'm too choked up to let the words slip past my lips, but I force myself to swallow, pushing past the pain. "But I don't want to party or travel... I want this—I want you."

"Please" I add, begging him.

Staring hopelessly back at me, he sighs. "You're young. You haven't really lived. We want different things in life and that's okay... We are better off separating before we get the girls too attached... You need to enjoy life."

I shake my head violently. "No. I don't agree," I spit out, refraining from stomping my foot like one of the children at work, frustrated from the situation. It would only confirm his thoughts that 'I'm young.' How did tonight go so wrong?

"It's what I want." His stare is hard, and he speaks with confidence.

I stand frozen, staring back. What can I say to that? My mouth drops open and my lip trembles. My eyes now fill with unshed tears.

His gaze flicks to the ground before returning, and I see a flash of pain, but just as it is there, it quickly disappears. "I'm sorry. I have to go check on the girls."

Nodding back, I say, "Okay."

Tears form on my lashes, but I refuse to let him see me break. If he doesn't want to be in the relationship, I will not force him. I don't need him to feel sorry for me and stay with me if it isn't for him. I wish he would fight for us, but I'm the only one fighting.

I spin and walk back to my house, my head swimming with the conversations that happened tonight, trying to make sure I didn't miss anything. I rip open the door and slam it shut behind me. The tears trail down my cheeks, and I pick up my pace as I aim directly for my room. I want to be alone. *I need to be alone.*

Mom is washing the dishes as I stalk past the kitchen in a hurry.

"Are you okay, love?" She talks softly.

I shake my head but don't speak, fearing the sobs will leave my quivering mouth. *I just want to be alone right now.*

I continue moving to my room, passing the table that is now cleared of dinner. I spot my dad's head above the couch, his face angled at the television. He doesn't get up or speak. He can hear what Mom asked but doesn't bother trying to apologize. That pisses me off. I just lost Thomas because of him. A simple sorry for his actions would be nice. I want to apologize for my behavior and actions but it's not the right moment, feeling I'm about to break, so I jog the rest of the way to my room.

I slam the door shut, leaning back on it. My head hits the wood and I close my eyes. Warm tears trickle down my cheeks, my body feeling drained and heavy. Pushing off the door, I take a few steps and throw myself onto my bed, my face landing on a pillow. I thrust my hands under it and let out the sobs I have been holding in. I don't know how long I cry, but I eventually pass out from exhaustion.

The next day, I struggle to get myself out of bed. The thought of having to face the day has me hiding under the covers until the last possible minute.

My feet hit the floor, and I walk to the door like a zombie, still tired, even though I slept all night.

When I arrive at work, I avoid bumping into Thomas as much as I can. I need some time to pull myself together. I was falling for him, and I thought he felt the same. *How stupid was I?* I know I loved the girls, but my feelings had developed for him as time went on. I could picture a future with us as a growing family. But he doesn't feel or want the same, blaming it on me to focus on my goals. With my job and social life, I was content before, but now I know what a taste of true happiness feels like, deep in my soul. I want more. *So much more.*

I see Emma preparing for the kids' activities, squatting and pulling out colored blocks from the activity drawer, and I wander over to her. "Emma," I whisper.

Her head tilts up at me. "Jen, what's wrong? Are you okay?" She drops the blocks and stands.

I take a deep breath. This will be the first time I speak about Thomas breaking things off. I wish I didn't have to, but it isn't my choice.

My gaze meets hers as I stammer, "Thomas, uh, broke things off with me." Why are the words so hard to say? *Maybe because saying it aloud makes it more real.*

Her eyes widen in horror. "What, no way. Why?"

Swallowing past the lump in my throat, I blink away the tears that threaten. I will not cry anymore. *I can do this.*

"He doesn't want me to settle and thinks I should go and be my age." I shrug my shoulders, trying to appear unaffected.

She shakes her head. "Oh, shit, Jen. I'm sorry."

"You have nothing to be sorry for, but I need to ask a favor."

"Yeah, of course, what is it?"

"If you could help me avoid him today and tomorrow, I'd appreciate it. I just want some space to think, wrap my head around it all."

She nods. "Yes, of course. When he comes in and out, you hide, and I'll deal with him."

"Thanks. Now, enough about that. Let's set up." I walk off to grab toys and place some fun activities outside.

Knowing Emma will cover for me for a few days before the weekend is a relief. I want the time to digest and discuss it with Katie and Olivia and get myself together.

On my break I pull my phone out and message Olivia.

Jennifer: *Are you free tomorrow night? Need to talk to you girls.*

Olivia: *Yeah, where are you thinking? Bar?*

Jennifer: *No, dinner. I'll book it and pick you up. Can you call Katie for me and let her know? I'll book Rosetta's. Will seven p.m. work for you?*

Olivia: *Yes. Will do. See you tomorrow.*

I slept on and off again. At work, I'm yawning and my actions are slow. My eyes feel heavy and sore, but I know even if I canceled with Olivia and Katie, I wouldn't sleep. I still have barely spoken to my family. I need to explain my feelings for Thomas to my parents, but I am not ready yet.

I only speak when I must, and neither Mom nor Dad brings up Thomas. I think from my messy hair and red eyes, they know I have been struggling.

Leaving work at five, I get home, shower, and dress in some blue jeans and a chunky knitted sweater. As I leave, I peer over at his house, wishing I could go over there for the weekend. My stomach drops, and I try to slow my breathing down. I rush to my car and drive off without taking another glance at his house. A few minutes later, I pull up to Olivia's house and send off a text.

Jennifer: *Outside*

Olivia: *I'll be right out*

A minute later, Olivia comes out wearing black leather pants, boots, and a white shirt. Her blond locks bouncing with every step. I smile a genuine smile. I'm feeling lighter for the first time in a few days. I relax, ready for the fun that is Olivia.

She pulls open the car door and climbs inside. "Hey," she yells.

A small laugh escapes my lips. "I'm right here, Olivia."

"I know. I'm just excited to be going out again. I feel like since you have been loved up, you went MIA. Also, Katie couldn't make it. She has to work."

My lips thin into a tight line, and my heart rips again—definitely not loved up now. "Sorry for disappearing. That's my fault," I mumble.

"It's fine. I get it, really. I would disappear if I had a guy like Thomas. I'd ride him all day every day."

I laugh at her, but it also punches my gut to think about how good of a lover he was. How insatiable and giving he was. God, I wish he wanted me as much I want him. This is so hard. My heart hurts. And talking about this is tearing me up inside.

"He ended things."

"What?" Her head whips around so fast I'm sure she almost broke her neck.

I drive toward the restaurant.

"Yep, on Wednesday."

"Why?" she asks.

"He said a bunch of things, but mainly, that he wants me to be out like other twenty-two-year-olds and not settle for him."

"That's nice, isn't it?" I hear the confusion laced in her voice.

"Yeah, I can understand he's concerned, but it's the way he chose my life for me, like I *should* be clubbing and traveling. When have I ever been interested in that? He didn't ask me what I wanted. I felt like it's an excuse, like there is more."

"Like he is hiding something?" she asks.

"I don't know. I might be overthinking, but I never found out much about his ex, just bits and pieces. I didn't want to push him. But it happened anyway."

"You need to go there and demand the answers."

I pull into a free parking spot at the restaurant. Turning off the ignition, I spin to face her. "You know I won't do that. I'm not you."

She opens her door. "I know, but don't you want to find out?"

Do I? Yes, of course. But it means nothing if he doesn't want to give it to me. Pushing open the car door, I climb out and slam it shut before walking around the car to her side. We walk side by side along the brightly lit path.

"I'm not forcing him to be with me or to give me answers. He should want to let me in," I huff.

Admitting that out loud was hard.

We walk toward the restaurant door.

"I agree, so unless he wants to sort his shit out, move on."

Our shoes click the same tune along the concrete as we approach the door. The air stills as I ponder her words. Move on? Do I want to? No, but I will have to, eventually. This was his choice. We arrive at the restaurant, but I pull on her arm to halt us, pausing to the side for a moment to talk.

"I think you're right. Wednesday, he came over for dinner and met my family. My dad lost it. Did not approve at all. We argued in front of Tom's girls. Dad is the one who mentioned how young I was, sparking Tom's decision. I'm sure of it."

"I'm shocked. Your dad lost it? Like I get it, but to lose it. I can't imagine."

"Yeah, Dad completely disapproves and doesn't even care about my feelings. I know he is just worried, but I wish he would have sucked it up at dinner and talked to me later about it when Tom and the girls weren't there."

"It's freezing out here," she says. "Let's go inside and talk more over alcohol. This discussion needs it."

We head inside and wait to be seated.

A moment later, a waitress sporting a blond ponytail with a large toothy smile on her face, wearing a white shirt and black dress pants, pauses in front of her desk. "Good evening. Can I help you?"

"I booked three under Jennifer," I say.

She skims the book, searching for my name until she finds it. "Yes, follow me this way, please."

We nod and trail behind her.

She stands in front of an empty table, gesturing toward it. We take our seats opposite each other, and the waitress asks, "Could I start you off with some drinks?"

"Yes, please, a Moscato." I need alcohol after the week I've had. "And also, just to let you know, the third person cannot make it. Sorry," I say.

"Make it a bottle of Moscato," Olivia cuts in.

"That's okay. I'll be right back with the bottle." The waitress takes the spare cutlery and glass from the table, giving us more room, then walks off.

"I'm driving, so I can't drink too much," I say.

"It's a Friday night. We are eating, and the bottle only has a few glasses. It's fine." She waves it off.

I shake my head. "I'll have two and that's all."

We scan the menu, and I decide on gnocchi and Olivia chooses fettuccine carbonara.

The waitress arrives with our bottle, pouring us each a glass of wine, then takes our food order before stepping away again.

"Back to what you said about your dad. Parents are annoying. Hence why I moved out. I like the freedom of my life. I know people think renting is a waste of money, but it's not. You grow and learn, and the freedom is priceless."

Sipping my wine, I mull over those words. What would it be like to live out of my parents' home? I haven't thought about my living arrangements. I hadn't been able to afford it, so I solely focused on my career, and getting the higher position took over everything. And with Thomas next door, I wouldn't have moved because of convenience. But now that I think about what I want, living out of home is something I want to try.

"I hadn't thought about moving out, but now with the promotion, I can afford it and I need my own space."

Just as I finish, Olivia blurts, "Move in with me. I have a spare room."

"Olivia, it's filled with your closet and makeup stuff." I laugh at her offer, envisioning the cluttered spare room.

"I'll get rid of it. I hate renting on my own. Please." She bounces and claps loudly.

"Shhh, no promises. Let me think about it. I want to do a budget. And I'll need to tell my parents."

"I'll start organizing the room so you can move in." Her face flushes pink and her mouth curves into the biggest grin.

Am I ready to move so soon? Away from Thomas? If it was up to Olivia, I would start moving tomorrow. I need a pause button on my life.

"Just let me think about it. I have a lot on my mind right now, so just give me time."

"Okay. I know. Sorry. You know me, I get excited. But just so you know, you won't regret it."

I tilt my chin. "I know it will be fun."

Our dinner arrives, ending the conversation, which I gratefully accept.

Changing the topic, I say, "And how are the guys in your life? Especially the one you went on the date with?" I stab the gnocchi with my fork and put a piece into my mouth. I chew as she talks.

She shrugs. "No one serious. I don't want to be tied down. I enjoy being single. He's nice but I have only seen him once."

"Look what happens when you try to settle down. Maybe it's best to be free and not tied down, to save the heartache." I stab another piece and chew.

Olivia picks up her wine and takes a sip. "We could totally fix that by heading out on a night out. Didn't Thomas say that?" She has a cheeky smirk on her lips, clearly mocking me.

"I only go out for events. You know that. That's why I was shocked by Tom's words. He assumed I'm like everyone else my age." I peer down at my pasta, my appetite disappearing. No longer hungry, I put down my fork, pick up my drink, and take a sip of the sweet fruity wine. I think about Thomas and what he would be doing right now. I wonder if he is missing me. I miss him. Having a heart sucks.

"You know I'm playing with you," she teases.

Flicking my gaze back to hers, I lower my glass. "Yes, I know."

When we leave the restaurant, she links her arm through mine, and we walk like that back to the car. The warmth from her is welcomed. She offers the comfort and safety I long for right now.

On the drive home, Olivia scrolls her socials and discusses her findings. I'm hardly listening but when I do, I'm enjoying it. It's helping pass the time and take my mind off Thomas.

I park in front of her house. "Thanks for listening to me tonight. I will let you know about moving in." Leaning forward, she unbuckles herself to meet me in a hug.

"Of course, I got you. Anytime you need me, call." She smiles.

"Okay," I mutter back.

I watch her climb out of my car, shut the door, and take the path back to the front door and into her house.

I scan her house more thoroughly. Could I live here too? It's a pretty brick home with a flower garden. And it's close to my parents. Olivia has decorated it already so I would only need bedroom furniture and accessories. It's a big decision, which I don't want to rush making.

Once she is safely inside, I head home. I keep throwing the idea of moving out around in my mind. But when I pass Thomas's house, the tightening pain in my chest returns. Pulling up outside my house, I park and take a few breaths before gripping the door handle and stalking the path. I push the key in and unlocking the door. When it's unlocked, I enter. The light from the television is on. *Crap. Someone is awake.*

I close the door and head straight for my dad. I can tell it's him because he sits in the same spot on the couch. Mom has her own armchair.

Walking into the family room, I whisper, "Hi, Dad."

He peers over the couch at me. "Jennifer, where have you been?"

I can see curiosity etched on his face. He wants to ask about Thomas and if I was out with him because I haven't said many words to him or Mom since the disastrous dinner.

"I went out with Olivia for dinner."

He shifts his weight on the couch, staring at me.

"Did you have a nice time?"

"Yeah, but I'm tired now, so I'm off to bed. I will talk to you tomorrow."

"Okay, darling. Good night."

A flash of something I don't recognize enters his eyes, but it's late and I don't want to have a discussion with so much on my mind. I want to have a serious talk about moving out when it's a more suitable time.

CHAPTER 28

JENNIFER

A LOUD BANGING OUTSIDE my room startles me awake. I groan and pull the covers over my head. It's the weekend, and I don't understand why my family insists on making noises before noon. It's been a week from hell, and I just want to sleep and drown my sadness in this bed, hoping it's all a bad dream and Thomas is still mine.

The banging continues and my covers don't drown out the noise at all. Thrusting the covers off me, I sit up to grab my phone from my bedside table, hoping for a call or text from Thomas.

My shoulders drop and a heavy sigh leaves my lips. Unfortunately, the screen only shows messages from Katie and Olivia. Opening the messages, I read Katie's first.

Katie: *Good morning. Have a good day. Today is a new day. Every day gets easier. Call me if you need anything.*

Olivia: *Boys suck. Hope you got some beauty sleep. Love you.*

Sitting here, I can't help but feel a little lighter today. Reading their messages makes me feel slightly less lonely and definitely loved. I can't thank the girls enough for checking in on me. Every day without fail I get a text from each of them, and if I haven't called them in a few days, they call me, wanting to hear my voice isn't lying when I tell them I'm fine.

I put the phone back down, stand and reach for a sweater in my closet, shoving it over my head. I mosey out of my room and follow the noise.

"Ugh," I call out as I enter the kitchen. The noise is louder in here, killing my eardrum.

Mom and dad have pulled all the contents from the cupboard in the food pantry. A frown forms on my face as I take in the sight. My dad is hammering at the shelves while Mom hovers over, inspecting.

"What are you two doing?"

Mom looks over at me, her lips turn upward. "Your dad is helping me put extra shelves in. Do you want some tea?"

"Sure," I mumble, moving toward a dining chair.

Mom brings over hot tea, lowering it to the table in front of me. I pick it up and blow on the top to cool it down, scanning the mess in the kitchen. The morning's wake-up call. This really solidifies how badly I want my own space. *It's time.*

"Mom, Dad, do you think you could come sit for a minute? I think it's time we talked." My tone is serious, which causes my dad to stop adjusting the shelves and turn his face toward me.

He doesn't say anything as he places the tool down and walks over, dragging out a chair opposite me. Mom joins in too, sitting next to dad. They stare at me in confusion, waiting for me to talk.

Clearing my throat, I quickly glance down at my tea before raising my gaze and flicking it between the two of them. "I have decided to move in with Olivia."

I hear a sharp inhale from my mom, and my dad's eyes share the same empty stare.

"When?" Mom asks.

"I don't have an exact date, but soon I would say," I answer honestly.

My dad shifts forward in his seat, his hands clasped on the table in front of him. "Darling, I hope you aren't doing this because of our fight. I like Thomas. He's a great man. I just don't think you're seeing the different paths you're on. You have so much life ahead of you."

I shake my head. "I'm not angry anymore at what happened with Tom. I'm just upset that you couldn't hold it until the girls and him weren't around. We should have had a discussion when they left. I'm sorry for yelling at you, Dad. That wasn't acceptable."

I take a deep breath before continuing. "As of now, he has broken things off with me. I really liked him and the girls. I'm not little anymore, and I think living here you're forgetting that. You live with me and should know I'm not like most twenty-two-year-olds. I enjoy my quiet space and being home. I just need to grow and be on my own. And with Olivia, I'm not far."

His gaze moves to the table in front of him. He can't stop me, and he knows it. I'm an adult and I can decide without his consent. I would prefer they accepted it.

He sits back. "I can't stop you, but your mother and I will always support and be here for you. And if it doesn't work out living out of the home, know you always have a home here."

I let out a shaky breath. "Thanks, Dad." I shift my gaze to my mom, who has tears streaking her red splotchy cheeks. "Mom," I say.

"It's okay. I'm fine, really. It's just as hard for your parents. We want only the best for you."

My lips twist. "Thanks, Mom."

I don't say anything else. I drink my tea and watch my dad stand and return to the kitchen. I didn't expect an apology. My dad is not sorry for protecting me; he would see it as his job.

But accepting my move is enough.

———

"What do you think about this bed?" I fall face-first into a display bed and roll onto my back to stare up at the ceiling, feeling the bed dip a few times beside me. I throw myself up, and my eyebrow perks.

Dad moves around the bed to inspect every angle. He stops in front of me, his arms crossed, and I'm expecting him to hate it.

"I think for the price it's good."

My face lights up, and I rub my palms together. "Let's get it."

My parents offered to buy me a new bed as a housewarming present. They didn't want me to take the existing bed in case I needed to stay over. I think they secretly hope I will move back. But I'm ready for this. Ready to stand on my own.

We move toward the registers. And I stub my toe on the bed.

"Shit, that hurts." Grabbing my foot, I flop onto the nearest bed. My toe pulsates in pain.

"There is a bed right there." My dad laughs at me.

"Well, obviously." I limp my way to the register.

After paying for the bed and arranging delivery, we walk to the car.

"I have scheduled the moving truck for the following weekend... But are you sure you want to do this?" Dad asks. "You can change your mind. Running away from him won't help."

Wide-eyed, I pause mid-stride. "I'm not. This is for me. I need to be more independent."

He stops when he realizes I'm no longer next to him. "So, you aren't doing this out of anger at me? Or avoiding Thomas?"

I continue walking to meet up with him and I keep walking, not wanting to look at him as I answer. Not trusting my face for giving away my true feelings. Of course, I'm avoiding Thomas. The guy dumped me. I'm pretty sure it's not something I should be excited about.

"No, Dad. I'll see Thomas at work and on the day I watch the girls for him."

It will definitely help my crushed heart by not having to live next to him. It will be hard enough facing him at work and Wednesday nights. But I can't bear to walk away from Rose and Lily. Those girls are too special to me.

We arrive at the car and slide in.

"Oh."

I laugh to cover the awkwardness and shake my head. "It's fine, Dad."

Missing the girls and Thomas is sad, but it's not my choice. I can't force him to be with me. I need to focus on myself and my future, even if I can't have them in it.

CHAPTER 29

THOMAS

THE SMELL OF BURNT batter wakes me from my daydream. It's Sunday morning and I'm standing by the stove, cooking the weekly pancakes, watching the wet batter bubble. But my thoughts drift to Jennifer and what she is doing this morning.

Remembering how good it was having her here for pancake Sunday, before I burst that bubble and broke things off. Now it's as if we are strangers. I can't even remember the last time I smiled. I flip the pancake into the trash and try again, imagining she's here so I can pull her close and hold on to her. Since I walked away from her that night, there has been a storm of emotions. My mind flips from I did the right thing to wanting her back. But my brain is telling my heart not to feel. But to have the numbness return after finally being free from it, rips me to pieces. All I hope is that she is doing fine and that I did the right thing. Because I'm fucking struggling. More than I would dare to admit out loud. Knowing I ended it, I need to push forward. She can't get hurt if she isn't with me. She is too good to be settling for a life with me and the girls. I can't offer her what she needs. I wish I could. She makes me feel alive again, and now I'm back to the empty, lost man like before.

I finish preparing the pancakes and then head to my room and strip my bed because her scent every night on my pillows and sheets isn't helping. It's making my nightly dreams harder. Wishing she was on my bed while I pleasured her until she was spineless and then have her tangled around me all night. How much I would love to wake up to her in my arms again.

Work has been the best distraction, but waking up on a weekend with nothing and no one to look forward to is tough. Jennifer's presence is everywhere in my home.

Walking to the washing machine, I switch it on and turn to see Lily standing there.

"Crap, Lily." My hand slaps my chest as I jump backwards.

"You said a bad word." Her face amused.

"Not really. Anyway, stop creeping up on me."

I encourage her out and back to the kitchen, where I dish her breakfast up.

"Is Jen coming over today?"

I'm surprised by her question, and I hesitate for a moment, trying to search for the best explanation. Coming up empty, I scratch my temple and blurt out, "No. Sorry, sweetheart. She is busy."

I spread her pancake, feeling nausea roll around in my stomach from the lie.

"Oh, I miss her."

My hands stop spreading and I peer up straight into her lost gaze.

So do I.

But I can't say that. My heart cracks for her. *Fuck.* This isn't just me who broke up with Jen. It's like I made the girls break up with her too. I can only wish it will get easier in time.

You chose this. You need to let her go.

"I'm sure she misses you too," I offer, trying to make her feel better.

"Don't you miss her?"

Damn it, Lily. Not today. But her innocent face has no idea about adult relationships or the turmoil running through me right now. And how fucking much I really miss Jennifer. So badly it hurts. I feel like I'm mourning a death again, which is fucking crazy. I have known her for much less time than I did Victoria, yet the feeling I have now that she is gone is the same. There is something seriously wrong with me.

I softly shake my head, "Yeah, baby, I do."

"Da-da, da-da," is being called out. Saved by the bell.

I give Lily her plate with pancake and walk to get Rose. Returning to the table with Rose, I dish her pancake up and we all sit and eat breakfast together. I can't help but sit staring at Jennifer's seat. *Fuck!* It's not even her seat but my mind is on overdrive. It's imagining her eating her pancakes moaning like it's me with my head between her legs. Fucking Hell. I need to get a grip on my thoughts.

My mind is going off the deep end really quickly. We sit quietly and eat our breakfast. The house definitely doesn't have the same vibrancy as it usually does... And I know it's because she isn't here. She makes a room feel happy and excited. Without her presence, it's quiet and dull.

I need to drink with the boys this weekend. Try to erase her from my brain.

It's Wednesday, and that means I will see *her* when I get home. Walking over to the window overlooking the city in my office, I stare out at the clouds and take a deep breath. I haven't been able to even send an email. My hands are sweaty, and my brain is foggy.

As I gaze out at the people below, a tapping sound tears my gaze away.

"Daydreaming about Jen?" Ava steps in and plops herself down in the chair opposite my desk.

I run my hands through my hair and walk back over to my chair and sit down. Leaning back, I glance at Ava before looking away. "We broke up."

"I don't understand," she splutters with surprise.

I move my gaze back to hers and watch as her head tips to the side, waiting for more details. I haven't spoken to anyone about that night and to be honest, it would be nice to rid some of this tightness that's been sitting in my chest from holding it all in. Feeling that Ava would be a good sounding board, I take a pained breath and explain.

"I was concerned that she was a bit too young... And well, she wants kids and I don't think I can do that."

"But did you talk to her about it?" Her brows pinch.

A wash of guilt rolls in my stomach. My mind went back and tried to replay the conversation. But I'm certain I didn't allow her to.

"No. But her dad doesn't approve of the relationship either," I add, rubbing my five o'clock shadow as I wait for her to talk.

"She is an adult. She doesn't need her dad to tell her who to be with. If you two aren't meant to be with each other then that's between you two. Not because of others. But are you sure that's all?"

Shifting my weight to the side of the chair, I say, "I don't want her to give up her life. She is so young and beautiful with her whole life ahead of her."

"I'm sure she wouldn't see it like that."

"And how do you know? Are you dating a guy with kids?"

"No, but I am a woman."

I shake my head with a chuckle. "Fair point."

Well, fuck.

"Just take some time to think about what you want. Don't make any further decisions until you sort your own head out."

Ava's desk phone rings, breaking up our conversation. "I better grab that."

I nod. "Thanks Ava."

I sit there for a few minutes, letting her words sink in. I can't sit at home this weekend and think about her the whole time. I need to get out and see what life is like without her. Can I live without her?

I push the knot that's formed in my throat down and pull my phone out of my pocket and call mom.

"Hi, sweetheart," she answers after a few rings.

Reclining back in my chair, I say, "Hi, Mom. Hope I'm not interrupting you. I just have a quick question."

"I'm just tidying the house. What's the question?"

"Do you have any plans this weekend?" I ask.

"No, why? Do you need something?"

"I was wondering if you would mind coming to stay for the weekend. I wanted to watch the game at a bar with the boys."

I need a distraction. Keeping myself busy is the only thing helping me to not allow my thoughts to drift. *Drift to her.*

"I would love that. It'll give you a break and I'll get my fix of the girls."

I smile. "Thanks, Mom."

"Anytime, sweetheart. I'm excited."

"The girls will go crazy when I tell them tonight. Well, I better go so I can get home."

"Okay, love. See you Saturday."

"Bye." I hang up and text the boys.

Thomas: *Guys, want to catch the game at a bar on Saturday?*

James: *Yeah, that works for me.*

Joshua: *Of course. I can't wait.*

Benjamin: *Bummer. I got practice, but I'll try to meet you after for a drink.*

I shove the phone away and finish the last few hours of work. Before I brace myself to see her face again.

CHAPTER 30

JENNIFER

"WHAT DID YOU DO on the weekend?" Lily asks. "Dad said you were busy,"

I chuckle. "I was. What did you do?"

I use this excuse to pry information out of her. It's not very mature but I don't care. I need to know what they did. Or what *he* did. Did he miss me? I shake my head. *Why do I care?*

"We went to the park and had a picnic," Lily tells me.

It's Wednesday and I sit with the girls, painting at the table before it's their bedtime.

"Oh, that sounds like so much fun." I glance down at the papers in front of me, writing their name on each paper. I missed them on the weekend. The tightness in my chest returns.

Needing a distraction, I say, "Girls, it's bedtime soon. Let's bathe you."

After the bath, I read the girls a book and tuck them in bed a little later than usual. I just wanted to spend extra time with them, so I offered more books until the girls were yawning and struggling to keep their eyes open.

I peer down at Rose and smile. Helen told me Thomas asked her for the list of doctors. That makes me happy because he cares so deeply for Rose and wants the best for her. He could have ignored our advice like so many parents, but he tried.

I'm nervous about seeing him tonight. The last time I saw him I had my heart crushed, so I'm unsure how to act with him. My leg bounces as I sit up straight on the couch, constantly checking the time, waiting for him to arrive home.

The noise of the television is on low, so when the click of the door happens, my heart accelerates, and I freeze. *Do I get up? Do I stay sitting? Shit. What do I do?*

I slowly rise, deciding it will be best if I get out of his space as soon as possible. I'll only be torturing myself by hanging around.

Taking small steps until I reach the kitchen counter, I grab on to the edge for support. His shoes tap along the tiles, and my heartbeat escalates, causing a bead of sweat to form on my brow with every heavy footstep. I suck in a sharp breath when he enters my view.

He is delectable in his black suit and tie with his white shirt. My throat dries when I glance up at his full lips, remembering the last time I felt them move across mine. We stare at each other but neither of speaks. He places his keys, phone, and wallet on the counter, his eyes razor-focused on me, not dropping my gaze for a second.

"Hi, Jen," he says in a smooth, controlled voice.

"Hi."

"How were the girls?"

He sounds so normal it annoys me, like I don't matter, like I don't affect him like he affects me.

I sigh. "The girls were great, as usual. We played, they had baths, read, and are in bed. No hassle at all. Dinner is ready for you. I'll see you next week."

Pushing off the counter, I walk around him, my body vibrating from passing his sexy frame. The magnetism of him is hard to resist. I focus on the door only, but he stops me by slipping in front of me, the intense stare stopping me in my tracks.

"I'm sorry," he whispers as he tucks a strand of hair behind my ear.

I close my eyes for a moment. *Please, don't.*

But when I reopen them, the warm brown glow staring back shatters me. I need to get out of here. *I need air.*

I slip out of his touch, looking directly toward the door and quickening my steps. I desperately need to put distance between us before I embarrass myself and beg for him.

"Jen," I hear him call, but I don't stop.

I yank open the door and quickly shut it behind me.

Running into the safety of my house. I make a beeline straight for my room, saying a quick hello to mom and dad as I pass the kitchen.

I close the door and dive straight for my bed, turning the TV on and when I flick on Netflix, the same stupid show Firefly is on. Taunting me of happy memories I had with Thomas. I flick the show off and toss the remote.

A knock on my door has me groaning and covering my eyes, before I sing out, "Yes?"

Peeling my eyes open, I slowly sit up. I flinch, expecting one of my parents, but I'm pleasantly surprised when the door opens to see Megan. "Meg. Hi."

"Hey."

I move over and she lies down next to me.

"Is everything alright? You are home early from his house."

I run my hand over my blanket, ironing out the creases, grateful she came to check on me because my heart hasn't stopped beating like it's on a damn treadmill since he came home. Seeing him again stirred up all the feelings again.

I wanted him to apologize. To say he made a mistake. That he wants me. That he loves me.

But when he was about to, his attitude didn't match his words. And I wasn't ready to hear them.

The only thing I walked away with was more confusion. The way his knuckles brushed my cheek to tuck the hair behind my ear sent my body lurching with excitement. My heartbeat throbbed in my ear when his hand paused there.

Peeking up at her, I see her watching me. Waiting for an answer.

"Yeah, he tried to say sorry, but I didn't realize how much he hurt me until now. The fact he didn't talk to me, just dumped me. Using the excuse of him not wanting me to settle just irks me. And I'm just not ready to hear it. I need more time."

"Yeah, it's all so new. But you should hear him out. I'm sure this situation isn't easy for either of you." She rubs my arm up and down in a soothing pattern.

I offer a small lift of the lips and mumble, "No, it's a lot harder,"

"Do you love him?"

Now that's a question I had the answer to tonight when he touched me. It's what had me running scared. What if he doesn't love me back?

"Yes. I love him."

CHAPTER 31

THOMAS

I CAN'T FOCUS SITTING at the conference room table in Joshua's office for an urgent project meeting. Murmurs can be heard around me, but I can't recall a single clear sentence. Since seeing Jennifer last night, my head has been filled with noise.

I want to kick my ass for reaching out and touching her, but I can't control my actions when she is around. It's the electricity whenever we are close. It causes me to rise and act without a second thought. My body remembers how soft her delicate skin is and how she reacts to my touch.

"Tom."

Hearing my name repeatedly and getting louder, I thrust my chin up and find Joshua staring at me. His face is a mixture of pissed, yet amused, his eyebrow peaked. When he realizes he has my attention, he repeats the question I obviously missed.

"Thomas, what do you think about the deadline?"

"For which project?"

Joshua rolls his lips, and Ava giggles beside me. Joshua becomes rigid and ruffles the papers in front of him. "For the tunnel we have just won. Will we meet the predicted deadline?"

Right, the tunnel. *Focus, Thomas. Don't think about her anymore. Concentrate on work.* Checking my papers, I turn toward Ava, who has a smirk, but nods.

"Yes, I think we can do it." I return my gaze to him as I answer.

He sits back in his leather chair. "Great. Well, let's get back to work. I'll arrange regular meetings for this project. We can't afford to run behind on it." I nod and shuffle my papers together. "Tom, can we talk for a second alone?"

"Sure." I turn to Ava. "Can you get a start on this? I won't be a minute." I hand her the documents and she stands.

"No rush, boss." She wanders out the glass door and toward the elevator with the rest of our colleagues who sat in on the meeting.

I return my gaze to Joshua.

"Are you okay, Tom? You aren't focused or acting yourself at all."

Clearly, my daydreams about Jennifer are seeping through to my real life. I really need to get my head back in the game and refocus on my job.

"Yeah, I'm good. Just a lot on my mind with the girls." It's a half lie. My mind is always on my girls, but he doesn't know that also includes Jennifer.

His face tells me he isn't sure, so I quickly redirect the conversation. "I see you blushing over Ava. Has something happened there?" I tease.

"Pfft. As if. Ava is not my type." He crosses his arms over his chest.

I don't buy it. The flush on his face tells a different story. He takes glances at her when he thinks no one is looking. But I am holding on to my own shit, so I can't really expect him to share.

"I better get back to work. I will see you soon," I say.

"Good idea. I will see you for the game Saturday," he replies, rising from the chair.

———

Saturday arrives and the girls are playing in the family room, and I'm in the kitchen, drinking coffee. Mom's chewing her lip off as she stares down at her coffee, clearly trying to hold back something.

"Spit it out, Mom. The way you're chewing your lip, I know you have something to say." I pop a brow.

Her eyes widen and she stops chewing on her lip and laughs. "You know I want to know what's going on with that sweet girl, Jennifer."

Hearing her name has me frozen still, and a pain shoots up my neck—the beginning of a headache.

I try to rub the pain from my neck before answering. "I told you nothing was going on. I'm focusing on the girls and work." I don't say anything else, not wanting to get into it any further.

But, of course, she won't stop poking. It's Mom. I should know better.

"Hmm, but you two have grown close?" She chooses her words carefully.

Glaring at her with a serious face, I say, "She needs to live, Mom. She's young, as you keep telling me, and I'm holding her back. She talks about more kids, and I can't—" I shake my head, the pain in my chest returning. Taking a few slow, controlled breaths, I attempt to calm my pulse down.

"So, she knows about Victoria?" Her voice is light, and I swallow past the uneasiness.

"No—" I say, not wanting to continue the conversation.

"But she might be happy to accept just the girls. She is only talking about kids, son, not asking for them. But are you sure that the door is completely closed?"

These are the questions that have been playing on my mind, so when she asks me, I can't really give her an answer. Having been through so much pain, I don't think I could handle anymore.

"I don't know, Mom," I answer honestly.

"I think you need to talk to her properly about this. You shouldn't cut out someone who you clearly like because it feels too much or too real. You don't deserve to feel guilty."

My mouth drops open. *How the fuck does she know?*

She laughs. "I'm your mom. I know everything." And with that, she winks.

I laugh softly and shake my head.

I deeply care for Jennifer. I know that in my heart. But to expose my past—I don't know if I'm ready to do that.

A knock comes at the door and it's James. He said he would pick me up.

I walk to Mom and kiss her on the cheek. "Thanks for watching the girls. I'll be home after the game."

"No rush, love. Enjoy yourself."

When I open the door, James, hands stuffed inside his dark-blue jeans, his white shirt undone at the top and rolled up at the sleeves, stands to the side staring toward Jennifer's house.

"What are you doing?" I ask.

He thrusts his chin in the direction of her house as someone walks out the front door. "They're loading furniture into a moving truck."

I tense from his words, panic swelling inside me. "What?" I push forward, moving James out of the way.

"Jeez, man. Calm down."

Stepping out into the entryway, my eyes widen. Sure enough, there is a moving truck parked out front in the concrete driveway. I can't tell who is moving, but a feeling of dread washes through my body.

"Maybe you should go over there and check," Mom says behind me.

"What's going on? I thought you two were dating?" James asks.

"Not currently," I mumble, unable to remove my gaze from the truck.

"Love, just go talk to her," Mom encourages.

Can I? I stand frozen, my legs unwilling to move. No, I have no right. I broke things off with her. I'm still working out what is going on inside my messed-up head. The other night, seeing her in my house again, touching her, I just wanted to go back. But we can't...

I shake off the thoughts. "No, let's go. We have to meet the boys."

"Are you sure?" says James.

I stalk toward his car without answering but hear his faint, "See you later, Mrs. Dunn. Yes, yes, I'll look after him."

I lean on his fancy-ass car, watching him with a blank stare, hiding any real emotion. He unlocks the car and looks at me with a knowing expression, shaking his head. "Get in, dickhead."

I pull open the door and slouch on his leather seat.

We have a twenty-minute drive where we talk about all things sports. Neither of us discuss women or work. James knows me well and understands when to back off and let me think.

A few hours later, James drops me off at home after the game.

He thrusts his chin at the front door. "Looks like someone wants to have one last goodbye."

I spot Jennifer, but as I watch, she swivels and turns to walk to her house.

Without thinking, I push open the door and race toward her, hollering, "Jen, wait."

She spins and her lips turn up and reveal her pretty smile.

She stops and I keep running until I reach her. I gaze into her magnetic eyes and try to catch my breath.

"Hi," she says. "I was coming to check on the girls before I move."

Hearing those words leave her mouth makes my heart feel like it's being ripped in half. "Moving?" I softly question.

She nods. "I'm moving in with Olivia."

"Why?" I ask.

She tears her gaze away from mine. "I feel it's time... And this is too hard." Her gaze flickers to mine and I see a tear sitting on her lashes.

My heart squeezes, and I can't speak. The words are stuck in my throat.

"I better go," she whispers. "I need to meet the truck at the house."

She is waiting for me to say something and all I can do is stare. Nothing leaves my choked-up throat other than a croaky, "Okay."

She hesitates before turning around and leaving., It's now or never. Do I want to open up and find a way for us to work? It's clear she wants me, and I want her.

But I just can't.

CHAPTER 32

JENNIFER

I TAKE SMALL STEPS back to my parents' house, holding my breath, hoping he'll call out my name. His voice cracked with his final words, so I hold a sliver of hope he wants me, that he'll give us a second shot. Focusing on myself has been good, but it doesn't change how much I miss him. Seeing him in casual jeans and a long-sleeve black shirt, smelling his spicy cologne mixed with alcohol, sent thrills through me. Obviously, he has been out with his friends. My mind drifts back to the night we met—the freedom, the fun, and the first kiss.

The simplicity of it back then. Now, it's a complicated mess and I don't know what to do. We can barely talk to each other. There is still chemistry whenever we are in the same room together. But where do we go from here?

"You ready, Jennifer?" My dad's voice breaks into my thoughts.

Rolling my shoulders back and faking enthusiasm, I say, "Yep, let's go."

Dad's gaze darting behind me, and he offers a small wave. Rotating slightly, I catch Thomas waving and smiling at my dad. Snapping my head back around, I concentrate on getting out of here and away from him as soon as possible.

Entering my family's home, I walk back into my bedroom and scan it for anything I may have missed. Doing one last sweep, I crouch down to check under the bed. I spot a piece of paper. Lying on my stomach and army crawling, I reach out and grab it. Clutching it, I retreat backward, exiting from under the bed, and lower myself down onto my heels. I unfold it and my face breaks into a wide smile.

Lily's drawing of me, Rose, and herself. She gifted it to me on one of the nights we spent together. I refold it and pop it gently into my pocket. With nothing else left behind, I move to the kitchen. Mom has stacked container meals higher than our heads.

Laughing loudly, I say, "Mom, you know I can cook, right?"

"I know, but I just wanted to help until you get settled in." Her eyes are red and watery.

"I'm just around the corner. You're welcome anytime, okay?" She sniffles, and I embrace her. "I'll miss you, but I *need* this."

"I know. I just hope I didn't force this because of the dinner with Thomas. I just don't really know if you're ready to be a stepmom to two kids. It's—"

"Mom, enough. We aren't together. It has nothing to do with you or Dad. But just know, I would never enter any relationship without wanting to or without giving it thought."

"I know, but I just worry. You're still my daughter."

"I know and I love you," I say, peeling myself off her. "Let me pack these too. We don't need to cook for weeks now. Thanks."

She composes herself as she scoops up the containers and helps me pack them into the car.

Ready to start my new life.

———

The dull ache in my chest won't ease up. It's been a week now, and I have unpacked and settled into the new house. It's been nice just having Olivia to hang out with every day. Katie has been coming over most nights too. We all sprawl out on the couch watching TV shows and eating Mom's dinners.

I don't feel different or any more grown-up. But I do miss Thomas. I thought by now it would be easier, but it isn't. I miss living next door. It surprisingly felt as if I was closer to him and the girls. Here with distance, I feel alone and lost. I can't keep this up. I need to figure out what to do with my life.

Olivia keeps pestering me to go out and I keep turning her down and using the excuse of next week. I'm certain she knows why I'm doing it but I'm grateful she doesn't push me. Maybe it would be better if I went out and tried to move on. Try to talk to another guy... But that thought makes my stomach harden.

No, I can't do that when the man I love is living around the corner.

Needing a drink, I walk over to the fridge and see the girls painting and tears instantly well. I miss them so much. I hung it on my fridge, thinking it was supposed to make me feel better, but it adds to my distress. I grab some water and sit back on the sofa.

I pull out my phone and sip my drink as I bring up his name in my phone. I type out a quick message.

Jennifer: *This is too hard. I miss you.*

But as I sit here biting my nails, I type a dozen different messages, but nothing feels right.

He needs to talk to me. I have given him all of me, but he hasn't given me all of him. I know he is holding back, and I can't be in a relationship with a guy keeping me at a distance just to protect his heart. No, it's either all in or all out.

I delete the message and toss my phone. I'm all out.

CHAPTER 33

THOMAS

IT'S SATURDAY MORNING, AND I'm sorting through the boxes in the garage. My mom is here so I can deal with the mess of what I have yet to unpack. When I moved in, I left a few boxes in here, and I have been meaning to sort through them. With nothing else to do, I tackled it today. Filling my days with jobs to do keeps my mind from wandering into thoughts of what she is doing.

In the last box, I find the belongings for the girls—Victoria's items. My ears thump, and I just want to stop and tape the box back up, but I need to man up and deal with this shit. I need to do what I came to do at this house. There will always be a gap where Victoria used to be, but I need to fill it with new memories, so I push the past the fear and pain and start sorting through the boxes with photos.

Pulling out a picture of the four of us crushes me. I dig through more pictures to find the ones I should have put up for the girls.

They deserve to have a few photos of their mom around the house in memory without it killing me inside. As much as I wanted to come here and move on, I know it's important to cherish the wonderful mother the girls had. Show them how much they were loved. How precious they were to her. The photographs shouldn't be stuffed in a box, forgotten. I'm angry at myself for letting my emotions take over my head.

With a collection of beautiful images, I turn to step into the house.

"Hello, Thomas?" I hear a deep voice call out.

"In here," I call out to Paul, turning around to face him.

"Whoa, look at this. You'll be able to park here now." He looks around the space.

"Right. About time I sorted the last of the boxes." I tilt my head in the direction of the last few boxes I emptied.

"What's in there? Need a hand?"

"Well, ah, it was photos and my wife's wedding dress. Just sentimental stuff for the girls."

Paul's face sags. "Oh, I'm sorry. I shouldn't have asked."

I shake my head, offering him a small smile. "No, it's fine, really... It's time."

"Do you mind if I ask how?" he asks softly.

I peer down at the top photo, a candid shot of her with the girls at the beach, hoping for the strength and courage to share. Her face staring back is encouraging me, smashing the wall I built to keep people protected, to keep my painful memories private.

The heavy question hangs in the air, and I'm still glancing down at the photo before gazing up into Paul's stare and answering quietly. "A car accident. I was driving, and a drunk driver crossed over into our lane, hitting us head-on. Victoria didn't make it."

My eyes are full of unshed tears. He stares back at me glossy-eyed, with a few tears leaking. He uses his thumb to wipe his eyes roughly. I glance away and move the empty boxes to the side with my feet to get them out of the way so I can park my car inside. I need the distraction before I let more tears go.

"I'm sorry. That's awful. I can't imagine," he chokes out.

I shrug. "Thanks."

He rubs his neck before stuffing his hand in his pocket. "I wanted to talk to you, Thomas... Jennifer hasn't said this, but I know she loves you. I didn't think she should settle, but my wife reminded me I fell in love with her when I was young. And if someone had stopped me, I wouldn't be as happy as I am right now. How can I take that away from my daughter? I haven't given her enough credit. She is smart and beautiful, and she wouldn't settle for anyone. We won't stand in your way anymore. You have our blessing."

I stand frozen in time; is this really happening? *Am I dreaming?*

Loves me?

Blinking rapidly, the few tears sitting on my lower lashes fall onto my cheeks. I don't have time to ask a question. He thrusts a piece of paper at me. I juggle the pictures with one hand and grab the paper in my other, then lower my gaze to it.

It's her new address.

My mouth moves a few times before any words spill out. "Thanks, Paul." I probably should say more but I am too stunned.

The emotions swirling through me right now are just too much. Jennifer loves me...

Do I love her?

The last few days are a blur. The words Paul said hit me like a bus and have been on repeat in my brain like a song on the radio.

I'm lifting weights at the work gym, trying to de-stress. I'm back to barely sleeping or concentrating. It probably doesn't help that I carry her damn address around with me and it's burning a hole in my pocket.

This was a new beginning for me, but instead of filling my days and nights being happy, I'm back to memories of a woman in a house.

The difference this time is I'm not moving.

"Bud, I think you're lifting too much. The vein in your head is popping out." Joshua's voice cuts through the music blaring through the speakers.

Squeezing my eyes shut, I push a few more reps out. I want to fatigue the muscles, hoping after seeing Jennifer tonight I'll pass out from exhaustion. After another three, I drop the dumbbells on the floor with a thud and swing myself up to a sitting position. Joshua is in sweats, doing bicep curls. I watch him with each curl as I catch my breath.

"Why aren't you with her?"

"Because I'm not." I'm not in the mood to be analyzed today.

"Don't fuck with me, Tom. Because why?" He glares at me through the mirror.

"I can't hold her back. I'm not ruining another woman's life."

"So, you broke it off for you," he argues.

"No, for her," I spit back angrily.

My lips thin as I drop back down to do another set. I suddenly found some new energy.

"Bullshit."

My jaw ticks, but I remain silent. Thinking about his words.

A few minutes later, I confess.

"What if she resents me in a few years because I don't want any more kids?"

"I don't know, but fuck, if you love her, don't let her go. Work it out because you and the girls deserve to be happy."

My mind ticks. His words cut deep. Just like he wanted them to. I broke it off for me... not her. I've been lying to myself.

CHAPTER 34

JENNIFER

IT'S WEDNESDAY AND I decide to teach Lily and Rose how to bake chocolate chip cookies. Both girls have a bowl and their own mixture. I brought them little matching aprons. They stand on stools on either side of me, looking as cute as pie. The smiles on their dough-covered faces are infectious.

I have to keep Rose from trying to eat the raw dough.

"Okay, let's take pieces and roll them up and put them on the cookie sheet like this." I show, then watch as Lily rolls some dough and puts it on the cookie sheet.

"I can't wait to eat them."

"Me too, but after dinner, okay?" I offer.

I hear the door open and pause. Familiar foot-steps cause my heart to thud. Panic spreads throughout my entire body. I still can't stop the desire coursing through my veins. My brain and body crave him.

"Okay," Lily says. "But I am having two." She throws two fingers up at me.

I giggle.

"Two of what?"

His voice sends tingles down my spine. My eyes focus on his handsome face as he steps closer.

"We're making cookies, Daddy," Lily says.

"Cookies," Rose squeaks.

He dumps his keys and wallet on the counter and steps beside Lily. He is in a charcoal-gray suit that fits like a second skin. The electricity buzzing between us is palpable.

I have to bite my lip and refocus on Rose to concentrate.

"Hi, Jen," he says in his silky voice.

"Hi, how come you're home early?"

Oh God. Shut up. How rude. I can't believe I asked that. This is his house.

I'm helping Rose finish the cookies and from the corner of my eye, I see him take his jacket off and throw it on a stool. He rolls his sleeves up, then helps Lily put the dough on the cookie sheet.

"I finished up early today. And I wanted to catch you. I'm taking Rose next week."

"Where is Rose going that I can't go, Daddy?" Lily asks.

"Well, sweetheart, you may need to go at some stage too. But the first session with the doctor is just for Rose, okay?"

Lily shrugs. "Okay." She returns to putting dough on the cookie sheet.

"That's great," I say. "I'm sure it will help a lot. Rose, are you ready to lick the bowl?"

She nods and layers her fingers with dough. I gaze over at Thomas and Lily who are doing the same. I watch as he brings his finger to his mouth and wraps his lips around it, sucking the dough off. My stomach pitches.

I'm jealous of the damn dough. I want his luscious lips and tongue on me.

His gaze flicks to me—caught red-handed perving at him. And I'm sure he knows exactly that I was thinking—dirty thoughts. *Shit.* I move to pop the cookie sheets in the oven and set the timer.

"Girls, let's wash your hands, and then go play," he says. "You can have one after dinner."

"I want two. Jen said we could, if we have dinner first."

I have to roll my lips in to prevent a laugh from slipping out.

His gaze shoots to mine. He arches a brow with humor written on his face.

"Okay, two then," he surrenders.

I help the girls wash their hands, and then they take off to play. I clean up, still sensing Thomas near me.

"Thanks for doing this with the girls. They love it. I wish I could do this, but truthfully, I'm an awful baker." He laughs. His sexy laugh is a sound I have missed.

As I wipe the counter and look up at him, I say, "I'm sure you're not that bad."

He raises his brows, amusement appearing on his face. "Want to make a bet?"

My lips lift, and a warm rush fills my chest. I push aside thoughts of us. I've finished cleaning up and with no other reason to stay, I gaze into his warm brown eyes, and say, "Dinner is ready and in the fridge. The timer will go off when the cookies are done."

Moving past him, I grab my bag off the counter.

"You sure you can't stay? You made the cookies."

I smile at the offer but shake my head gently. "They're for the girls. I better get home."

"If you're sure. I would say I would save some, but with us three, there is no way."

"Good. Enjoy them."

"Girls, Jen's going," he says.

"Bye," they call out.

Feeling my body tensing with anticipation. I walk to the door with an erratic pulse. I pull open the door, then step out, not allowing him close.

He waves, so I wave back at him, admiring his solid body as he leans against the doorframe, then I go next door to visit my parents. I don't want to hope and have my heart crushed again. But there was a little spark in him tonight, a spark that ignited a fire in me.

It's Saturday, and Olivia is out shopping for a new outfit to wear tonight. She has been begging me to go out, but I really just want to stay home and have the house to myself.

I'm tidying up the house before I cook lunch when the doorbell chimes. I bet it's my mom. They normally stop in on the weekend. They like to check on me, but really, I'm sure they believe Olivia corrupted me.

I pull open the door, suddenly feeling light-headed at the sight of Thomas.

What is he doing here?

"Hi. Sorry. Am I interrupting?" he asks.

I blink. "No, uh, it's fine."

I look around him, wondering where the girls are.

"My mom has the girls at her house for the weekend," he says.

I nod, staring back. His messy brown hair looks like he's been running his hands through it a million times. Why can't he look bad for once? Here I stand in my baggy sweats and my hair in a messy bun on top of my head, definitely not expecting visitors. And visitors that look like *him*. He wears a pair of jeans and a V-neck black shirt. Everything looks made for him, showing off his delectable body, making me burn up inside.

"Can I come in and talk to you for a moment?" he asks, his forehead creasing in question.

"Uh, yeah, I guess so."

I stand back, bringing the door with me, allowing him to pass.

He steps into the house and his spicy scent hits me full force. I briefly close my eyes before trailing behind him.

He takes a seat on the couch. "Nice house."

I sit down opposite him on the other couch. "Thanks, Olivia's."

I can't seem to form flowing sentences, feeling tongue-tied. But also, he needs to explain why he is coming here and asking for time.

With a quick realization, I ask, "Are you and the girls okay?"

"Yes, it's nothing like that." He takes an audible breath. "I owe you some answers."

I nod. "Okay."

His hands rest on his thighs as he leans forward.

An empty feeling in the pit of my stomach hits as I wait for the news he wants to share. "I want to tell you about my late wife, Victoria."

His eyes stare through me with a blank expression. I blink rapidly and offer a small tilt of my head.

"Victoria died in a car accident. I was in the car with her."

I gasp, covering my mouth with my hand. Staring at his pained face, I know there is more.

He scoots forward on the couch. "We were driving home from an ultrasound. She was twelve and a half weeks pregnant with our third baby. I was driving around the corner from home when a drunk driver hit us head-on. Both Victoria and he died on the scene."

Hot wet tears stream down my face, but I refuse to remove my eyes from him. Even with blurry vision, I can see his lashes have tears sitting on them, waiting to fall.

"I was in the hospital and when I woke, I had all these ugly wounds and learned Victoria was gone..." He touches his chest with a wince. "It was a nightmare, and I covered them up a few months later. I was still furious at the world."

He pats his chest. "The lion is Victoria." He points to the center over his heart. "This was a rose I was drawing the first day we met in class, and the other is her and the kids' names. We didn't name the baby, so I had the footprints instead." His voice is low and tormented.

I saw the footprints, but I assumed it was one of the girls. Definitely not that.

My heart squeezes in pain with the shock of the story. I don't know how to make this better.

"When I met you, the connection I had with you was so unexpected and so magnetic. I never thought I would see you again let alone be your neighbor." I can hear the lightness in his tone.

I smile to myself as he speaks.

"I never thought I would meet someone that would make me hope. Hope for happiness and love and a future as a family. My worry is that you're young, and I don't want to make you settle down and not live the life you deserve. I don't want to hold you back. Take it from me, life is too short."

I open my mouth, but he interrupts. "And I don't want another baby. I love my girls, but I don't want to be in a situation where I am left with another child to raise on my own—the thought kills me. I realize how unfair that is to you. You're twenty-two and you haven't had kids, so that's why I broke things off. It's a lot for me to take away from you. Totally selfish. I felt like I needed to come here and be open and honest with you."

A few tears leak from his eyes, and I crack. I stand abruptly, moving to sit beside him. Reaching out, I grab his hands, breaking the vise-like grip he has and twining my hands through his fingers. I have missed his touch, so warm and strong. He watches my thumb rub across the top of his hand.

I take a breath, knowing there was something special about him from the very beginning. "That's a lot to digest. I wish you had told me about the accident, the baby, and your fears. It would have been nice to understand back then, and we could have prevented a break."

His gaze lifts to mine, his brown eyes gentle and understanding. "Sorry, my feelings for you overwhelmed me, and then your father agreed to my thoughts about you being young and how you shouldn't settle down right now, and then you spoke about children of your own and I freaked out," he says.

"It's okay. We all have different ways of coping with emotions. I'm glad you're opening up now, but I do want to make one thing clear. You and the girls are my family. If I never had a baby, I promise you I would still be the happiest woman alive. The break proved to me how much I love you, Tom... and I want us to be a family."

"I can't promise you I'll change my mind," he whispers honestly. He reaches out and strokes my face in the softest caress. I blink rapidly. "I love you, Jen. You were a piece of sunshine I never knew I was missing until I met you."

"I love you too." I thrust my fingers through his hair and pull his face down.

His dark gaze meets mine and my heart turns over. His large hand cups my face, and he brings his lips down to capture mine.

I push his shoulders back, making him fall back onto the couch, then I scurry over and sit on top of him. Feeling his desire hit my core, I rub my sex hard along him.

He lets out a groan and captures my lips in a desperate kiss. My sex fills with desire, my body on fire for him.

I pull back, panting, and he tugs his shirt off, then lets my hands explore every ripple and muscle.

He removes my top and my bare breasts are on display. "Fuck, princess," he moans.

Thank you for being too lazy to throw on a bra or t-shirt, Jen.

My nipples are erect from need, my body burning up from his heated glare.

"I *need* you," I plead.

He snaps, lifting me off him quickly. I stand on shaky legs. He rises and pecks my lips. "Where is your room?"

A wicked grin breaks out on my face. I walk on wobbly feet, dragging him by hand.

We rush through the hall and enter my simple room. I'm excited he is in my space. But the thoughts are short-lived when he pulls my gray pants down.

"I've missed you," he grits out.

"Clearly." I giggle.

"Sorry." He winces.

"No, no, no. You go back to what you were doing, Mr. Dunn. I'm still wearing panties and I expect you to remove them with your teeth."

His eyes flare, and I want to high-five myself for being ballsy, figuring I need to be the grown-up I want people to treat me like.

A flash of fire hits before he leans forward and bites down on my panties and drags them down my legs. I climb higher just from the sight of his naked back, rippled with muscles, on display. My mouth waters. *I need him now.*

I lift my legs when he taps each foot. He sits back, clearly waiting for instructions.

"Up." I'm barely hanging on. I want him inside me.

I unbutton his jeans and tug them down along with his briefs.

Once they're off, I push him down on my bed and straddle him. Grabbing him, I rub his cock along my dripping folds. His fingers dig in my hips, and I slowly lower myself down, acclimating to his size. It's bordering on painful, but I can't stop.

Condom.

My eyes snap open. "Condom."

"You said you're on the pill." He grunts, lifting his hips.

I nod.

"Then don't worry, I trust you."

He enters me and my eyes close, already close to coming.

I brace my hands on his rippled stomach and move up and down. His hands are still on my hips, guiding me, but he allows me to set the pace.

At first, I go up and down slowly, but as I feel my orgasm building, I pick up the pace.

Feeling myself climb, I say, "I'm close."

He growls, letting me know he is too

Thank God.

I fall apart and continue moving until I feel him pulse and then fill me.

Falling down beside him, I drape myself on his side. His chest rises and falls at a rapid rate that matches my own. We cuddle, panting, until I hear...

"I love you, princess."

I turn to look at him, smiling with satisfaction. "I love you too."

EPILOGUE

Jennifer

Six months later

DRIVING TO ROSE'S DOCTOR appointment as a family has been a regular pattern for the last few months.

Rose has been attending weekly sessions. At first, the doctor requested individual meetings with each of us.

And then we started attending them as a family.

I still can't quite believe Thomas is my family or that I am a part of his. But it has been the best few months of my life.

He still can't take his eyes off the road or hold my hand when driving, but it all made sense when I found out Victoria died in a car accident.

When he drives, he needs total concentration.

I still live with Olivia at her place, because keeping my newfound independence was super important to me. I only stay with Thomas and the girls on the weekends. I still want time for us to grow as a couple, and I think living together too quickly would ruin that.

We need to continue the pace we are going. It's comfortable for all of us.

After fifteen minutes of driving, we arrive at the doctor's office.

"Hi, Amber," I say to the receptionist.

She beams. "Hi, Jennifer. I'll check you in. Take a seat. We are on time today."

"Okay, thanks."

Thomas and the girls are already playing with the toys in the waiting room.

We don't play for long when Rose gets called in.

"Hi, everyone. Come in." The doctor ushers us into her office, which is huge—all cream walls with brown-stained trim. And her desk is a large chocolate-colored desk. There are toys at the back of the room, which the girls gravitate to as soon as we arrive.

"Hi, Doctor Davis," I greet as I step in.

Thomas follows, greeting her too.

"Good morning," she says. "Take a seat. I'll get the girls set up with their activity. I'll be right back."

We each drag out a chair and plop down into it.

A few minutes later the doctor takes a seat at her computer.

"Any concerns this week?"

"No." We shake our head in unison.

"Any improvements?"

I turn my head to look at Thomas before facing back to the doctor.

"Not that we noticed," Thomas answers.

"That's okay. She has made massive improvements so far. It's normal for some weeks to make no progress. I'll book you in for next week, but soon we will reduce them to every other week. I don't feel she needs to be here weekly now."

My mouth curves. That's wonderful news.

"I'll go work with the girls, then I'll bring them over before you go."

We nod and she wanders off to interact with the kids. We watch them draw. After a good ten minutes, they all come over. The girls jump over to us with their pictures in their hands held out toward us.

"Well, both Rose and Lily have drawn a picture of the family."

Looking at the girls' pictures, I still. It's us but I'm holding a baby. *What the?*

I know I'm not pregnant.

"Are you two expecting?" the doctor questions.

"No, we definitely aren't," I answer quickly, worried Thomas is thinking that I am.

"Okay, just checking."

For the rest of the session, as she asks questions, I zone out. I wonder where Lily got the idea. I never talk about children of my own—ever. I'm happy and fulfilled with the girls.

It's time to leave so I shake my head, trying to clear my thoughts, and follow them out.

We get back in the car and I remain quiet. I just don't understand why the girls had me holding a baby. I'm still so confused.

"Are you okay, princess?" Thomas asks, rubbing my thigh before buckling himself in and starting the car.

"Yeah, I'm just thrown off by the picture."

I stare out the window as he reverses the car.

"Do you still think about your own baby?"

"No, I haven't thought about it until today, honestly."

I've been so busy with the work promotion and minding the girls, and I really haven't thought about it.

"Listen, if it would make you happy, then I would have one with you."

I gasp loudly. "What? You're not serious."

He laughs. "Deadly. I'm not saying let's go home right now and make a baby, but maybe in a few years?"

"How do you make a baby, Daddy?" Lily asks.

I cringe. I'm not answering that question.

"You're too young to understand, okay?" Thomas says. "When you're older, I will talk to you about it, okay?"

"Okay, Daddy," she replies, happy with his answer.

Settling back into the seat, I watch the cars drive by, the new information Thomas just shared with me circling inside my head.

This is huge, but for now, I love being a mom to the girls. I have found my family. I feel whole.

Two years later

Thomas
"Jen, are you ready?" I shout.

We are going on a family trip away to the ski resort. The girls and I have always talked about it, but I never had time to do it. This year, I put in leave and booked us a getaway.

Rose has been asking every day if today is the day we go. Lily, my sassypants, still likes to remind her it's not. But today she finally said yes. Rose was delighted with the answer.

She's improved tremendously with therapy. We visit every six months. We can request a visit for any emergencies, but so far Rose has had no setbacks.

"Okay, I'm ready, everyone," Jennifer says.

"Let's hit the road. We have a long drive ahead of us."

I packed the car earlier this morning while everyone was asleep to save time.

The four-hour trip isn't going to be fun, but everyone has books, snacks, drinks, and iPads.

The drive up is smooth and relaxing. There aren't many cars on the road which helps my anxiety. I relax and listen to podcasts in the car.

We arrive at the cabin, and it's stunning. Surrounded with snow, the brown wood building shows off its character. I carry one bag up to the cabin and unlock the door. We walk into the cabin pre-warmed with the fire.

The cabin is all set up to make it cozy for my girls. They deserve the best. I had James help me arrange this. I needed the perfect location, and he found it.

Then I hired a local to set it up, and it's perfect. Better than the pictures I was sent.

The girls run for the couch in front of the fireplace, and Lily flicks on the television.

I return to the car and bring all our belongings inside. When that's done, I take a quick shower before I start dinner.

When I come back out, Jennifer has already begun cooking. I come up behind her and wrap my arms around her middle. She leans back, sighing.

"What are we cooking?" I ask. Kissing her neck before slipping out of her hold, I look at what she is chopping.

"Italian. I'm going to make some pasta. I'm just starting the sauce."

"Sounds good, princess. I'll make a homemade garlic pizza."

I feel relaxed working alongside her in the kitchen. She has always had this calming effect on me and the girls. She makes everything better.

We cook in comfortable silence before we take a seat in the family room with the girls, waiting for it to be ready.

When it's done, we enjoy the meal. Then we bathe the girls and tuck them in bed.

I grab a glass of red wine, and we sit in front of the fireplace, watching the fire flicker.

I take a big pull of alcohol for courage, then place it down gently before I reach for her bottle of water.

Her brows furrow. "What are you doing?"

I place it down next to mine.

Sucking in a deep cleansing breath, I grab her hands in mine and drop to one knee. I look at our joined hands and then back up at her.

"Jen, I feel so lucky to have met you. Our worlds collided on more than one occasion, and I will be forever grateful. You make me and the girls so happy, every single day. You are kind, beautiful, and caring. I can't live a day without you. Will you do me the honor and marry me?"

I pull out the box I had hidden, flicking it open, and she covers her mouth with her hand while tears slip down her cheeks.

"Yes," she whispers.

I was confident she would say yes until I had to actually propose. I've said the words over and over in my head in preparation, but it wasn't the same.

I pull the ring from the box and slip it on her finger before she looks down at the emerald-cut diamond with fascination. Her gaze flicks to mine, and I smile. I stand and kiss her before taking her into my arms. And rubbing my hand over her pregnant belly.

My life changing accident brought me a second chance at love.

The End.

BONUS SCENE OF VICTORIA AND THOMAS

15 years ago- Flashback

Today is the first day of my final school year before heading to university. After the first half hour sitting in biology class, the teacher began talking, and I knew right away this subject wasn't for me. Standing up, I walk to the teacher to gain permission to leave and never return to her class. I walk straight from biology into the director's office to discuss switching classes. Lucky for me he agrees to swap as they have a few gaps. They assign me to business which I know I will enjoy and it will help my future; I was never going to be a doctor or a scientist.

Leaving the office, I look down at the paper with directions and I find the portable room within a minute. Knowing I am interrupting doesn't bother me. I knock hard on the door and I hear a "Come in," screech from the other side of the door. Gripping the handle, I swing the door wide-open and step in. I have twenty-five students staring back at me with wide eyes and gaping mouths. There are a few whispers between the students, but I keep my eyes in front on the small middle-aged woman conducting the class.

"May I help you?" Her eyes assess me.

Striding over to her desk where she is standing, I hold out the paper that explains the swap; the director handed me the form to give Ms Buckley. She takes it out of my hand and reads it before nodding and points to the room. "Take a seat," she says in a dull, bored tone.

I gaze up and take in the room, noticing only a few spots in the front row available, and I decide on the empty seat on the left. I will never hear the end of this; James, Benjamin, and Joshua will have a field day knowing I was in the front row of the class. The rumors will spread quickly. I have been part of the popular boys' group from the start due to hanging out with the richest and most attractive boys in the school. I put my head down and try to stay hidden. Halfway through the class my pen runs out of ink. Fuck. *Lifting my gaze up from my drawing that I have almost completed on my notepad, I lean down and rummage through my bag but I cannot find a single pen. I sit back up in my chair and I turn to the person sitting next to me. "Excuse me." The blond girl turns and my heart sings. I completely forget all my words and just stare, the beauty in front of me with wavy blond hair has the palest skin and the most dazzling hazel eyes and full plump lips. My heart* beats faster in my chest and my stomach has a swarm of butterflies. I notice a flush of pink appear on her nose as her eyes avert my stare. "Yes?"

Right, I spoke to her. Snapping out of my trance state, I clear my throat.

"Do you have a spare pen I can borrow?" I watch her as she chews mindlessly on the end of her pen. I don't even think she is aware she is doing it.

"Sure but..."

"But what?" I question.

"If you tell me what you're drawing." She nods in the direction of my paper.

"It's none of your business. Do you have a pen or not?" I don't know why I'm being so snappy other than the raging hormones that have awoken feelings I haven't experienced before and are making me un-comfortable in my school pants.

Her face has gone like stone as she snaps, "Don't talk to me like that."

"Sorry," I mumble back apologetically. "Can I have one?"

She thrusts the pen she had been chewing in my direction and I stare at it. She wiggles it in my face and I reach out and snatch it.

I finish the drawing using her pen, and I leave that class in awe. I have never had a girl give me attitude or awaken me like she had. The issue in my pants is agreeing. Every class after that I find some way to talk to her. I find out in the next class during a roll call that her name is Victoria, reminding me of a queen.

I do anything to start conversations with her during business class. In the last class of the first semester, I ask her out on a movie date. Surprising me, she agrees instantly.

The date is that weekend, and I am a bundle of nerves. Victoria is not only striking but fierce like a lion. She scares me a little and at the same time, she excites me. I wait for her to arrive at the movie theater because I don't have my license yet, which meant I couldn't pick her up in a car. I was another semester from turning eighteen. Watching her walk toward me in wedges, a navy off the shoulder top, and blue jeans is like getting my own personal model on a catwalk, strutting toward me. My mouth hangs wide-open.

"Hi, Tom. You ready?" She winks.

Rearranging myself in my pants, I nod vigorously. "Yes. Hi. You look beautiful." It comes out like a pant.

"Pick your jaw up off the floor and let's head inside." She laughs.

Snapping myself out of it, I take back control, then I take her hand and lead her to the movie. Keeping my hands and lips to myself is extremely hard but I was taught to respect women so I need to control the urges. The movie that we watch is Harry Potter and the Prisoner of Azkaban. *I am distracted from my raging hormones the entire time. We share a big box of popcorn and hold hands and when we leave the cinema, I walk her to the bus stop and pause, spinning her around and kissing her full lips. It is the best kiss I had ever had. I had kissed a few girls before but nothing like Victoria. I have lust at first sight. I ask her to be my girlfriend right there and then. And from then on, we are together.*

Also by Sharon Woods

The Gentlemen Series

Bossy Mr. Ward

White Empire

The Christmas Agreement

Saffron and Secrets- Novella

Stand-alone

Doctor Taylor

BOSSY MR WARD EXCERPT

Joshua

Staring across an old wooden desk into my father's gaze, my head thumps inside my skull as I watch my dad's small, thin lips move. I can't understand his words; it's as if he is speaking underwater. I scrunch my forehead, trying to concentrate on reading his lips, but I can't for the life of me lip-read.

I shouldn't have drunk so much scotch last night at the party. It was a regular boys' night that quickly got out of control. As usual, I let myself get loose. With no work commitments or girlfriend to answer to, I don't know when to stop. I'm not complaining. I love my easy, free life. But the hangovers every week are getting harder to bounce back from.

I'm slumped in one of his worn office chairs. I watch as he rubs his eyebrows with his hand, rests his elbows on top of the desk, and blows out his cheeks, frustration written on his face. I haven't had the best relationship with my parents. They wanted the so-called perfect child, not the rebellious party boy they got.

If they gave two shits about me, they would have talked to me. But I was invisible to them. I think I was born for the society picture, not out of love.

Love—what is that?

I wouldn't know what it feels like to be truly loved. People see the outside, the pretty face, the family money, the carefree attitude I put on, but underneath the façade is darkness. Deep loneliness hidden deep under layers.

I scan the office, noting the mess, the papers piled up on his desk. I shrug it off, blaming my drunken state that I must be seeing shit.

Rubbing my hands over my face, I say, "Dad, what did you call me here this early for?" Irritation is laced in my voice.

He rises, snatching his glass full of whiskey off the desk and taking a big swig. "It's eleven in the morning, for god's sake. Look at the state of you. Every week, you do this to yourself. You need to grow up."

I sigh, leaning back, taking in his profile. He looks out the window, talking to it instead of me. He barely looks at me. I shake my head. He seems to have aged, his gray hair more white, his black suit a little big for his small frame.

My head throbs and I snap. I would rather be on my couch, recovering, than sitting here. "What did you call me here for?"

He picks up a piece of paper and shoves it out to me. I move a little too quick and wince. I want to get the fuck out of here. I snatch the paper from his hands.

I peer down and my brows furrow. *What the fuck?*

I blink rapidly. *Surely not.*

It's a contract.

For the business.

The family business.

He transferred it.

Into my name.

Joshua Ward.

Effective immediately.

My mouth slacks and I try to think of what to say, but nothing is forming coherently in my mind.

I thrust my hand to the back of my neck and squeeze the tension that's building up, hard and fast.

I clear my throat. "Why?" I whisper.

I want to say more, but that's all I can think of right now.

My heart is beating erratically at the news and the contract that I'm currently glaring at.

"Why?" The words leave my mouth again as I lean back into the office chair in shock and take in my old man. I squint as I try to read his face for answers.

"It's time, son. I'm not young anymore. I can't do this forever." He continues looking at the window and not at me.

Lie.

He is hiding something. I'm certain. I lean into the right side of the chair and rub my hand along my chin, trying to figure out what it is. As if glaring at him long enough will make him spit it out. *I wish!*

I lift my chin in a sudden thought. "It's sudden. Effective immediately? Why not prepare me—show me how you run the business?"

My dad stands and rounds his chair to the drink trolley. He turns and lifts the glass into the air in a silent offering.

Bile rises in my throat. I shake my head. *Fuck, that hurts.* I cease immediately and he shrugs before pouring himself another large helping of whiskey. He takes a large gulp of the amber liquid.

He cradles the glass as he returns to his chair. I notice his eyes appear red and dull.

Maybe it is the right decision. I just wish he hadn't thrown me into the business like this. A little warning would have been nice.

"Your mother and I are taking a trip for six to twelve months. Change of scenery." He stares out the office window and takes another large sip. Something is on his mind.

I shift, sitting up in my chair. Raising a brow, I say, "You're serious?"

His gaze meets my hard eyes. "What is your issue, son? I thought you would be happy taking over the business."

I think about his question. Am I happy? I sigh. "Of course I am. Just not like this. And this soon. But it's not like I have many choices. How much time do we have before this...trip?" I ask.

"Six weeks."

I slap my hands on my thighs, not giving a fuck about my head. "You expect me to learn everything in six fucking weeks? You're crazy, old man...Gahhhhh," I growl, sitting back in my chair.

His body straightens and his eyebrows draw close together as he says, "Do not speak to me like that. You will show some respect. You will be fine. You're young; you will find better and new ways to run the ship."

My jaw thrusts as I hold back another outburst. We don't speak as he drains his glass. I watch him stalk toward the alcohol trolley and lower his empty glass. He swings around and walks over to me. He stands beside me, resting his right hand on my shoulder, and squeezes.

"I'm tired. It's time I get home. Your mother will be expecting me."

I nod, scared that if I open my mouth, I'll disrespect him. And I'm not wasting my breath. My sore head is quickly turning into a migraine.

I hear him walk to the door. It creaks open before I hear the click shut. *Asshole.*

I inhale a deep breath through my nose and stalk around the desk, dusting my hands across the top surface. Papers fly in every direction.

I take a seat in my new chair, scanning the room. Old white paint, dark brown carpet, and a small window looking outside at houses. It's a small, run-down building. The computer needs an upgrade desperately. My dad insisted that upgrading was a waste, but I don't agree.

Now that I am to take over, things need to change.

As I scan the office, I think about the recent projects we have lost to our competitors. My gut twists and I need to dig deeper.

I tear open the drawers and pull the paperwork of all our current jobs out and pile everything onto the desk. Some papers hold on top of the pile, but a few slip straight to the floor.

Once all the papers inside the office are on top of the desk, I sift through, making two piles. Keep or throw. My stomach grumbles, reminding me I skipped dinner with a fling I have been seeing this week.

It's close to two in the morning by the time I finally get ready to leave the office. I've been here all day, trying to make sense of everything, and I pick up one final paper that had slipped off the desk and landed on the other side.

I crouch down and scoop it up. As I stand, I scan the contents. "You asshole," I say out loud. So this is what he wasn't telling me; I knew he was hiding something... Scrunching the paper in my hand, I pull out my phone and click on James' name, bringing the phone to my ear. It doesn't take long for him to answer.

"Josh?" His voice is gravelly and I wince.

"Shit. Sorry. I didn't even think about the time when I called you."

"No, no. It's fine. What's up?" he asks.

"My dad left me with the family business, effective immediately. The asshole is going on a holiday in six weeks for six months, maybe a year. I don't know how to run a business, James—a failing one at that." I squeeze my eyes shut at the last statement. The paper in my hand has angered me further.

"It's okay. I got you. I'll be there in five minutes. You at the office?"

I sigh loudly. "Yeah."

I hit the end button and shove the phone back into my pocket.

I step to the drink trolley and pour myself a good three fingers of scotch, the one thing he still had—expensive liquor.

I move over to the chair and pull at the drink, the amber burning my throat before my head reminds me I'm still hungover.

I lower the glass to the table and sit down again while I wait for my friend James. I crinkle the paper and stare at the eviction words. Staring back at me. Mocking me.

Fuck!

Chapter 1
Ava
Six months later

My desk phone rings, scaring the crap out of me. I work as a receptionist for a printing company. "Good morning. Ava speaking. How may I help you?"

"Ava, it's David. Could you see me in my office when you finish with the orders?"

"Of course. I won't be too long," I answer.

"Take your time."

I hang up. I've been working with David for a few years now; I enjoy the peace of the small town I live in. And there are only a few of us who work here, so I can be myself.

Twenty minutes later, I rise and wander over to David's office. I knock on his doorframe.

He looks up from his computer with a half-assed smile. Uneasiness churns in my stomach. "Ava, come in. Please take a seat."

I frown at his comment. He doesn't ask me to sit down. Ever. Sweat forms on my palms and I rub them quickly down my ripped blue jeans.

"Okay." I step inside and sit down on the chair opposite him. I sit straight, waiting for the reason for his call.

He rubs the back of his neck before gazing at me. *Shit. He looks serious.*

"Ava, I'm so sorry to have to say this, but we have to close the business."

My hands cover my gasp. "What. Shit. Why?" I mumble through my fingers.

He hangs his head. "I know it must shock you, and trust me, I tried to avoid this, but financially the company is now in the hands of administrators."

I blink rapidly, trying to process his words. *What the fuck am I going to do for money now?*

Feeling my heart beating in my throat, I try to concentrate on breathing in and out, trying to calm the panic that's rising. My breaths are shallow yet audible. I'm unable to talk, my mind going over the same thoughts. How am I going to get through this? I can't go back there.

"Are you okay, Ava? Would you like a glass of water? Ava?" He asks again, louder this time.

I would rather have alcohol, but I know we don't have any here in the office. I nod slowly. His chair drags across the floor as he rises, and heavy footsteps walk to the water fountain. The water trickling sounds like my bleeding heart. The footsteps begin again as a shadow appears in front of me. I slowly raise my head to see David has the cup held out in front of him. Grabbing the cup slowly out of his outstretched hand, peering down at the clear liquid, I raise the plastic cup and chug the water back, draining the cup. The cold water coats my warm throat. *So good.*

David steps back around to his chair.

I offer a small smile and talk in a quiet voice. "Thanks." I continue to concentrate on breathing in through my nose, out through my mouth, feeling my shoulders relax with every breath and my heartbeat regulating.

He clears his throat, gaining my attention. "I'm giving you two weeks' notice. If you find another job before that, I will understand. You're a fantastic worker and I'm happy to be called as a reference."

My lips tip up. "Thanks, David. I appreciate that." I hesitate before adding, "What will you do?"

He takes a deep, audible breath and leans back in his chair. His gaze meets mine. The sadness there makes my cold heart break.

"I don't know, Ava. Truthfully, I don't know."

"Well, shit." A nervous smile appears on my lips.

He laughs, but it's not his carefree laugh. It's a broken cackle. "I will miss you. You kept this place in order. Hell, you kept me sorted. I just couldn't keep this place afloat. I'm sorry."

His eyes return to his computer and I swallow. "You are a significant person and boss. I'm sure something better is out there waiting for you."

He raises his chin to glance at me, offering me a genuine smile. The surrounding air is quiet, so I stand. "I better get back to work."

He nods and also stands, walking around the desk and toward me. I instinctively take a step back, not wanting any physical touch. I cross my arms, spin around, and wander back to my desk, lost in my thoughts about my future.

The next few hours drag. I work, but it's not as productive as I usually would be. Not like I have to try very hard now. I will be jobless in two weeks. *Fuck. What will I do?*

A few hours later, I clear my desk and make my way home. I pick up the cheapest bottle of wine from the store, not giving a shit that cheap wine causes the worst hangovers. I need alcohol tonight. It might help this numbness I'm feeling disappear. That, or it will help me sleep.

As soon as I enter my apartment, a lump forms in my throat. I hate that I could be looking at moving out of here. *My home.* It's a warm and safe place. Entering the kitchen, I pull open the cupboard and scan the contents. I don't have the energy to cook a fancy dinner, nor do I have the funds.

I spot a packet of noodles. *Bingo.* I grab them and begin preparing them. While they cook, I connect my phone to the Bluetooth speaker so I have music playing softly in the background, then I open the bottle of wine and pour myself a decent helping. Taking a sip, I scrunch up my face. *This shit is awful. Fuck.* I stir the noodles, which are almost done, and take another large mouthful of my shitty cheap wine.

My phone rings as I lower the glass and choke on the awful shit, then twist the volume down on the speaker so I can answer the call. Pulling out my phone, I check the display. Mom's name is flashing. Even though I hate myself right now, and I hate that I could disappoint her, the need to tell her about my day has me answering it.

"Mom, your ears must have been burning. I was going to call you tonight." I step back to the kitchen.

"Oh, no, they weren't, darling. What did you want to talk to me about?"

Raising the wine, I take another large sip, needing the liquid courage. I stir my dinner before flicking the stove off. "Are you sitting down?" I ask quietly.

"No, but what happened?" Concern is laced in her voice.

A sour taste hits my mouth. I am hating how I'm about to let her down, that David sacking me is a disappointment to her. A heaviness enters my heart and I blow out a breath I hadn't realized I had been holding until she speaks.

"Darling, tell me. You have me worried sick here," she begs through the phone.

I squeeze my eyes shut, then open them. "Sorry. I was turning my dinner off. David called me into the office today and said he is closing the business." I hear her gasp. Tears form behind my eyelids. I'm glad she isn't here because I would be a basket case.

"Oh, darling. I'm so sorry."

"It's not your fault, Mom." Pinching my lips together for a moment, I finally say, "I have two weeks to find another job."

As I glance around my one-bedroom apartment, my heart hurts. I love this place. I'm settled here and my paychecks keep me living here independently.

"No wonder you're upset, darling. But there is a reason. Things happen in your life for a reason. There is a better opportunity out there. I believe that," she offers.

My eyes fill with tears. I still don't believe this is happening. I love how she always believes in me, but right now, I'm feeling numb and not optimistic.

Desperate to change the subject so I don't start sobbing on the phone, I say, "Thanks, Mom. I hope you're right. Anyway, enough about me. What are you doing?"

"I was going to see if you wanted to come for dinner Sunday night? Darling?"

I am having trouble responding; my mouth is opening but no words are coming out. After a beat, I sigh, "Yes. That sounds good." I would rather be by myself. Alone. But then all I will do is think about my jobless situation. And she would insist she comes to visit. At least this way, I won't have to cook.

"Okay, good. I'll cook one of your favorites."

I close my eyes at her sweet gesture. Any food is my favorite, but there are definitely a few dishes that stand out. I feel weak, like I need to sit down. "Mom, I better eat my dinner before it gets cold."

"Good idea. Are you sure you will be okay tonight? Do you need me to come over?" she offers.

"No thanks; I'll be fine. I'm tired and will crash soon."

"Okay. Call me if you need anything. I love you."

My heart thumps at those words. "I love you too...Bye." I hang up and retreat to the stove to serve my noodles. Scooping up my bowl, fork, and glass of wine, I carry them into my living room, lowering my butt to the floor, my food on the coffee table and wine beside it. I stab the noodles with the fork. I try to eat but my throat thickens, making it hard to swallow. Deciding against eating, I push the bowl aside and drink the wine instead.

A few glasses of wine later, my veins are now filled with alcohol. It's warming me from the inside. Feeling hot, I peel off my sweater, leaving me in my tank top and leggings.

I search the television, looking for a show or movie to watch tonight. Scrolling aimlessly through the stations, I find nothing. I flick it off and open my mom's old laptop. I power it up and continue to drink. By now I have had too many, but I'm cradling my last glass as I scroll through job ads. I stop on one that sounds simple enough. I sit up straight and the wine sloshes around in the glass and over the edge. *Fuckin' hell.*

I lift my finger up the glass and wipe the wine up, sucking the residue into my mouth. I don't want to get this over my white couch or rug.

I squint as I read the job description.

Personal Assistant required for an expanding electrical company. That sounds easy.

I shrug at myself on this cozy night. Scrolling through, I read each duty.

Able to work as part of a team
Facilities management and maintenance
Schedule management and meeting coordination
Coordinating and organizing project manager
Office management including stationery, mail, greeting clients, couriers, and more

It all sounds easy enough. I can support a project manager with daily tasks. *Piece of cake.*

Feeling a little buzzed, I set the wine down on the coffee table. A little smirk plays on my lips. I fill in a new version of my résumé. I'm smiling to myself as I add some cheeky extra words and side tasks. I have never done them, but it makes me sound more experienced.

I need money and a job desperately. With no other options and only two weeks to find something new, I laugh at how ridiculous I sound on this résumé. But the website has nothing else that's suitable.

An icy shiver runs through my spine. The thought of getting kicked out of here has me hitting send. I close the laptop, drain my glass, and my eyes become heavy. Unable to concentrate on the TV, I switch it off and climb onto my sofa, snuggling in as my exhaustion takes over, and I pass out.

When I move the next morning on the couch, my head feels like it's about to explode. I groan out loud at no one. *Fuck. I feel sick. Stupid cheap wine.* Without lifting my head up, I reach for my phone.

I can't remember a thing about last night. I seem to have lost all recollection of events. My fingers touch my cell. *Yes. Found it.*

I lift it up in front of my face and squint as the light from the screen blares back at me. *Ahh, so fucking bright.*

I blink rapidly until my eyes adjust. My thumb moves aimlessly over my socials and I catch sight of my email icon, showing one new message. Frowning, I click on it and open my emails, sucking in a breath as I read the subject line to the one email.

Job Interview from Ward Electrical and Infra-structure.

I rub down my face, trying to wipe away the sleep and foggy brain. *What?*

Shifting my weight on the couch, sitting up a little, I try to understand if it's a spam email. I need a closer look. I haven't applied for any jobs. *Right?*

I open up a browser and google the company's name. Sure enough, a website pops up. And as I scan, it seems legitimate.

So, the next question is how?

I rub along my brow, trying to remember and finally deciding to check my sent emails. I have a niggling feeling in my stomach. *Did I apply last night?*

Clicking the folder, it opens up and sure enough, there is the application I sent off. *Fuck.*

Moving back to the inbox, I reopen the email and read the contents. Job interview means I'll need to look professional. I groan. But my stomach grumbles, reminding me I also need money for necessities. *And better wine.*

As I continue to read, I see a comment stating it's a phone interview. *Thank fuck.*

The interview is scheduled for ten a.m. on Thursday. If I'm successful, I start Monday. Maybe Mom is right about her signs. If I get this job, then I'll know for certain that it was meant to be...but at the moment, I'm not convinced. Surely someone is going to come busting through my door and tell me I have been punked.

My shoulders drop and I relax back onto the couch with a loud sigh.

Closing the application, I swing my legs off the couch and sit up. I grip my head with both hands, wincing from the movement. Waiting for the waves in my head to settle, I stay still before getting up and sorting myself out with some food before work.

Thursday arrives, and after work, I sit at my dining table, waiting for the phone to ring. I chew the end of my pen. I hardly slept last night, tossing and turning. Not having much experience with interviews, I was mulling over all the questions they might ask me. I stayed up and googled all the standard interview questions, as well as the business.

My pen repeatedly taps on the paper, my stomach fluttering with nerves. The phone rings. *Shit. It's time.* Ipick it up and stare at the screen, not answering until a few rings. I don't want to seem desperate, even though I *need* this job.

I swipe the pad of my finger across the phone, bringing it to my ear. "Hello. Ava speaking."

My tone is the sweet professional one, not my regular, relaxed tone.

"Hi, Ava. This is James calling from Ward Electrical and Infrastructure. How are you?" A deep voice speaks into the phone. It's rich, confident, and sexy. I'm still nervous, but now a tad of excitement shrills through me.

"I'm good. Thank you for asking. And you?"

"I'm excellent, thanks. Now, I'm calling about the job for the assistant position you applied for."

"Yes," I say back.

"Are you okay if we begin the job interview now?"

"Sure." I shuffle to the edge of the chair and twirl my hair around my finger. I stare down at my paper. My heartbeat picks up speed.

"Why do you want this position?" he asks.

My mouth drops open. Straight to the point, no bullshit approach. I like that. I like it a lot.

"My previous company is closing. Having previously worked for them for the last eight years, I need a job and I'm experienced in the position you require."

"You are, and you have had no other workplaces?" He seems to be taken aback.

"No, my previous employment was the one and only. Oh, and the odd jobs when I had spare time."

The add-ons to my résumé have returned to haunt me. I really could kick myself for making that shit up right now. Hopefully, I don't get caught out by the lies. Surely I would have been interviewed on my work with David alone. I don't know why I lied. *The booze, you idiot. This is why you don't drink so much. And especially with no food.*

"Very good," he mumbles. I can hear the faint scratching of a pen gliding across paper.

I sit back a little, my shoulders still tense and sitting up around my ears. I'm waiting for the next question.

"What do you think you can bring to the company?"

I answer, "I'm creative, timely, and organized."

A pause and then he chuckles, "Perfect. Thomas, who you will potentially be reporting to, needs that. A lot," he drawls.

Oh god. I hope this Thomas isn't a slob; I'm not a cleaner. I can organize the office for a better system for working. But I don't want to be cleaning up after a male. I shake my head at the thought. *Gross.*

Luckily, David was tidy and understood my quirks.

"What do you know about the company?" he asks.

I hear a rustle of papers in my ear. When it stops, I answer.

"Ward Electrical and Infrastructure specializes in the electrical design, cabling, project management, information technology, and technical services. They provide these services to the construction industry, public transport, and the corporate sector," I answer without a pause.

"Impressive," he mumbles. "Are there questions for me?"

I rub my brow with my free hand, not expecting that question and feeling a tad stupid for not being able to think of anything. My brain is coming up blank. "Ugh, no. Not at this stage, thanks."

"Well, you sound like you would make the perfect assistant to Thomas, so congratulations. I'll email you now with a formal letter of offer and more important details about the company. If you can come to the address on the date provided, someone will welcome you in."

An enormous smile appears on my face. *I did it. I found a new job.*

"Wow. Thank you," I breathe.

My mouth opens and shuts, but nothing else leaves it, so I just slam it shut again. I wish I could talk, but I'm shocked by how I scored a job quickly after David sacked me.

"You're welcome. Goodbye, Ava."

"Goodbye." I rip the phone away from my ear, hanging up and staring at it out in front of me. I take a few big deep breaths as relief washes through me. Then I call Mom.

DOCTOR TAYLOR EXCERPT

Alice

"Ready to pretend you're a millionaire?" Blake says as we exit the Uber.

My heels click on the concrete pavement as we take a few steps toward the entry for Luxe, the hottest new club in the city. Blake, from my course at college, has been begging me to join him for weeks, and I finally caved. It's been a really long week of finishing my final exams, and though my eyes feel heavy, and I have a constant throbbing pain in my temples from the constant late nights, nothing will stop me from celebrating the completion of my nursing degree with my three best friends.

I'm so excited I'm bouncing on my toes while waiting to get inside. I love the light-hearted pleasure of a club. The mix of dancing and drinking gets me feeling more relaxed and self-confident. Tonight's club is even better; it's a club I haven't been to before, but I'm now a member of.

Luxe is a club for the elite. Only the most successful and disgustingly rich men and women secure a membership to Luxe. It's a secret club where you must earn a minimum of a million dollars a year—with proof—in order to get a membership. But Blake scored us all one from his dad's work connections. His dad worked on the construction of this club, which has allowed us to take advantage of the perks of a lifetime membership.

They hid the club off the main road, and you wouldn't know it's here unless you're a member, as only members get the address. Shuffling up to the front of the line, I rub my hands together, trying to warm myself up, but it's not working. The fresh air on my skin raises goosebumps all over my body. I stopped by the local department store to pick up a new dress on my way home from work today. It's different from my usual style of jeans and a top. My wardrobe is usually a mixture of sweats or jeans, along with the occasional dress. I have my regular clubbing dresses, but I needed a statement dress for Luxe.

I feel super sexy for a change, and I love the way I am feeling tonight. I have been getting a few eyes raking over my body, just while standing in the line, so I know it was the right choice of outfit—the little black dress, paired with black strappy heels that wrap delicately around my calf, adding height to my small frame. Smoky gray eye shadow makes my blue eyes pop, and pinning all my hair back in a sleek high pony completes the outfit.

I never wear this much makeup; I'm usually a mascara-only girl. But thanks to YouTube, I have slain my makeup game tonight and look older than my twenty-three years. We strut past the two suited bouncers and step through the doors into the moodiest club I have ever been to. I take in the packed crowd. There are men in three-piece suits and a woman for every man, who are all dressed in designer gowns. I tug nervously at my dress, wishing it was an inch longer after seeing all the elegantly dressed women in the room.

Blake grabs my upper arm with his soft fingers. "Leave it, Alice. You look hot as fuck. If you had a dick, I'd totally fuck you."

I bring my hand up to stifle my giggles.

I had a few vodka, lemon, and lime drinks with Blake back at my house, so we already have a warm buzz coursing through our veins. The alcoholic drinks at clubs are too pricey for us students, and I barely make enough money at the coffee shop to pay my share of the rent.

Blake's hand drops from my arm. "My treat. Let's find the bar!" he shouts above the loud music blaring all around us.

On the right, just behind the crowd, the abstract gunmetal bar with servers in suits comes into clear view. We amble over the white stone floor to the front of the bar to order.

"This is incredible, Blake. I have never seen a club like this. Check out this bar. It's so luxurious." I skim my hands along the smooth surface. It's cool to the touch and completely opposite to how the alcohol is warming me.

Blake orders our drinks while I finally take in the whole club. It's a lot bigger than I had imagined. The dark-gray walls are softly lit by down lights; 3D sculptures are popping from the ceiling, and there are white couches lining the walls, leaving a large dance floor in the middle. Men and women already occupy every seat, so we have no choice but to stand. There are no fluorescent lights or nasty sticky floors in sight. Everything here is in immaculate condition.

When I turn back to the bar, the server is putting a peach-colored shot in front of each of us. I frown, touching the glass between my fingers, and shout, "Blake, what is this shot?"

"Just shoot it." And with that, he taps the shot on the bar and downs it.

Without giving it a second thought, I lift the cold shot glass to my bottom lip, and closing my eyes, I chase mine back. The shot burns my throat, making my eyes pop open, reminding me why I detest shots, but the aftertaste from this one is scrumptious. I lick my lips to pick up any remaining residue.

"Oh, peach. Yummy. What are these, Blake?" I question.

Before Blake can answer, the bartender speaks up. "Wet pussies." He winks and I flush, but he collects our empty glasses from the bar and takes them away before I can respond.

I turn to Blake. "Let's wait until the girls get here to order more drinks. I've got a good buzz going already, and I don't want to be drunk too early, especially since we had a few at home." I hiccup. We're waiting on my two roommates, Maddison and Tahlia, to get here. Tahlia had to work later than usual today, so they should join us soon.

He shakes his head. "No chance. They take forever getting ready. We are ordering now."

I giggle at his impatience. He swivels slowly on his heel and orders another round of our favorite—vodka, lemon, and lime. Blake hands his credit card across the bar to the flirty bartender to pay for our drinks.

The bartender shakes his head. "A fellow patron has already paid for these. Enjoy."

My lips shut into a flat, thin line. *What?* "By whom?" I ask.

Blake and I stand frozen before spinning around, trying to find the person responsible for paying for our drinks and, more importantly, why? The bar is full, and everyone is either in groups chatting among themselves, dancing on the crowded dance floor, or waiting in lines at the bar to be served. None of them are by themselves or seem to be paying attention to Blake and me. *Weird.*

"Who the fuck cares? Thank you to whoever paid for these." He picks up his drink and toasts the air.

I shake my head, reaching for the glass. Clutching it in one hand, I stir the alcohol with the black straw in the other. Wild doesn't begin to describe Blake. Meeting Blake three years ago was like finding another sibling. He sat down in the empty chair next to me in our first biology class for our nursing degree, and he kept distracting me with his constant outbursts. We both got warnings that very first day for disrupting the class, but we still achieved the top marks out of the entire class by the end of the three years. He always keeps the girls and me laughing at his weekend antics. It's like living in a real-life episode of *The Bold and the Beautiful.*

"You're crazy. We can't accept them. The person could be a weirdo."

"Honey, have you looked around the club? He would be a rich, successful weirdo. Drink his money. I'm sure he's swimming in it." He drinks it without a care and pushes off the bar, nodding to the dance floor. "Come on."

I peer down at the drink, thinking and watching the lemon bob around on the surface. *No one has ever bought me a drink before.* It sends a slight chill through me, but I shake off the feeling and walk over to stand beside Blake, taking a swig of my drink. No words leave either of our mouths, both of us happy just to peer at the patrons dancing on the floor in front of us. We have a good view of the entire dance floor from where we are standing. The music blaring from the speakers is R&B and the latest pop.

I take my last sip and drain the glass. My stare lands on a man standing across the dance floor directly opposite us, leaning his large frame against the arm of a white couch full of men. My gaze meets his and I let out a shocked gasp. My grip on the glass loosens and the smooth surface slides straight through my fingers to land on the stone floor, where it smashes into tiny fragments with a popping sound.

"Shit." I crouch down, but Blake pulls my arm, preventing me from picking up the glass.

"Alice, don't. You will cut yourself. The cleaners are heading over now."

Allowing Blake to help me up, I push up on my heels to straighten myself out. I spot a cleaner in a suit holding a dustpan and brush strolling over in our direction. I swallow and glance down at my twisted hands.

Remembering why I dropped the glass, I raise my head and look around for the handsome man with scorching blue eyes, but he's no longer standing there. I close my eyes, squeezing them shut for a moment, wishing I hadn't been so clumsy in front of him. He is probably used to elegant women, not a clumsy mess like me.

I have never had a reaction like that to a man. His eyes and the way he stared at me set my whole body on fire. Then the sexy smirk at the corner of his lip that rose when I dropped my glass sent chills down my spine. He must have seen what effect he had on me. I open my eyes, grimace, and hurry to the bathroom to clear my head. I need to forget about that man and focus on having a good night.

I hurry through the crowd of people, weaving in and out as I make my way toward the ladies' room. Not paying attention and keeping my gaze on the sign above the door with the word 'bathroom,' I collide with a hard chest. I bounce backward, stumbling on my heels. The stranger reaches out, grabbing on to the back of my arms to steady me, saving me from falling flat on my ass.

"Shit, I'm so sorry." The voice is smooth and rich, making me take a step back.

My eyes flick up and I meet the same magnificent blue eyes from before. I smile to myself as he stares, feeling heat spread across my cheeks. He stands there, devilishly handsome, his brown hair gleaming in the club lights. His lips part in a dazzling display of straight white teeth. He holds an air of authority and has the appearance of one who demands instant obedience.

I nod, fighting the overwhelming need to be close to him, to feel his tongue tangled with mine.

My tongue slides out between my lips, and I skim it across the lower one, moistening it. He makes no attempt to hide the fact that he's watching me with a heated stare. The air around us crackles with electricity.

"Can I buy you a drink?" The double meaning in his gaze is obvious.

I stand frozen, and my heart jolts inside my chest.

But as I stand there staring into his glowing eyes, I give in, and I lean forward and kiss him. He kisses me back, and it's a slow, all-consuming kiss. Not the hungry kiss I expected. I can taste the liquor on his tongue and the delicious sensation of the touch of his lips. When we pull away, I'm panting, staring up at him under heavy, hooded eyes.

The air becomes thick, overwhelming me. Clearing my constricting throat, I try to suck some much-needed air into my lungs. "I have to go to the bathroom. I'll catch up with you later," I whisper before I rush off to the ladies' room.

After using the bathroom, I collect myself. My breathing is now regulated, and my body temperature seems to be returning to normal. I wander back out and stand by the entrance to the bathroom. Scanning the club, I can't see him in the sea of faces. My heart constricts as I look around a few minutes more before giving up and walking to meet Blake. I spot him, so I quicken my pace. I notice my roommates, Tahlia and Maddison, have arrived, and they are standing around talking.

"Hey, girls," I yell, moving between them. Draping one arm around each of their shoulders, I squeeze them closer in a hug.

Chuckling at my affection, Maddison asks, "Where did you go? You sound happy."

"That's because you girls are finally here, so we can dance now." Just as I finish the sentence, my skin prickles. I glance toward the spot the man had been standing in before, and he is back in the exact same position. He's staring at me, but this time he is clutching a glass of amber liquid that he brings to his lips. I watch his Adam's apple bob when he takes a sip. His eyes don't falter; they drink me down with it. A delicious shudder heats my body, and before I can register what's happening, Maddison squeals.

"O.M.G. Yes! I love this song! Come on, let's go dance!"

"This Is How We Do It"by Montell Jordan plays, and I lose eye contact with him when Maddison drags me by the hand to the dance floor, pushing through the crowd of people to get to the middle. I'm almost tripping over my feet, trying to keep up with her. My tight dress only allows me to take short, quick steps.

Maddison, Tahlia, and I met during high school. Tahlia and I were working in a local coffee shop as waitresses after school. Maddison would come every day after lessons to have coffee and study. After a few months, I began talking to Maddison about college applications and she offered to assist me in the research and also with applying to my top three preferences—which I accepted. We hung out every weekend, all becoming fast friends before moving to the city and renting a house together. Blake was the final piece that completed our friendship group.

"Maddy, slow down. I'm going to break my neck in these stupid heels!" I shout.

She stops suddenly in the center of the dance floor, and, spinning my body to face her, she dances. The entire floor is packed with sweaty bodies touching and grinding against each other. I can't see past the people dancing to see if the man has moved or if he is still standing there. I'm strangely flattered and intrigued by his interest.

A few songs later, the crowd surrounding us has thinned. I'm having a blast. My knees ache and the balls of my feet are burning with pain from all our dancing, but I'm too buzzed to care. Tahlia and Blake join us, and we all dance together. I can't remember the last time I had this much fun. Recently, my life has consisted only of work or study. To be so carefree in this moment makes my heart sing. I sway my hips from side to side to the beat. I look around again for the sexy stranger and I note he is standing near the bar. A woman with rich, long brown hair, and wearing a black sequined dress, is engaged in conversation with him, her fingers wrapped around his bicep. They are standing relatively close to each other, and she is whispering in his ear.

My heart sinks at the sight of them, so I tear my gaze away. I'm about to ask if the others want to call an Uber soon, when I feel a body slide up behind me. A masculine arm snakes around my waist to pull me back flush against his hard torso, and he rocks our hips slowly to the beat.

The body hugging mine is tall and seems to be built of solid muscle. I can smell his deep sandalwood and caramel scent, which is intoxicating. I sigh audibly at the memory of when I was last being held in a man's embrace. I feel his breath tickle the tip of my ear, pulling me from the memory as we continue to sway into the next song. I close my eyes and get lost in this moment, forgetting everything and just enjoying his warmth.

He whispers, "You're incredible. I couldn't resist." His tone is soft and sensual, totally different from the smooth, rich voice of the man I kissed earlier in the night. I grin from ear to ear at the memory. The warm embrace is pulling a deep longing from me that I don't want to lose. I don't reply, but I continue to dance with him.

"Turn around, beautiful." I stop and turn in a circle, curious to see what this man looks like. Raising my arms, I lay them on his shoulders and step back, leaving a decent gap.

His eyes close and his hands are on my hips, moving them to the sound of the beat. I seize the opportunity to take him in—he has short brown hair, tanned skin, and his jeans, t-shirt, and blazer are all black. My lips lift at his classically handsome features. As I finish scanning him from head to toe, his eyes suddenly pop open and his blue eyes meet mine.

He is beaming, which makes me grin back. However, his beauty and presence don't hold the same power and control over me as the other man's did. It doesn't stroke the deep desires and feelings that have awoken in me. My gaze drops to his solid chest. And I sigh. *I'm not feeling it*.

Before I have the chance to speak, he leans forward, closing the gap until his lips meet mine. I gently push on his chest and take a step back, which breaks the seal of our lips.

I swallow hard, with a soft shake of my head. "I'm sorry," I whisper.

Then, in the corner of my eye, I see *him*. His fine tailored suit and crisp white shirt with no tie stand out in the crowd of dark clothes. He stands motionless, a dark, angry expression on his face, his hands deep in his pockets. The brunette is still talking to him, but his icy gaze is focused entirely on me. My eyes widen and I turn away to gaze back at the man in front of me. An easy smile plays at the corners of his mouth. He hasn't noticed the other man or my sudden loss of focus.

"I didn't intro—" he begins.

Tahlia comes over, her presence cutting into his speech. "Hey, Alice, can we head home soon? I'm pretty tanked and I have work in the morning." Her smile widens in approval as she glances between me and the man I had just been dancing with. A lump forms in my throat because my mind was elsewhere, and I couldn't get into him.

I twist to face her. "Sure, T." I swing back to face the man in front of me. "We have to go. Thanks, err, nice to meet you, I guess."

His posture is relaxed as he stands there, chuckling. "Yes, and I'm Alex, by the way. It was my pleasure. Are you going to be okay getting home, or do you need me to call you girls a cab or an Uber?" He is being so nice, making me feel a twinge of guilt in the pit of my stomach. I almost wish I had felt a small connection to Alex, but I shouldn't be surprised at my lack of interest. After all, I was with my ex for two years without feeling real love for him.

"No, thank you. I already called an Uber, and there are another two people coming with us. Thanks anyway."

"Okay. Well, if you're sure. It was lovely to meet you both. I'd better head off now to find my group of friends before I'm left here. Hope to see you here again sometime. Bye." He nods at Tahlia, and the beginning of a smile tips the corners of his mouth before he moves away.

I let out a shaky breath. I was petrified he was going to ask for my number, and I would have had to turn him down in front of Tahlia, but he didn't, so maybe he read the same signals I did. Even though he was nice, there was no spark.

Oh well. I won't have to see him ever again, except maybe when I come back here, so I don't have anything to worry about.

Linking my arm through Tahlia's, we slowly wander off the dance floor. "Let's find the other two and get out of here. My feet are killing me," I moan.

"Me too. What a great night, though, celebrating the end of your studies."

My smile widens. "The *best* night. Thank you."

Chapter 2

Alice
Six Months Later

It's midmorning and Blake is driving me into the city. Both of us need to pick up our parking passes for our graduate year. We decided to do it together and make a day of it. Neither of us has work today and we want to do a test run of driving into work to see how long it will take. Blake didn't get placed at the same hospital, but he is around the corner, within walking distance.

I gaze down at my Google Maps, noticing the hospitals are close by. "Let's park here," I say and point to the parking spots along the curb.

"Good idea," he mutters as he pulls in and parks.

I dressed in my comfortable clothes—jeans, a cream crewneck, and sneakers. My hair is thrown up in a sleek pony, opting to pin all my fringe back. We exit the car and peer around before I throw my phone inside my bag, then walk up to read the sign. "It's free all-day parking and we can walk up. Your building is farther away, so let's do yours first and then mine."

"Sweet. Let's get to it. I just need to find the information desk. They should have the pass ready."

I nod and we walk along the sidewalk. I link my arm through his, and we walk in sync as I peer around, admiring the trees and tall city buildings. The buzz of the people and cars surrounding us has me grinning wide.

"I still can't get over the fact we have finished our studies. All that hard work is finally paying off," I exclaim.

"I know, right? No more exams or studying, thank fuck. Here we are." He motions to the entry to his glass building.

I scale my eyes up and down the tall building, noting people standing outside smoking and others talking on their phones.

"You go inside. I will wait here." I point over to a spare bench outside the building.

"I'll just be a minute."

I watch him enter the doors before I walk over and take a seat, then I take out my phone to send a picture to Mom.

My phone vibrates after I hit send.

I smile and answer. "Mom."

"Hi, love. Are you at work today?"

"No. Blake and I are picking up our parking passes."

"Oh, how nice. Say hi to Blake for me."

I watch as Blake comes out, waving his pass in victory. I laugh loudly.

"Mom, I gotta run. I will call you tonight. Love you."

"Okay, have fun. I love you too."

I end the call and stand up.

"Ready?" Blake asks, nudging his head in the direction of my building.

"Yeah, let's go." We link arms and wander slowly down the path. "Mom called to see what I was doing. I sent her a picture. She said hi."

He throws his spare hand on his heart. "Aw, I love her. Let's go get your pass now before we find somewhere for a drink—I'm parched."

I giggle. "Okay."

Blake waits outside on the sidewalk while I enter the building, locating the information desk on my phone.

It takes me a minute to get mine, and when I exit the building, Blake jumps up.

"Drink time?" I ask.

"Are you talking alcohol?" He winks.

"No chance." I look around us and locate a shop across the road. "Hey, there is a smoothie bar across the road. Let's go there."

"This could be dangerous. I could waste all my money here when I'm working so close."

I nod in agreement and loop my arm through his. We cross at the lights and enter the smoothie shop. It is surprisingly quiet, with only a few patrons inside.

"Let's sit there in the booth," Blake says, motioning toward the brown leather booth in the corner. We walk over and slide into the seats, across from each other. I shiver from the cold leather before I pick up the menu and scan it.

"What are you thinking?" I ask Blake.

"Mango dream."

"Oh, that sounds good. I'll order them. Stay here. I will only be a minute."

Blake smiles and pulls out his phone. I round the booth and walk to the counter, then order two mango dreams.

I stand to the side and wait for them to be ready.

The door chimes, signaling people entering. I peer up and watch as a group of four men in tailored suits walk through.

But it's the last one that walks through the door that catches my eye. *Fuck.* He is taller and broader than the others, but that's not what captures my breath. It's the eyes I haven't been able to forget and the lips. His gaze holds mine and his jaw is tight from him clenching.

The black suit, fit to perfection, shows off his large shoulders and lean body. I shudder at the memory of his soft, controlled lips on mine and the taste. How I would love a taste again. My mouth dries. *Where the hell is my order? Did they pick the mangos off a tree themselves?*

He owns the room and I stare after him as he takes a seat opposite me. The guys around him are talking, clearly oblivious to his distraction.

He leans on the table, brows furrowed, rubbing his jaw—staring at me. The electricity in the room crackles, and the heat level makes my crewneck sweater feel restrictive. I bring my finger up and pull on the neck of it, trying to get more air.

"Two mango dreams."

I jump with a squeak. I spin around, breaking my intense eye contact with the sexy suit guy, and scoop up the drinks. I turn to see him still watching me. I dip my head with a flush and suck the drink up through the straw immediately, and his eyes darken. The cold sweet drink hitting my tongue helps to cool me down.

I reach our table and peer at Blake as I slide his drink to him.

"Thanks, hon."

I nod, just sucking the drink as I squeeze back in the booth. I peek over. He is still staring. I tear my gaze away again, overwhelmed by his presence.

"What's the plan tonight?" Blake asks.

"Let's grab something for—" I lose my train of thought as I hear the screech of a chair dragging on the floor. I look over and watch *him* on the phone, practically running out of the shop. Once he is out of my sight, I drop my head, sadness washing over me.

Twice I have missed out on finding out *his* name.

ARE YOU A SHARON SWEETHEART?

To keep up to date with new books releases, including title's, blurb's, release date's and give-aways. Please subscribe to my newsletter. www.sharonwoodsauthor.com

Want to stay up to date with me? Come join my Facebook reader group: Sharon's Sweethearts This is a **PRIVATE** group and only people in the group can see posts and comments!

ACKNOWLEDGMENTS

To my true love, my husband, you are my biggest cheerleader and supporter. Without you, my dreams would not exist. I love you.

My two blessings, my children. Thank you for allowing me to write and watch you grow at the same time. One day, it will be me pushing you to chase your own dreams.

All my friends and family, without each of your support, I would be awfully lonely. I'm so happy to be supported by a tribe. Just know, I will be forever grateful. Love you all.

Tee or some of you know her as T. L Swan. Thank you for always supporting, encouraging, and giving me advice when I need it. When I picked up your stanton series years ago, I had a dream, and I reached out and you answered me. I will always be forever grateful to you, my Margarita loving queen. Love you!

My readers, thank you for supporting me and purchasing my books. You are supporting my dreams and without you, my career wouldn't exist. Thank you.

ABOUT THE AUTHOR

Sharon Woods is an author of Contemporary Romance. She loves writing steamy love stories with a happy ever after. Born and living in Melbourne, Australia. With her beautiful husband and two children.

http://www.instagram.com/sharonwoodsauthor

http://www.facebook.com/sharonwoodsauthor

https://www.tiktok.com/@sharonwoodsauthor

http://www.sharonwoodsauthor.com

http://www.bookbub.com/authors/sharon-woods

Printed in Great Britain
by Amazon